NOT JUST SEX
(Volume 1)
Formerly Titled "Unprotected" – (Part 1 & 2)
David Theodore

visit – NotJustSEX.net

Thank You Very Much for Purchasing My eBook and Thank You So Much for Supporting all Our Authors and Writers:

Feel Free to Contact and Email Me:
DavidTheodore@DNAeBooks.com

NOT JUST SEX
(Volume 1)
by - David Theodore

Visit – DNAeBooks.com

The Place to HangOut for all Reading Groups and for all of Us who Enjoy Reading...

The DNA eBooks Publishing Group Can Bring Authors / Writers to Your Events...

email us: Events@DNAeBooks.com

MEET OUR WRITERS and AUTHORS, WATCH VIDEOS and MUCH MORE:

Check Out – DNAeBooks.com

**Special Offers, Exclusive Content and More...
Sign Up and be on Our VIP Email List**
email us: VIPList@DNAeBooks.com

http://www.dnaebooks.com/short-form/

For information:
The DNA eBooks Publishing Group
P.O. BOX 314
New York City, NY 10037

Info@DNAeBooks.com

Any similarity to persons living or dead is purely
coincidental. But then again, what is a coincidence? Is it
a coincidence that you are reading this book right now and I
am sleeping, eating or taking a crap? LOL.

Forgive me I got jokes. But I really want to thank you for
purchasing this book. I need the money because
the rent is due and baby needs some new shoes.

Unless you are reading someone else's copy in which case
you better buy my next book or be cursed with the itchies
and short arms. Now stop reading the copyrights
section because the story inside is much more interesting.

Have a good mother"#$%&* day.

DNA eBooks Publishing Group

DNA eBooks Publishing Company

Published by
DNA eBooks Publishing Company
P.O. BOX 314
New York, NY 10037

www.DNAeBooks.com

Publisher@DNAeBooks.com
and **Co-Published by**
DavidTheodore@DNAeBooks.com

ISBN - **978-0-9832476-9-2**

Special Thanks to:
my Mother, my Sister, and My Grandmother, Barbara Davis,
Warren Thompson and
Marlene author of Island Beauty, Making It On My Own,
and Babies Daddies .
That's all folks…
Dedicated to Donald Goines and Iceberg Slim
They made a nigga want to read

Indahood Books
185 McClellan street
(Suite 3A)
Bronx NY 10456-4811
indahood@optonline.net
917-915-2026
****

Rip
Poncho and Leo

David Theodore

About The Author

David Theodore is a product of the Bronx and has been creating stories for over twenty years. A Psychology graduate of Paine College in Augusta Georgia and Forensic Psychology at John Jay College in Manhattan, he intends to one day pursue his doctorate. Life's journey has allowed him to hold down many jobs including father, teacher, cab driver, cashier, fast food cook, vacuum salesman, construction worker, government worker, video jockey, counselor, and more. Still each day has its ups and downs, and for a short period he was homeless and sleeping in the tunnels under New York City. Through all the good and bad times, writing remained a passion.

Having the doors of the major publishers and agents repeatedly slammed in his face, he decided to self publish. Ultimately he has found the very people who share in his struggle have become his biggest supporters. Now when he gets on the subways or walks the streets of NYC he is armed with his books and a desire to share his literature with the world.

To find out more about David Theodore or his novels:

Visit:

www.NotJustSex.net

and

www.DNAeBooks.com

Not Just Sex
(Act I)

Formerly known as "Unprotected" – (Part 1 & 2)

Contents

(Chapter 1)
WOLLER

Inside the covers, Don is warm and cozy. Outside the covers it's nippy and cold even though the radiator is hissing. It's just another morning for Don where his worst fear is a day closer. He is up early because he is going jogging before he heads to school. He wants to try to cleanse some of the filth from his bloodstream by running. He feels yucky in the pit of his stomach as he reminisces about the night before.

Don was at his part-time job at the Shiny Apple Supermarket on 15th street and Third Avenue. It's called part-time but he works between 28 to 36 hours a week including his weekend hours. Don likes his job. He is in charge of the produce department, which he keeps rotated and watered. He also helps himself to everything and anything in the supermarket. The truth is, about eighty percent of the stores shoplifting is an inside job. Don fits in well and is liked by most of his co-workers.

Don looks up to Mike, a brother who works stock, along with working two of the cashiers that are employed at the Shiny Apple. Mike and Don became friends when he caught Mike puffing a blunt in the freezer. Mike was surprised when Don asked, "You know what a quarterback does in football games?"

"Yeah he makes the passes." Mike

"So pass Nigga!" Don

They bust out laughing and Mike passes Don the spliff. Since then, they have puffed plenty of choke together. This Thursday however, they get paid on Thursdays, Mike wants Don to try a wooller.

Looking at the time, Don snaps out his thought, jumps out of bed and shivers as he walks quickly to the hamper. He picks out a dirty long john set and puts them on. He puts on his sweat pants, torn hoody, and sneakers. He takes a piss, brushes his teeth and washes his face. He puts on his windbreaker, Chicago Bulls cap and, most importantly he scoops up his MP3 player with FM radio. The music helps to soothe the pain. The running helps to drive the pain away. Down the elevator and out the door, the cold air hits him. He likes it that way because he knows he'll have to run in order to stay warm. Don appreciates the incentive. Stopping for a moment to stretch, he clicks on the radio and hears Tom Joyner talking about the senseless deaths of Tupac and Biggie and then playing one of Tupacs new songs. He starts to run and the music is quickly lost in his own thoughts of the previous night.

After work, Don and Mike ride the train up to 110th street. They buy two fat twentys of hydro from Mr. B's, and begin to troop it uptown. Headed to Mount Morris Park, they decide to split up and meet at the park. Don goes to get a pack of white owls while Mike goes to get the powder. To Don's surprise, Mike beats him to the park and is sitting on a bench with an unopened quart of Golden Champale by his side, just lounging. Don strolls into the park and they walk up the stairs to the top of Mt. Morris and have a seat on a rock that overlooks east and downtown Manhattan.

Tapping the bottom of the quart, Don passes it over for Mike to tap it. Mike smacks the bottom. While Don opens the sweet Malt Liquor, Mike splits open a white owl with a box cutter and let's the insides fall out. He pulls apart the two layers of skin and then peels off the cancer paper from the inner layer. He puts the two layers back together and glues them in place via saliva. He takes one of the bags of weed and dumps half into the open skin of the owl. After spreading the ism evenly around, he dumps about ten dollars worth of cocaine on the ism. With three flicks of his index fingers and thumbs he twists the blunt, gives it one sloppy lick across and glues the cigar shut. It is almost as fat as the original state the owl was bought in. Out of nowhere Mike holds a lit match towards the wooller, looks up at the three quarter moon, and lights it.

After six to seven puffs he hands the spliff to Don. This is Don's first time smoking a wooller, so on his first puff he jokes about the minty taste. By the fourth toke, he is very quiet. He begins to feel as if he is trapped in a box, even though he is clearly out in the open. Without even thinking about it, Don passes the spliff back to Mike and takes a guzzle from the quart. His throat remains dry. His whole body goes numb. He begins to feel that his soul has left him and although he wants his soul back, he continues drinking and puffing till the blunt is gone.

Mike on the other hand was feeling quite at home as he split another white owl and began to roll another wooller blunt. "Ya Know" Mike said while standing up and holding out his hands to the city, "One of these days I'm gonna be at the top of this world. All of this will be mine." Then he began to run off at the mouth about how he did one of the cashiers in the storage room and how she gave him head.

Don could hear Mike talking, but he was having internal conflicts. He was experiencing a great amount of anxiety within. He still felt it as he grasps the second wooller and takes four hard pulls. For the past year he has been smoking and telling himself he should stop. Weed is the only comfort he needs, yet he always finds it hard to say no to other drugs. He thinks about getting some wood root tonic to help cleanse some of the poison from his body just as the wooller is being passed back to him.

Before Don realizes it, he has run a mile. He stops to stretch as he switches the station to 107.5. As cold as it is, the sweat still runs down his back. Running home should be much easier since most of it is downhill. Stevie Wonder comes on with 'My Love Is With You' as his mind slips back to the previous night.

Don and Mike must have been zonin for hours before they heard the glass breaking behind them. Apparently a bum who had been sleeping on the rocks behind them knocked his half full Night Train bottle to the ground. At that moment Don and Mike saw the beam of a flashlight coming up the stairs. Then they see two more beams behind the first. Don was the first to notice that the bum had quietly slipped into the darkness.

"Hey!" A voice yelled! It was the cops. About two stories down, with jagged edges on the way, Mike is the first to jump. His jump is graceful and almost perfect. Don jumped next. He doesn't want to jump but he is not going to be left up there alone with 5-O. Unfortunately, his jump is not at all graceful. He lands on his butt and cuts his arm on a piece of glass. Don wanted to just lay there because of the pain, but when he heard the shots being let off, his feet cut on automatic pilot and he quickly caught up to Mike.

A few blocks later they stop to catch their breath. All Don wants to do is get on the bus and go home. Mike on the other hand is having fun and wants to smoke more woollers.

"Come on D. Let's get some more of that good shit."

"Nah Mike, I don't think so. I have to get up in a few hours. It's after two and I want to spend the rest of my dough on some gear," Don.

"Aight" Mike said, "I guess I could crash at one of my bitches crib. Let's at least puff the rest of this wooller before we break."

Even though Don felt as if he could get no higher, he agreed. They walk to Monroe projects and go to the top floor in the stairway of a building. There, they light the wooller. Halfway through the blunt Don knew he couldn't smoke anymore. "Mike," Don said, "I'm there. I'm totally fucked up. I don't need anymore."

"Ya sure" replied Mike. "We could get us a couple more quarts and a twenty of blo. It's on me nigga." Mike acts as if he has just woke up from an extremely restful sleep. He is hyped up and ready to get blasted as he smokes the wooller

till it burns his fingers.

"A yo nigga." Don says, "I got mad shit to do kid. I needs to boogie."

"Aight" Mike said, "I'll get up later."

"Peace" they say in unison.

Don walks to the bus stop and watches Mike walk down the block and disappear. After waiting a few minutes Don begins to get impatient. He is feeling paranoid as it is, and the only people out on the streets seem to be riffraffs and chickenheads.

Don goes to hail a cab and right away one stops. Just as he touches the door handle, he hears a voice behind him.

"Hey You!" It was the cops from the park. "Don't even think about getting in that car." Don turns to face the four cops. Three are white and one is mulatto. "Come here boy! Get the fuck over here now!"

Already having to piss pretty bad, and feeling gassy, Don walks over to the cops and is quickly slammed against the wall. He can't believe it. He knows he is a dead man. He feels the urine trickling down his leg.

"I saw you in the park boy." Don couldn't see their faces because he was pinned to the wall, but he could sure smell the stink breath of the one talking. Then he heard the laughter. The cops were laughing because they discovered Don had urinated on himself. The one who had Don pinned against the wall had not caught on yet and began screaming at his fellow workers. "What the fuck are you'se laughing at!" One of the cops pointed to the puddle, there was a few seconds of silence and they all broke out laughing.

It was while they were laughing that Don got a good look at all of them. Especially the short stubby red neck that had him against the wall. "Face the fucking wall," the red neck managed to say between giggles. After a few minutes the amusement died down and it was back to business. First, they made Don empty all of his pockets. Then they patted him down and joked about his wet right leg that they refuse to pat. When one of the cops finds an empty plastic dime bag

11

in Don's coat pocket, they put him in handcuffs and the mulatto reads him his rights.

Reading Don's high School ID the tall officer speaks for the first time. "Are you Donathan Breyer, student at Malcom X High School, Social Security 917-915-2026? "Yes" replies Don.

"There's nothing but books and a camera in his bag sir," the red neck tells the tall officer. Don could read the tall ones tag. It said Gomez. Don is surprised because he thought the man was white.

"What were you doing on Mt. Morris? Trying to get some shots?" Gomez said as he held up Dons camera.

Before Don could speak, the red neck retorts in an evil tone. "I was trying to get some shots too." Don could feel a chill run through him and he would have sworn he saw the same chill run through Officer Gomez. But why would the red neck's words put fear in Gomez too? Don had his own troubles to worry about.

Don felt the pain on his wrist ease away when Gomez took the handcuffs off. "Look here Don," said Gomez, "I never want to see your face again. And believe you me, you never ever want to see my face again." Don is relieved that they let his hands free but he still feels in danger. His bowels are heavy and he breaks a loud wind. "What are you a fucking wise guy?" The red neck is ready to put his foot in Dons ass. "I didn't mean it," Don pleads.

Gomez grabs his partner and tells him to chill because Johnson is coming. Quietly another police cruiser pulled up took all four of the officers away.

Don is still in shock when he hears his name being called. "Don, Don," It was Mike. "Yo Nigga, I saw the whole thing. It was fucked up. Those niggas played you. Oh shit you pissed in your pants." And Mike begins to laugh. He laughs so hard that all Don could do was laugh too. But Don didn't laugh long. He told Mike "Peace," and jumped in the next cab. He hears Mike say "Yo, I got the shit, and we could hang." As the cab drives off.

12

So rapped up in his thoughts of the previous night, he jogs two blocks past his house. Once he gets home, he does his stretches so he won't get cramps and, eats some oatmeal. Don looks at the time and sees he has twenty minutes to take a shower and get dressed. "Fuck it," he says to himself, "Who the hell goes to school on time anyway."

Don lives with his father and grandmother. His father works the graveyard shift and usually doesn't get home till almost noon. Because his dad is normally asleep when he gets home from school, they hardly spend much time together. And since Don has been working, they rarely see each other at all. On the other hand, his grandmother is a great influence. She was the one who encouraged him to get a job in the first place. Because she is a teacher, she understands the educational system and is pushing Don towards college. She feels Don is headed in the wrong direction and needs guidance. If she only knew how much trouble he is headed for, she would take him out the city now.

"Don, I'm leaving" his grandmother says through the bathroom door. "Eat some fruit before you leave and don't be late. I already got two letters from the school saying you were late last month."

"Yes Grandma," says Don. "I love you, be careful and have a good day."

"Bye Baby," replies his grandmother. The front door slams and locks. Finally, he is alone. "Now how did grandma get those late slips?" Don thinks to himself. "I've been checking the mail and I interceptive four last month. I guess I have to check the mail twice a day."

Getting out of the shower, Don lights a charcoal for his incense and blasts Mary J. Bliges' latest album. He knows he will be late again and wishes he had a cutie coming over this morning. He is in need of some loving. However, he is in the doghouse with the ones he is able to hit. He knows it is his fault, but he always ends up playing or disrespecting

13

the honeys after he sexes them. And if he doesn't diss them, they diss him.

At the present time though, Don is only temporarily lonely. He has quite a few girls who love to share his company. Even after being dissed. He also has a few prospects to dog in the future. Dropping a few pebbles of frankincense on the charcoal, Don puts on his clothes. He takes special care with his jeans and boots, to make sure every sag and every shoelace is in order. Throwing on his wind breaker and Yankees cap, Don is ghost. He is headed to school. Just another day of his senior year. Yeah right!

(Chapter 2)
JACKIE

Don suffers from very mild anxiety attacks whenever he is on his way to school. No one but him knows and he is the only one who can tell when he is having one. The anxiety is in the pit of his stomach and increases the closer he gets to school. Usually by the end of 1st period his anxiety is gone, but at the moment he is feeling it. At the root of the anxiety is that he seems to never know when trouble will approach.

It seems that things he'd done months ago had a way of smacking him in his face. He sometimes would even get the blame for things he hadn't done.

Since 1st period has already started, the outside of the school is deserted. Don has to walk around back to fill out a late slip. All of the late comers have to use the lunch room entrance in the back, fill out a late slip and drop it in the box.

There are about twenty students scattered throughout the lunchroom. Some are hurrying to fill out their late slips and get to class. Others are socializing and taking their time in an effort to miss first period.

Don spots Jackie among the talkers. Jackie is Johnny's girlfriend. Johnny is a wanna be gansta. Don can't understand why Jackie is with Johnny but he has never expressed his thoughts about it. She and Don are friends because she fills out late slips for him whenever he is not going to attend school. Since Jackie is a chronically late student, Don can usually call her in the morning and ask her to fill out a late slip for him. While his home room teacher marks him absent, the main office changes him to late after first period because of the late slip. So Don would be marked late when he really is absent.

"Good morning Jackie" Don says, as he kisses her on the cheek.

"Hey Don, I'm surprised to see you here," She says with a smile.

"Well ya know, a brothers got to get his edubication," they laugh.

"So you heard the latest gossip?" Jackie

"No, but like Craig David fill me in" Don

"Well Mellisa, You know Mellissa, the one with the short hair, who goes with Curtis? Well she's pregnant and it's not Curtis's." Jackie

"How you know it's not Curtis. He told somebody I know that he be hittin those skins on a regular."

"Well she says it ain't Curtis. And you know how niggas be lying on their dicks. Anyway you know Roberto? Smart, intelligent, herb Roberto? Well, they just charged his parents with child abuse." Jackie

"Word!?" Don

"Yup, there was a reason why he would never get dressed for gym. Apparently his father was beating his ...."

When Jackie stops talking and starts packing her books, Don knows it can only mean one thing. The Dean is very close by. He is a man not to be played with. It isn't just his six foot two, 245 pound frame. His shiny bald head, piercing black eyes or thunderous voice that makes mortal students give him respect. It is the combination of those traits along with the air of authority the Dean possesses. He can talk you into believing you can capture the world. He can also embarrass or belittle you into the laughing stock of the school.

So far Don and the Dean are on good terms. But the Dean has mentioned Dons lateness to him on two occasions already. Finishing their late slips Don and Jackie get up to put their late slips in the box. They try not to look in the Deans direction but they have to pass by him to get through the doors to the stairway. Just before they go through the doors, they catch his eyes and stop in their tracks expecting a speech. Instead the Dean shakes his head in disgust and looks away as if he no longer acknowledges their presence.

Once in the stairway, Don and Jackie face another dilemma. With only 15 minutes left to the end of 1st period, should they roam the hallways and take the chance on getting caught by the Dean. Or go to class and possibly get yelled at by an angry teacher.

"Come with me," Jackie says, and Don goes along. Instead of going up the stairs toward their classes, they head down the stairs to the basement. Don has never been down there, but it is obvious that Jackie has as she meticulously picks the lock to the door of the boiler room. They walk into the dark room and have to duck under some pipes while they make their way to the back of the room.

Conveniently, there is an old couch at the end of the room. Jackie sits down and immediately lights up a philly. Don is feeling nervous and really wants to take a leak. Jackie passes him the phil and Don takes some puffs. Not only doesn't he feel like smoking but he had every intention of going to class. Now he is in the basement of his school, smoking weed with a gangster niggaz girlfriend and cutting class. "Its gonna be a rough day," he thinks to himself.

"I have to take a piss so bad I'm gonna burst." Don says "There's a drain over there" Jackie points. Don walks to the drain, and as soon as he pulls out his penis he begins pissing. He doesn't hear Jackie creeping up behind him, but he knows she is there when she grabs him from behind and starts massaging his chest.

"What are you doing?" He asks.

"Something I've wanted to do for a long time," whispers Jackie in his ear. She then takes his penis in her hand and shakes it off when he finishes urinating. She gently strokes his cock till it is hard as granite. Then, towing him by his jimmy, she heads him back to the couch where she gets on her knees and begins kissing and caressing his private member.

All the while she is pleasing him, Don is wondering how this sexy girl could behave like this. And the fact that she knows that very often when he has asked her to drop a late slip in the box for him, he was having a girl come over to his crib. Most of the time not the same girl. She knows of five

17

to six girls that he has done. Yet she wants to get with him anyway. And to top it off she already has a boyfriend. And a crazy one at that. Don doesn't want to, but he feels he has no choice. Before he can say anything, Jackie is sliding a condom on his penis. She mounts him and for the first time Don realizes just how beautiful she truly is. Jackie has a wonderful brown complexion at 5 foot 9 with legs that won't quit. He has a thing for nice butts and she has an ass the feels soft as butter.

Without even thinking much about it, he starts to caress her breast as she rides him and sucks on his neck. He can feel her juices began to drip down his balls. Her pounding begins to get wild and she digs her nails in his back, something Don hates. But at the moment he is too caught up in his own ecstasy to care. They explode together, and hold each other for what seems like hours while trying to catch their breath.

Don is already beginning to feel guilty, and he wants to tell her that this could never happen again. The last thing he wants is to have Johnny find out. He doesn't want any beef with that niggah.

"Jackie I......." Don starts to say something but is interrupted by her finger to his mouth.

"Look Don, I just wanted to see what all these girls been talking about. And you know what?" Jackie

"What?" Don

"They were right." Jackie

Don suddenly feels gassed up and on top of the world. His ego blows up 100 fold. But he doesn't let Jackie in on his bewilderment. "You're so beautiful," Don says switching the attention back to her. "But I would never want to hurt our friendship."

"I won't tell if you won't tell." Jackie

Luckily Don has on a T-shirt under his sweater because they need something to wipe up the juices that flowed between them.

Dried and dressed Jackie lights up what is left of the blunt. And even though he doesn't want to smoke, he smokes.

18

"Damn it's almost third period, we gotta go." Don

"Just wait a few minutes, we'll leave when the bell rings so we can blend into the crowd with the rest of the students."

"Well since we have a minute, tell me why you would cheat on Johnny like this?" Don

"First of all we did this. Secondly you and I both know Johnny does not believe in fidelity. Since he has a reputation of being such a so called bad motherfucker, girls be sweatin him hard every second. And finally, Johnny knows nothing about making love to a woman. He's a two minute disappointment." Jackie

"Well Jackie, not only don't I want to lose your friendship and trust but I don't want no pork or beef with that nigger." Don

"Don?"

"Yeah Jackie," Don

"You really are sweet and have nothing to worry about. By the way Fatima was looking for you."

"Fatima, when did you see her?"

"You must have just missed her when you came in." Jackie

"So what did she want?" Don

"She just asked if anyone saw you. I think she likes you." Jackie

"You think so." Don

"Yeah" Jackie replies.

Don could sense the sadness in her eyes. "And how do you feel about her liking me Jackie?" Don

"Look niggah what I wanted from you is totally physically. I know you're a hoe so let's leave it at that. As far as Fatima, I feel sorry for her cause all you are gonna do is dog her out."

"Damn Jackie that is harsh." Don

"You just remember one thing, what goes around comes around. So don't hurt these girls anymore than you have to." Jackie

"Jackie." Don

"What." Jackie

19

"I'm scared of you!" Don

They laugh. "The bells about to ring, let's get up on out of here!" Don

(Chapter 3)
THIRD PERIOD

Thirty seconds before the bell, Don and Jackie are peeking out the boiler room door. The bell rings and they start upstairs as a wave of students fill the stairways. Don takes a last look at Jackie who winks at him as she is carried by the crowd in one direction and he is carried by the crowd in another.

"Allah, please be with me." Don thinks to himself. He prays coming and going. It is his way of asking the infinite powers to protect him.

"Hey Don, what's up?" It is Answar, a fellow student.

"Just chillin G. Where are you headed?" Don

"The same place you're headed. Psychology class." Answar

Don and Answar have had a lot of classes together. They've studied together, did reports and home work together. They even cheated on test together. But outside of school they never hung out together.

The two became friends in the tenth grade. They started studying and buddying together in the 11th grade. Towards the end of the 11th grade however, Answer let Don in on a secret. Answar is androgynous. He was born without any sex organs. His parents had to make a decision on whether they wanted a boy or girl. They choose a boy. He has a penis but cannot obtain erections. He is impotent.

"So why did you miss math this morning?" Asks Answar.

"We had a test!"

"I forgot all about it. My mind has been on other things lately."

Nobody else in the school knows about Answar. Since he has small breast and some female features, there have been rumors that he is gay. Although there are no basis for these rumors, except that Answar doesn't have a girlfriend, Don keeps his relationship with him to a minimum and strictly business.

They take their seats in the back of the class just as the late bell rings. Professor Pavlove is taking attendance. Since he has taught all of the thirty students at one time or another he silently takes roll call.

"Now class, I am confident that you all have done the reading I last gave for homework! Who can tell me who and what chapter three is about?" The whole class is silent. Don knows the answer but doesn't raise his hand. Since the beginning of the school year, he has consistently answered most of the questions. Although he knows the answer he does not want to be labeled as a teacher's pet. But he really likes psychology and being able to use it on people.

"Come on now, I know at least one person did the reading!"

Sheena, a very smart girl from Indonesia raises her hand. "Chapter 3 is about Sigmund Freud and his theory on the ego, id, and super ego." Sheena

"Excellent," remarks the professor as he writes Sigmund Freud's theory on the board.

"Now," replies the professor, "The ego, id and superego is according to Freud what makes up our unconscious behavior. Can anyone tell me the functions of the ego?"

Answar raises his hand, "The ego is the need and want part of our personality."

"Almost but not quite." Professor Pavlove

Don raises his hand, "The id is the part of one's personality that wants and has to have. The ego is the part that says no you don't need that and, the super ego is like the mediator between the two."

"Very good," Professor. "Now can you give the class an example of how these functions work?"

"Sure" replies Don, talking more to the class than the professor. "Say you wake up in the middle of the night with the munchies." The class laughs but the professor doesn't get it. "And you know there's a whole sweet potato pie in the kitchen. Well your id would say to you, let's get a fork, grab the pie and eat every crumb! Then your ego would say It's too late to eat, and there are other people who might want some pie. Just leave the pie alone. Now your ego and id will be fighting over whether or not to eat the pie, when your super ego comes along and says, Ya'll need to chill. This is what we're gonna do. You wanna eat the pie and you don't. So we are gonna compromise and eat just one piece. One piece and get back in bed."

"Wonderful, Don! Freud couldn't have done a better job explaining it himself. Now are there any questions?" Professor Pavlove looks around the room.

The class is silent. Although Don generally tries to be a quiet student who knows how the majority of students treat the so called intelligent nerds, he still decides to speak one last time.

"I have a question," asks Don. "We have all heard the expression that guy has a big ego or he's an ego maniac. But since we know it's the id that kinda pumps you up, shouldn't we be saying that person has a big id or that person's an id maniac?"

The professor is quite amused but the rest of the class don't get it. "Yes yes, I see what you mean. But for all purposes of the test next Friday, you will need to learn the functions as they are in the text book. Now I would like everyone to turn their books to pages 72 and 73 on defense mechanisms."

Don does not speak for the rest of the class. Before the class started he was feeling guilty for missing the first two periods. But here in psychology he feels as if he is redeeming himself.

Freud's defense mechanisms are particularly interesting to Don because he can see people using them in everyday life. Halfway through the defense mechanisms the bell rings. That's the way time is, whenever you are doing something you enjoy, it goes by quickly.

"So when can we study for this class together?" Answar asks Don

"I don't know maybe next week Tuesday." Don

"How about this weekend? You could come to my house. You've never been to my house and my parents want to meet you." Answar sounds real gay to Don. Don is embarrassed because he feels as if Answar is coming on to him. How gross.

"Sorry Answar, I have to work Saturday and I'm going to the studio Sunday. Monday, I'm working after school so it will have to be Tuesday in the library." Don

"Fine," says Answar as he storms out the room. Don finds himself alone in the room with the exception of Sheena and Professor Pavlove who are engaged in a deep conversation. Don becomes mesmerized by Sheena. Her back is to him and he is hypnotized by the view. It is as if he is having an awareness of the beauty around him.

Sheena must have felt the beams coming from his eyes because she turns around to look at him. She smiles so beautifully that Don feels his heartbeat speed up. She is more lovely than he had every noticed. He feels like he could stare at her forever.

"Don you're gonna be late for class." He can hear someone speaking to him, but it isn't Sheena or Professor Pavlove. "Don. Don!" It is Fatima. She must have come in while Sheena's ass had him in a trance

As cool as he can, he walks over to Fatima and kisses her. They walk hand and hand towards the exit, but just before they make that ninety degree turn out the door, Don takes one last glance at Sheena. Sure enough, she is looking his way. "She's next," Don thinks to himself. "After Fatima, Sheena is next."

"Damn Fatima. Were not even married yet you already boss me around." Don knows marriage is a word that always softens a woman's heart. As they enter Social Studies Fatima has a huge happy smile on her face while Don has a big sly grin on his face.

(Chapter 4)
LET'S DO IT AGAIN

"Well Ms. Sadae and Mr. Breyer. So glad you could join us," remarks Mr. Cohen the Social Studies teacher. "Unfortunately Mr. Breyer your presence is needed in the Dean's office."

"Huh, what did I do!?" Don

"I have no knowledge of the matter. I am simply relaying a message that was given to me. It's a request that you report to the Dean's office. M'kay."

Without another word, Don backs out the door. "Damn," he ponders to himself. "What am I guilty of now?"

His heart is beating profoundly as he nears the Dean's office. The first person he sees in the office is Jackie. Because of the way the Dean's office is situated, Jackie sees Don before the Dean does. The moment she makes eye contact with him she begins yelling at the Dean, "I was in the girls bathroom 1st and 2nd period with a bad case of diarrhea, is that a crime?!"

"Shut up!" Screams the Dean as he gets up from his seat. "I was looking all over for you second period. I know you went to class third period, but where the hell were you second period?"

At that moment Don enters the office. "Oh I see," says the Dean. "You decided to speak up now that this shit bag is here. I know both of you did not report to your second period classes. I honestly believe you were together somewhere in this school.

"I was on the toilet," says Jackie in a very stink tone.

"Where were you Donathan Breyer?" Dean

Think Don. Think Quick. Nothing. "I, I, I was on the toilet too."

"Bullshit," screams the Dean. "I checked all of the boy's rooms looking for you. So where were you taking a dump?"

"I, I, I..." Don

25

"He was taking a dump in the custodians' room." Jackie
"And how the hell would you know that?" Dean
"I opened the door for him." Jackie
"You did what? I don't believe none of this shit. But if that's the story you want to tell, you're both suspended."
"Suspended?" Cries Don and Jackie in unison.
"What for!?" Yells Jackie.
"You, you little thief, ought to be kicked out of school for what you did. Picking locks is a criminal offense."
"Fine," says Jackie. "But what is he getting suspended for?"
"Him!?" Screams back the dean. "You are more worried about saving his ass that your own. I am suspending him for using facilities that were not his to use."
"You know the boys bathroom toilets don't have doors. If he took a shit in there, the whole school would be snapping on him by lunchtime." Jackie continues Dons defense.
Don can see the Dean is taken back by Jackie. It's the way she speaks to him that seems to take the fight out of him.
Don begins to feel pity for the man.
"Okay" says the dean in a low voice. "Three days suspension for you Ms. Michaels. Starting tomorrow. And Don..... you better watch your back cause I'm a be on you like white on rice. Now both of you get out of my face!"
As they exit the deans room Don fells like scum. Jackie just saved his ass. What a strong woman she is. She talked back to the Dean. And what kind of man he is. "I couldn't even speak up for myself," thinks Don.
"Wow Jackie, thank you so much. I have really seen a new you today. I'm impressed." Don
"Shit" said Jackie. "You couldn't come up with a better lie than that. What the hell am I gonna tell my moms? Suspended Again!?" Jackie
Jackie pushes the door to the stairway so hard that it slams against the wall. She knows her reaction went too far so she looks behind her to see if any of the authorities are around.
Luckily the hallways are deserted. They walk into the

stairwell but instead of going up she starts to go down.
"Jackie," Don says in a whisper "Where are you going?
The classes are upstairs." Don
"Just shut up and come on." Jackie
Once again Don finds himself going to the boiler room with
Jackie.
"Look Jackie," Don says once they are in the back of the
boiler room. "Don't you think this is crazy? We just got
busted for spending second period here and now we're back
here fourth period?!"
"Shut up and strip," Jackie says with a laugh! "You ought
to be thanking me for covering your ass? So don't give me
no lip and do what I tell you to do!"
Don is stunned, he feels like she is playing him cheap.
Here he is being order to give up the goods and he feels as if
he has no choice. Jackie sits, lights up a joint and stares at
him as if she wants to eat him alive.
"You know" says Don. "This is sexual harassment. I
could have you arrested for this."
Jackie passes Don the joint and Don takes it.
"Don, you have to learn to relax. Come here." Jackie
Don goes to her and sits on the couch next to her. She
begins massaging his shoulders. After a few minutes the
chocolate tye and Jackie's rubbing takes effect. He starts to
relax. Jackie's roaming hands go lower and lower. She
unbuttons his shit, his belt and jeans with such ease that
Don's in awe. "Women are so graceful," thinks Don. "Men
fumble on buttons and belts while women do it so casually."
Caught in Jackie's web, Don begins to kiss her ferociously.
He decides that he wants to please this woman and give her
the pleasure she is giving him. He starts by caressing her
neck, her shoulders and breast, kissing her all over. Within
moments they are both semi naked in the back of the boiler
room, entirely engrossed in each other. If the whole school
was down there watching them, they probably would have
not noticed.
When he touches her womanhood, it is so juicy and

27

swollen that his manhood grows even harder. This turns her on more because she has her hands on his oysters and feels how hard he gets. Don is no Don Juan or super lover, but he has been with older women who taught him the joys of satisfying another.

"Oh Jackie," Don says in his sex voice. "I wanna be in you so bad it hurts." He can feel her tremble. He rubs on her clit with one hand and gently pulls her hair with the other." She is cumin and he has not even entered her yet. He can feel the wetness soaking his fingers. "She has such a sweet smell," thinks Don.

Jackie gets up and stands in front of Don. His manhood is sticking up like the empire state building. Still facing him, she sits on his lap and wraps her legs around his back. They kiss passionately as they do a slow grind. Don feels strong so he stands with her still wrapped around him and they continue to pound at each other.

Then he lies on the couch with Jackie on top. Her moans get deeper and her friction harder and faster. Don can feel himself about to burst and knows she is on the verge of an orgasm. He grabs her butt, squeezes and pulls it up and down. She screams with the ecstasy of her climax as he explodes inside her.

It is at that moment that Don realizes he is not wearing a jimmy hat. "Oh well it's much too late now," thinks Don. Jackie is spent, as she lays limp in his arms trying to catch her breath. Before they can recuperate the bell rings and brings back Dons anxiety. "Jackie it's lunch time, we should bounce."

"Love them and leave them, that's your style." Jackie
"No Jackie I just don't want to get you in any more trouble."
"I'm just kidding Don, besides I'm starving." Jackie
"Cool" replies Don. "Just do me one favor."
"Anything." Jackie
"Do something with your hair, your doo is beat girl," and they laugh. As Jackie gets up Dons dick slowly slides out of

her vagina and they both moan as it comes out.

"We didn't use any protection," Don. "And I don't have anything to wipe up with."

"Do you have a condom?" Jackie

"No." Don

"Well alright then, and besides I want you to smell like my pussy for the rest of the day." Jackie says as she starts fixing her hair and putting her clothes back on. "Oh by the way how did you get that bruise on your arm?"

"Oh shit my arm. I forgot all about it." Don takes his first look at the scabby gash on his arm, it begins to hurt. He knows it has to be mental because it didn't pain him until he takes notice of it.

"So what the hell happened?" Jackie

"I jumped off of Mt. Morris!" Don

"You jumped off Mt. Morris?! For what?" Jackie

"5-0 was coming." Don

"You're crazy," says Jackie as she kisses his lips. "But don't expect me to kiss that thing," she points to his cut. "You really need to clean that out before it gets infected." Jackie

It doesn't take her long to get dressed and finish fixing her hair. "So how does it look?"

"Much better, much much much better" Don. They laugh. "Ya know Jackie I don't think I have any pictures of you." Don takes out his camera and Jackie poses sexily. "Say cheese."

"Cheese." Jackie. Click.

(Chapter 5)
READY TO RUMBLE

Don and Jackie decide to exit the boiler room separately. Don leaves first, two minutes later Jackie makes her way out. Luckily they both get to the lunchroom undetected. There is a line of students waiting to get their lunch. Don gets on the back of the line behind Bruce, a fellow senior. Bruce is a big sports fanatic. Although he only plays baseball he can answer damn near any question about football, basketball or baseball. If sports were a major he would be valedictorian.

"So who you going for in the super bowl this year?" asks Bruce.

"Who else?" Don comments, "Pittsburgh. They have so much talent I think they'll do it for the next few years."

"True, but don't sleep on Dallas or Greenbay." Bruce

"Did you see the Lakers the other day?" Don

"Hell yeah, did you see how Kobe dunked that alley-oop?" Bruce

"Word it went Boom!" They say in unison and slap each other a high five. It is then that Don notices Jackie in front of the line getting her lunch. "That girl is something else," says Don.

"Who?" Bruce asks looking around to see who he is talking about. Clearly Jackie stands out in her skin tight skirt and leather boots.

"Yeah she's definitely butters. But don't look too hard because Johnny's ready to catch a body over her. Just give him a reason." Bruce

"And what the hell is that supposed to mean?" Don

"Johnny be bugging. He got mad skills in basketball, so he thinks even if he doesn't graduate, he'll still get picked up. He thinks he's the shit. And he has a big shank."

"Word?! How do you know?" Don

"He showed it to a couple of us last period. He's an

accident waiting to happen." Bruce

With fifteen minutes left to eat and get to their next class, they get their lunches and take seats in a fairly deserted part of the lunchroom. In between chomps of his burger, Bruce runs off at the mouth about sports, and Don just listens when Fatima approaches.

"Hey Don" chimes Fatima as she kisses him on the cheek and takes a seat next to him.

"Hey cutie," replies Don.

Fatima puts her face next to his neck and starts sniffing. She sniffs around his face and chest like a hound dog picking up a scent.

"What are you doing Fatima?" Don

Fatima sniffs "You smell like.." sniff. "You smell ..." sniff. "You smell like..." She grabs his hand sniffs his fingers and screams out loud. "You smell like pussy!" Now the whole lunchroom becomes quiet and focused on the drama at hand.

"You've been fucking. Who have you been fucking?" She stands up and yells. "How could you do this? Don't you have any respect for me to even wash your funky ass before you come to school?"

Don is speechless. And he really does not even want to say anything. All he wants is for the earth to open up and swallow him. He takes a look at the crowd around him and through everyone he sees Jackie looking and grinning in amusement. He pans around and sees Johnny staring with the ice grill standing next to the dean.

"Look bitch," Don hears himself say. "I haven't been hitting any skins and you ain't been giving up no ass, so get the fuck out of my face with that weak shit!"

Fatima stands stationary as the tears rain from her eyes. Don gets up and walks out of the lunchroom. He can hear the murmuring behind him but he never bothers to look back.

Straight to the gym he goes. He has gym the last two periods of every Friday. He likes it that way because he believes it is a good way to end the week. He can play ball and lift weights just before the weekend begins.

Don should be hungry but he has lost his appetite. He walks through the empty gym, into the locker room and puts on his gym clothes. He does some stretches and goes to the weight room. It is empty. He adjusts the bench press to 200lbs lays down and starts pressing. He closes his eyes as he tries to escape from the pandemonium he feels inside.

What seems like a second to Don is almost half an hour. When he opens his eyes he feels as if he can't move his arms. He is sweating and there are other students in the room working out.

"Dam Fool, I thought you would never stop. You did way over a hundred presses." Daz a transfer student from L.A. remarks.

Don just lays there. Too weak to even reply.

"So can another nigga get strong too?" Daz asks waiting to use the bench press.

"Help me up fool." Don says in a mocking west coast drawl. Once up Don can really feel the strain in his arms, chest, stomach and neck. He has to stretch. After stretching he does some laps around the basketball court. Beginning to feel loose, he joins in on a game of twenty-one already in progress.

Don has one of those rare moments in basketball where he doesn't seem to miss a shot. It's not that he usually stinks, he just isn't a Michael Jordan or Reggie Miller. He concluded at an early age that he would never go pro. This time however, he is hustling, playing defense and, having one of his best games.

When he enters the game, Drew has sixteen, Tony has 9 and Gary has 4 points. Don hits eighteen straight points before anyone else scores again. Then another player steps into the game. It is Johnny. Tony is at the foul line. He shoots. The ball hits the rim and bounces off. Everyone jumps for the rebound. The ball is tapped in Don's direction. He grabs the ball and heads to the basket for a layup. All of the players put up defense. Don's warning light goes off when he sees Johnny coming to his left with his elbow in full

32

effect. Don takes a big step back just in time to miss the elbow as he shoots a jumper. Gary who is also d-ing Don unfortunately catches the end of Johnny's elbow to his jaw. It is a bit funny because the crack noise of Johnny's elbow to Gary's jaw sounds simultaneously with the swish of Don's jumper.

Johnny looks around like he is totally innocent and unaware of what just happened. Gary bends down holding his jaw in pain. Don feels nervous. The last thing he wants is to have to fight Johnny.

After a few minutes Gary walks off the court with a busted lower lip.

"Later Gary!" Johnny Yells

"He doesn't even apologize," Don thinks to himself. "I know that elbow was meant for me." He goes to the foul line and without giving it much thought he shoots. Swish.

"Game."

"Game?!" Johnny screams. "Run it" he says as he passes the ball with hated force back to Don.

"Nah, I'm straight." Don says passing the ball back to him. "I'm a jump in the pool."

"Yeah a-ight punk!" Johnny replies, "But I will be seeing ya." The tension is in the air. Even the other players can sense it.

"Cool," Don says taking it more like an invitation than a threat, "Take it easy." But he knows exactly what Johnny means.

Don walks straight to the pool. There is a rule that anyone entering the pool has to shower beforehand. Don doesn't follow the rule. He just takes off his shirt, socks, sneakers and jumps in the pool. Being a decent swimmer, he swims from one side of the pool to the other without coming up for air. He is beginning to relax. "Hopefully" he thinks to himself, "I can get through today in one piece." Back under he goes to swim to the other side. The water is warm and refreshing. He almost wishes he could stay under forever.

As he gets closer to the other side of the pool, he sees a

figure approaching. As soon as he comes up for air he is hit by a flying kick to the shoulder that sends him back under. Without seeing exactly who is attacking him Don knows it is Johnny. He can see Johnny coming closer for another attack.

Without going up for air Don quickly swims to Johnny's feet. He grabs Johnny's ankles and flips him under.

With Johnny under the water, Don frantically tries to get out of the pool. He makes it to the side of the pool only to be taken into a headlock and pulled back into the water.

Johnny's grip is so tight that neither air nor water can get through Don's lungs. Don knows that he will surely die if he does not fight back hard. Using all the strength he has, Don is able to loosen Johnny's choke hold and lift his arm up, just enough to bite it. Johnny immediately releases him. Don comes up gasping for and tries to get out of the pool. Again he is pulled back in, hitting his head on the side of the pool before going under once more. Kicking furiously as Johnny tries to grab his legs, Don manages to get a good kick into Johnny's groin. Still gasping for air, Don manages to get out of the pool. For the first time he notices the small crowd of students forming. Then he sees Johnny getting out of the pool.

Without knowing what has come over him, Don runs toward Johnny and kicks him dead in the face. As Johnny flies backwards into the pool, Don can see the blood trickling out of Johnny's mouth. Feeling the job isn't done, he jumps into the pool on top of Johnny and holds his face under the water.

Johnny would have certainly died had not some students jumped in the pool and pried Don off of him. Don is more afraid of what Johnny will try do to him, than he is afraid of Johnny himself. He knows this is not over.

Before Johnny can regain his senses, Don is out the pool headed toward the locker room. He wants to get dressed and get the hell out of there quickly. He feels very nervous as he dry's off and puts his clothes on. He expects something to jump off at any minute. He knows the authorities will soon be around. He is actually surprised that none have showed up all the time he was fighting.

"Don!" Don hears his name called and jumps up ready to fight or take flight.

"Hey I've been looking for you," it is Answar. "After that commotion with Fatima, I heard you had a fight with Johnny and oh my God Don your face is all bruised."

Answar sounds so gay that Don can't take it anymore. "Listen to yourself Answar. You sound like a faggot! I don't swing that way so don't come off to me like that!" Hastily grabbing his knapsack, his camera falls out. As he picks it up to look for damage the camera accidentally goes off in Answar face. Answar thinks Don did it on purpose.

"Fuck you!" Answar says in a manly tone that surprises Don. He is slightly relieved to see the man come out of Answar. But those feelings are quickly crushed when Answar breaks down crying. Without another word Don is out the back doors of the school in a flash.

"What a way to start the weekend," he thinks to himself, "Anu please continue to guide and watch over me."

(Chapter 6)
FAMILY TIES

Don arrives home in less than thirty minutes. As he walks by his dad's room he can hear his dad snoring through the closed door. Upon entering his own room, the phone begins to ring. Looking at the caller I.D., he recognizes that it's his school. Using a deep voice he answers it. "Hello"

"May I speak to a parent or guardian of Donathan Breyer." Don recognizes the principles voice.

"Yes, this is Mr. Breyer." Don replies

"Your son has been involved in a fight today. The other student is hurt pretty bad. He has a broken nose and, he was almost drowned by Don. Of course you understand that disciplinary actions will have to be taken. I'll need you to come in A.S.A.P. Preferably Monday morning. Don cannot continue his classes until you come in," says the principle.

Knowing damn well who it is on the other line, Don asks "Who am I speaking too?" Just for effect.

"This is Ms. Castilla the principle."

"Thank you" says Don, as he hangs up the phone, grateful that he caught the phone call and not his dad or grandmother.

"Now how the hell am I going to get out of this jam," he thinks. "Stay positive Don. Jesus please show me the way through this," he prays.

Minutes later he is in a hot shower feeling the force of the water massaging his back. He tries to relax and he feels very sleepy. He quickly washes, rinses and jumps out of the shower. After drying off, Don ties the towel around his waist and proceeds to exit the bathroom.

"What is this?!" His grandma yells, surprising Don with a sudden verbal attack. "It's another late slip," his granny continues. "For the rest of the school year I want you to leave before me! You didn't come all this way through school to not graduate because you are constantly late. You can't get into a good college by being late. You better get it

36

together and stop trying to be like those stupid niggers you hang out with." Without another word she storms away.

Feeling as if all the life has been sucked out of him, Don retreats into his bedroom. He crawls into bed wanting only one thing....to sleep!

Five minutes in the bed and he is fast asleep. "Ring, ring, ring," goes the phone.

"Hello," says Don groggily.

"Damn nigger, you ain't woke yet?" It is D.J. He is a DJ who lets Don rhyme in his home music studio.

"What up D.J." Don

"Just wanna know what's up for tonight. Do you still wanna do this?" Asks D.J.

"Yeah of course. You heard from Nate?" Don

"Nah, but he knows we've been meeting every Friday to cipher." D.J.

"I'll be there." Don

"True. And yo, bring a bag of that good shit." D.J.

"Indeed. Check ya later" Don

"Out." D.J.

"Peace." Don. Click

Sleep once again comes easy. Rapid eye movement steps in when "Ring, ring, ring," off goes the phone again.

"Hello" says Don

"Daddy"

"Damian? Is that you?" asks Don

"Dadd-dee," Damian repeats wit a giggle.

"I love you. I miss you." Says Don

"I wuv you daddee," Damian says and laughs.

Damian Is his son. He is almost two and a half and very bright. When Damian was first born, Don didn't know how to react to him. All Damian seemed to do was cry and want Lydia, his mother. Before Damian turned one, Don stopped going to see him and Lydia. But he couldn't get it out of his mind that he had a seed. About six months ago Don went to see them. It was a Friday. Since then Don has spent nearly every Friday with his son after school. About three months ago Damian started calling him "Daddy." The joy he receives from that one word has been immense. Now Don looks forward to spending time with his son and he likes to dress Damian in the latest gear.

"Hello Don." Lydia takes the phone from Damian.

"Hey honey how are you doing?" Don

"Fine, you sound tired." Lydia

"Well I was trying to take a nap." Don

"Oh does that mean you are not coming over today?" asks Lydia

"Of course I am. I was just gonna catch some z's first. Why what's up?" Don

"Well I wanted to fix a nice dinner and I needed someone to watch Damian while I ran to the supermarket. If you will watch him for an hour you can sleep here while I'm cooking."

"Hmm, whatcha cooking?" Don

"Pork chops & black eye peas."

"You know I don't eat no pork and how you gonna be feeding that poison to my seed?"

"Gosh I was only kidding. I'm making baked chicken, mash potatoes, and greens."

"If you throw in your delicious cornbread I'll be there in a half."

"You Got It." Lydia

"In a minute" Don

"Bye" Click

Don takes a minute to reflect on how much Lydia and Damian means to him. Even when he stopped coming around, she still called him every other week or so to see how he was doing and to tell him how Damian was. She is a beautiful woman whose only flaw in Don's eyes is her body type. She is very petite at 5 ft 1and a buck even. She is also ten years Don's senior. However he is happy it was her who got pregnant out of all the honeys he went into raw. Since Lydia became pregnant Don has worn his jimmy hats religiously. That is up until today with Jackie. "Never

again" He says to himself. "Never again," as he jumps out of bed throws on the Notorious B.I.G. and proceeds to get dressed while singing along to suicidal thoughts...
When I die Fuck it I wanna go to hell
Cause I'm a piece of shit it
It ain't hard to fucking tell...

(Chapter 7)
NUT

"Grandma, I'm sorry about being late. I was just trying to get in a good breakfast and I was no more than five minutes late both times," swears Don. "And I promise it won't happen again."

Don is the apple of his grandma's eyes. Everything that her son wasn't she hoped and prayed that Don would be. She has already secretly mailed out dozen of college applications for Don. Letters, transcripts, fees, the works. She is determined to make sure Don is given a chance to go to college. "Okay baby. I didn't mean to yell. It's just that you can do so well if you put your mind to it. You can become a man and stand on your own two big feet and be proud."

"I love you too mom." Don says as he kisses his grandma on the cheek. "And I probably won't be back home tonight."

"Your starting to spend the night out more times than not. Who is she?" Granny inquires.

Under pressure Don blurts out, "Nicole, her name is Nicole." Don doesn't like lying, but his grandmother doesn't know about Damian. He just doesn't know how to tell her. So he likes to stay as far away from the subject as possible. He knows it would bring her great pain. Then it would hurt her even more because it took him so long to tell her.

"Where did you meet her?" Grandma

"At work" Don lies even though there actually is someone there named Nicole. "We're going to hang out tonight and then go to work together in the morning. But mom, you see its top secret because we don't want the other workers in our business. We hardly say anything to each other at work."

Grandma laughs. Don throws on his backpack.

"Love you grandma bye." Don

"Bye Baby, take care and call me from work tomorrow so I

know you alright." Grandma doesn't like Don spending the night out, especially at some unknown female's house. But she knows Dons hormones are running overtime and she does not allow that hanky panky stuff to go on in her house. She says a prayer for Don and sits down to watch Oprah's new network.

It's a nice afternoon, and under the circumstances Don is feeling sort of good. He thinks about Monday and knows he will have to pray for a miracle to keep today's incident away from his Dad. This is something his dad would definitely blow out of proportion. He hates when his dad gets all loud, even though it seems to be the only way his father communicates. Otherwise they hardly speak. Deep down Don feels that his father blames him for his mother's death. In a way it kind of was his fault. It was about four years ago that he begged his mother repeatedly for a new pair of Jordan's.

The day before his fourteenth birthday she went to foot locker and charged over $130.00 for one pair of Jordan's. Half a block away from the store, right on 125th street a teenager tries to snatch the bag from her hand. There was a struggle, he pulled out a gun, shot twice and ran off with the kicks. This happened in the late afternoon and the culprit has never been caught nor had anybody seen a thing. Needless to say, Don has not celebrated a birthday since. While his father, on the other hand, chose to climb in a liquor bottle for safety and comfort.

Without even thinking about it, Don walks to a weed spot on 156th street and buys 2 dime bags marked 'Arizona'. He takes his MP3 out of his knapsack and prepares for the 12 block walk to Lydia's house. He puts on his downloaded copy of Joe. It is one of his favorite CD's. The player automatically goes to his favorite song called 'Alone'. As Don crosses the street, Joe sings
"It's like being in a crowded room with no familiar faces, It's like thinking I can see your face in unfamiliar places....."

He walks about five blocks when someone starts calling his name. Unfortunately he cannot hear the person because Joe is bumpin Better Days into his headphones. Then someone taps him on his shoulder. Don is startled and almost drops his MP3.

"Yo! Yo! What up!" Don gets ready to throw blows.

"Hey chill Bro. I was calling you for two blocks. But I guess you couldn't hear me because you had your headphones on."

Don knows he knows the guy speaking to him but he can't quite remember his name. Nut?" Don inquires. Thinking he may recognize the cat.

"Yeah it's me, Nut from 151."

"But, but they said you were dead. I remember you supposedly died right before my mom died." It shocked Don to hear himself say his mom died. He couldn't remember actually ever verbalizing it.

"Hey little brother I'm sorry to hear about your moms. I just wanted to say what up to you because I haven't seen you in so long."

"Yeah I remember you. You use to get all the honeys. That's why they called you Nut. I also remember you use to ride me down the hill on your skateboard. Man that was a long skateboard. Three people could stand on it. Whatever happened to that skateboard?" Don

"That Damn thing! Man it was split in half by a bus!" Nut

"A Bus?!"

"Hell yeah. And praise Saint Mary, K-ci and Jo-Jo, I fell off of the board or it might have been me split in two too!" Nut

They laugh.

"So what you been doing with yourself Don?"

"I've been chillin trying stay out of trouble, but it follows me everywhere I go." Don

"Damn Nigga you too young to be singing the blues. I was just headed to the park to smoke a joint." Nut

"Say word!" Don

"Word. Do you doobie?" Nut

"I doobie do. You want me to get a couple of cold ones?"

"Nah I don't drink alcohol. But I wouldn't mind a Snapple." Nut

They get two Ice teas and walk to the park. They find a bench not far from some fellows playing a game of two hand touch football. Nut pulls out a pack of easy wider.

"Are you really gonna roll a joint?" Don

"I thought you said you puff?" Nut

"I do smoke. But I don't smoke joints." Don

"I don't puff nothing but weed duke, so I don't know what you are talking about." Nut

"I smoke white owls." Don

"White owls?" Nut

"Yeah nigga, blunts." Yo, put your shit away. I'm a roll a blunt." Don pulls out a bag of weed.

"Yo is that a nick?" Nut

"Nah it's a dime." Don

"Word, I thought it was kinda fat for a nick. Damn homey, you put half the fucking bag in there! That's a five dollar mega joint!"

"It's a blunt. Ain't you ever smoked a blunt before?" Don

"Nah man. I only smoke weed from bongs, pipes or paper."

It takes Don about two minutes to break up the buds and roll a fatty. He lights it and takes about seven deep pulls before passing it to Nut. "Take light pulls because you inhale more smoke than a joint."

Nut takes a hit. While holding the smoke in his lungs, he says "Not Bad" then he starts to cough, gag and spit.

"Yo dude you alright?" Don

"Strong shit." He says as he passes the blunt back to Don. Don takes about seven more good pulls of the blunt and passes it to Nut again. This time Nut is able to keep his composure. "So Nut where you been anyway? What happened to you?"

"I'm surprised you don't know. You haven't heard any

rumors?" Nut

"Nah. Actually all I remember was someone saying you caught the bug and passed away!" Don.

"Half true," said Nut while passing the spliff back to Don. "Remember Tara from 154th? She had twins. A boy and a girl." Nut

"Tara?!! Yo is that the one who died of AIDS. Didn't her kids die too?" Don

"Yeah that's the one." Nut

"I remember after her babies died, she started smoking crack and selling her ass. A few of my homies ran a train on her. It was more like a rape scene. Niggas called me pussy cause I wouldn't join in." Don

"It's good that you didn't. I used to hit it though. She was really a nice girl. She just liked to have sex. She liked to cum." Nut reflects on the past.

"Yo! Yo! What you mean you use to hit it." Don

"Yeah man, I hit on a regular for some time. Way before she started hoeing. Still, a few years ago one of my other girlfriends told me she was HIV positive. At first I didn't want to believe it. I continued my rampage doing the honeys raw. After about six months I knew things weren't right. I could feel it inside. I felt like my insides were decaying!" Nut

Nut now has Dons' full attention. He wants to know how Nut has risen from the land of the dead. Nut continues, "Luckily I have an uncle who is an herbologist. He studies herbs and uses only natural medicines. I became his trainee while he took care of me," Nut says while taking the blunt

"How did he treat your HIV? And how do you know you are cured?" Don asks as he realizes he is smoking a blunt with someone who had or has AIDS.

"It's sort of complicated so I'll just break it down slightly. My uncle put me on a very rigid diet of oranges, pineapples, and lemon for breakfast. Sesame butter or toasted grain bread for lunch. And alfalfa, soy protein burgers, and green algae for dinner. Occasionally I had sugar cane for desert.

44

No drinking with any meals, and I only drink water or fruit juices. There are also exercise and breathing routines involved." Nut

"So how do you know you are really cured?" Don

"A couple of months ago I went and got tested for the first time. The test came back negative. Man I was elated. The first thing I did was go to Mickey D's for a Big Mac." Nut

Don laughs

"Let me tell you, I'll never eat it again. Halfway through my burger I start feeling sick. For the rest of the day, I was out of it with mad stomachs problems. I've learned how important it is to eat right!" Nut

By now the blunt is gone and Don begins to faintly recollect that he is supposed to be doing something. "A yo what time is it?" Don

"It's a quarter to five." Nut

"Damn man, I gotta go. I'm a get up with you next time we bump heads." Don

"Take it light little brother and remember to think five times before you make any moves." Nut

"Peace." Don

"Later." Nut

(Chapter 8)
DAMIAN AND LYDIA

As Don hot foots it the half mile walk to Lydia's house he throws on the new Jay Z and Kanye album. He especially likes 'The Joy'. Don is in front of Lydia's door before the song is over. He is jammin to the track when Lydia opens the door on her way out.

"Hey Lydia!" Don says trying to kiss her lips, but she turns her face and he kisses her cheek.

"Damian" he yells as his son jumps into his arms and gives Don a big hug. "I'm so sorry about being late I got caught up in something important."

"I'll bet," says Lydia. "You could have at least called. I didn't know if you were coming or not. Now you can stay and we'll be back in about a half," she says in mockery of Don.

Don gives his best sad puppy dog look and pleads, "Can I please go with you?"

Lydia wants to say "Hell No" but when she sees Damian replicating his father's sad face, she decides to say, "Come on" instead.

"Hey let me leave my bag here." Don

Lydia opens the door and Don steps in, passes the kitchen into the living room. He puts his bag on the floor against the couch and senses something is different about the living room. He looks around. Most of the pictures of him are gone. There use to be lots of pictures of him. Now the only picture with him in it is one with Lydia and Damian.

Don quickly gathers his composure and puts on a smile. As he exits he tries to look as if he had not noticed a thing. While Lydia locks the door she gives him a look that makes him think she knows what he thinking.

As the trio walk towards Bravo's supermarket, Lydia begins feeling like a family. She really wants Don in her life more. But she will beg no man. And she believes it will just be a matter of time before another man sweeps her off of her feet. There are a few guys already hawking her, yet deep down she wants nothing to do with them. None of them make her feel the way Don does. "Still" she thinks "Don better be good to me and recognize what he got before I'm gone."

When Don is with Lydia and his son, he feels like a family. He acknowledges the possibilities of losing his family. Without much thought he says "Lydia, no matter who you see never keep my son away from me. Always allow me some time in his life."

Unsure where all of this is coming from, Lydia grabs Don by the arm and says, "Damian is your son and you can see him whenever you want. But don't expect me to wait for you forever."

As they near Bravos gunshots are heard about a block behind them. Quickly they dash into the supermarket for food and shelter. Damian demands to stand in the cart and refuses to sit in the part made for kids to sit. Lydia leads the way picking out items and putting them in the shopping cart. Damian points to everything he wants while Don pushes. He is deeply contemplating the whole scene. He feels that he could actually settle down with this woman. He thinks about his son calling another man daddy and he can feel himself getting heated. He is so caught up in his thoughts that he runs the cart into the aisle and knocks some cans of Hawaiian punch over.

"Don are you okay?" Lydia

"Yeah. But I think there's something wrong with the steering column on this cart." Don

Lydia smiles, "I'm still gonna have to give you a ticket."

Don really wants to be able to love Lydia the way she should be loved. He knows however that she would have to be his only. And he knows that he cannot continue to be a part-time father to his son. "Take it step by step and day by day," Don tells himself.

They get to the checkout counter and surprising don't have

to wait on a long line. Don starts packing the items as they are being checked out. After all of the items are scanned he pays the cashier before Lydia has a chance to take her money out. "It's the little things Don does like this, that makes me love him so much," thinks Lydia, as the nuclear family leaves the supermarket.

A block away from Bravos a crowd is gathered around an ambulance. As they get closer Don can see the crowd standing around a body. Telling Lydia and his son to wait for one moment, Don walks closer to the body. What he sees is someone who has been shot dead. A young man about his age. Caught like so many of us, in a crossfire that he had nothing to do with. A victim of the gun fire that Don and his people had missed by minutes. The very bullets they heard ringing out as they ran into the supermarket. Don feels a sadness overcome him. Although he did not know the young brother, just the thought of the grief this unfortunate death will cause a family makes him want to scream out. Instead Don turns to walk away, saying a silent prayer in hopes that the brothers' soul is able to rest in peace.

Lydia says nothing to Don because his face seems to say it all. She wonders if Don knew the victim but decides she will wait to see if he wants to talk about it later. Don appreciates her silence, and they all stay quiet for the rest of the way back to the house.

Damian falls asleep within minutes of arriving home. Lydia starts to cook and Don takes the portable boom box that he leaves there out on the stoop. There he twists the second and last blunt out of one of the dimes he purchased earlier. Halfway through the blunt Lydia walks out onto the stoop and lights a Newport. They are both silent as they watch the sun disappear behind New Jersey.

Lydia is looking extra attractive this evening. He's feeling lonely and she seems to have a radiance about her. He longs for the comfort of his mother. For the comfort of a woman who could give him the warmth his mother gave him and more. He is feeling so vulnerable that he knows he has to check himself. He does not want to say anything he doesn't mean or would regret later because of his need for passion. He remembers that Lydia has tried a few times to use her pussy as bait to a promise. What man in his right mind can tell a woman "No I don't love you," while he's deep inside her.

"Dinner won't be ready for at least an hour. Would you like to play some cards or scrabble?" Lydia

"Nah, but I wouldn't mind watching a movie or something." Don

"Okay. Look through the DVD's and pick one." Lydia

Don gets up to go to the video stacks and Lydia steps in his path. With her looking up to him and him looking down to her she asks, "Are you okay? You look sad."

Without saying a word, he pulls her into his arms and gives her a long, passionate french kiss. After the fiery kiss, he says, "I feel fine, how about you?"

Caught completely off guard by his actions, she feels turned on and giddy. "I'm fine thank you." Lydia

Don walks over to the DVD collection. There are lots of movies and most of them are badly made bootleg copies. "I haven't bought any new movies in a while. I haven't really watched a whole movie in a long time." Lydia

Don looks through the selection. "I've never seen 'Waiting to Exhale'" he replies. "I remember when you let me read the book."

"I could watch it again." Lydia "I just hope they make a movie of 'Disappearing Acts' one day."

"I think they did. You know, you would make a wonderful Zora." Don

"And you would be a typical Franklin." Lydia

"Oh low blow. But then again he wasn't so bad. He did make honey with the bees." Don

"Oh really. And just what is that supposed to mean? Making honey with the bees?" Lydia

"You know, he made the ladies cream." Don

"Oh so you think you make the ladies cream?" Lydia

49

"You're the one who said I was a typical Franklin. All I'm saying is that women found him attractive, so if you compare me to him I'll take it as a compliment." Don

"Well just like Franklin you need to work on your constitution." Lydia

"Work on my constitution?!" Don

"Yes you have to come to grips with what it means to be a man." Lydia

"So a woman is gonna tell me what makes a man? Well let me tell you what makes a woman!" Don

"You don't have to tell me what makes a woman. I am a woman. I have responsibilities and I take care of them!" Lydia

"And I don't take care of mine?" Don

"I didn't say that." Lydia

"So what are you saying?" Don

"All I'm saying is that a real man makes commitments and sticks to them." Lydia

"So that's what this is all about. You want more commitment from me?!" Don

"I don't need commitment. You need commitment or life is gonna pass you by." Lydia

"You're not saying what you really mean but I know what you are trying to say. You miss me when I'm gone and you would like me to spend more time with you." Don

"I used to miss you. But since you are gone more than you are here, I don't miss you as much. But, Damian misses you and that bothers me." Lydia

Don begins to feel as if he is being cornered. He knows that Lydia wants him to make a promise that he will come around more.

She is thinking that she may be pushing him too fast too soon. Don is not perfect but he treats her a lot better than some of the other knuckleheads she has dated. She also thinks about how young he is and how she does not want to scare him away.

"Maybe we should just watch a different movie." Don says

breaking the silence. "How about Space Jam or Set It Off?" It is then that Don notices that Lydia has her hand over her face. She is crying. "Tears," thinks Don. "The oldest trick in the book."

"Lydia what's wrong?" He asks as he sits next to her and puts his arm around her. She cries for about ten to fifteen minutes without saying a word. Don doesn't know what to say so he just holds her in his arms and rubs her back. The more he rubs, the closer she cuddles into him. The more she cuddles the more his hand begins to wonder. Then her lips begin to roam around his neck and somewhere in between, their tongues commence to do battle with one another. Passion flows between them as his hand caresses every part of her body. Things are getting pretty heated when they hear "Mommy I'm hungry." It is Damian, awake and ready to eat.

"Dinner will be ready in about 15 minutes." Lydia jumps up while trying to regain her composure.

"Group hug!" Don yells. Grabbing Damian with his left arm and holding Lydia with his right. With both of them in his grasp he squeezes till they scream with delight.

"Maybe," Don thinks "I can get used to this family stuff.

(Chapter 9)
MY SISTERS KEEPER

Shortly after the meal Damian falls back to sleep. Lydia and Don pause the movie so they can clean up the dishes. "I'm going to stop at the store while I'm taking out the garbage, do you want something?" Asks Don

"I don't know, what are you going to get?" Lydia

"I'll probably get beer and popcorn."

"Well yeah, get me a Heineken and a pack of Newports."
Lydia

On the way to the store, Don contemplates taking a detour to the nearest weed spot on 145th street. He checks to see how much cash flow he has and decides he must stop at an ATM. While crossing the street to the bank, Don notices there is a full moon out and it's barely 8:00 P.M. Just before he reaches the bank, the door fly open and out runs two young men. Hesitant to walk in he contemplates going somewhere else. All of a sudden a young lady stumbles out of the bank holding her stomach. She reaches toward him and falls into his arms. Bleeding and smearing blood all over him.

"It's gonna be alright," he says as he helps the woman to her feet. "I'm gonna get you to a hospital." Quickly he hails a cab "Columbia Presbyterian emergency entrance and step on it!" The woman is not making any noise and he is worried that he is losing her. Her eyes are shut and it looks as if she is not breathing. "I must keep her awake" he senses. "Ms, Ms please wake up" Don says while slapping her face softly and firmly. He is about to panic when she opened her eyes. "Hold on for a bit longer miss, we'll be to the hospital shortly." Before he has to worry further they are pulling in front of the emergency entrance.

"That'll be eight bucks," says the cab driver. Don reaches in his pocket and pulls out his last twenty. He gives it to the driver and jumps out of the cab. Having a hard time holding the woman up, he tries to turn around to get his change from the driver when the cab speeds off.

"Hey asshole!" Screams Don.

At that moment a security guard approaches. "Is there a problem here?" Guard.

"Yes this woman has been hurt. She is bleeding from her stomach," Don. Within seconds paramedics have her in the emergency room receiving treatment.

" I'm going to need you to fill out these forms," says a nurse to Don.

"Well I don't know the woman. I was about to use an ATM when she fell into my arms."

"Oh. Well hopefully she will have some kind of I.D. on her. Please wait here," nurse.

"Wait here?" thinks Don. "Why I got to wait here? What more can I do?"

After a long few minutes, Don is ready to be ghost when a boy in blue approaches.

"Are you the man who brought the unidentified woman into emergency?" Don is surprised that the cop called him a man. A respect he seldom receives, especially not from 5-0.

"Yes I brought in a woman with a stomach wound," replies Don. "How is she doing?"

"Shes in critical condition," answers the cop who looks more like a homeboy in a uniform. The way he walks and the way he wears his clothes is that of a street cat. "Can you tell me what happened?" Asks the officer as he flips out his pen and pad. Don tells the officer everything except that he saw two guys running out of the bank just before the woman came out. In so many ways Don wants to tell the cop, but he just doesn't want to get into it any deeper.

"If that's all, I would really like to be on my way," Don.

"No doubt," the cop says making Don smile. "But, I would appreciate a name and number from you in case I need to ask you a few more questions." Don gives the cop his real name and number and kind of wishes he hadn't. He really doesn't want to get involved.

"Hey Donathan," the cop calls. "If you still need to use the ATM I could give you a lift."

"Nah that's alright," replies Don. Thinking about his cash flow and the long walk to Lydia's house he quickly changes his mind. "Well alright," says Don feeling somewhat nervous to be in the presence of po po. But as they drive down Broadway Don begins to feel important. Here he is in a police car and he is not under arrest. He is even in the front seat no doubt.

"I was going to drive over to that bank to see if that woman left any I.D. Behind. You know you probably saved her life. So what do you do for yourself Donathan? Work or go to school?" inquires the officer.

"I do both," answers Don. "Why did you become a cop?" Don asks switching the attention toward the driver. "And what is your name?"

"Well my name is Butler. And please don't call me Butt. My friends call me B.J. I became a cop because it has a decent salary and I didn't see many other options for a guy like me. I know police officers can have a bad rep. I just put in my days work, pay my bills and try to keep my woman and kids happy." B.J.

"So you don't have no save the world complex?" Don

"Nah. Man has been committing crimes since day one. But take a case like today. I wouldn't think twice about arresting whoever shot that woman." B.J.

"She was shot?" Don

"Yeah, what did you think?" B.J.

"I thought she was stabbed or something." Don

"Nope. She was shot with a low caliber weapon. Still she lost a lot of blood. And you got a good amount on your coat. Soak it in cold water as soon as you get home." B.J.

"There's the bank," Don points as they drive slowly past. B.J. makes a quick u-turn and is doubled parked in front of the bank.

"Well Donathan, I'm going to go in and check things out in the bank. I hope to see you around. You play any basketball?" B.J.

"Yeah I do a lil something on the court but I don't expect to go pro. My friends call me Don and I would like to use the ATM. Which was what I came to the bank for in the first place." Don

"Aright Don, let's go kick some ass." B.J.

Don takes a liking to B.J. B.J. seems like the kind of guy he could look up to. He wonders if he too could be a cop. "Nah I couldn't arrest another brother," he thinks to himself.

Inside the bank, they find the woman's pocketbook, I.D. and paraphernalia scattered all over the floor. Picking up and an I.D. card Don comments "I Believe this is her." He passes the card to B.J. Together they pick up the rest of the woman's belongings and put them back in her pocketbook.

After they are done, Don goes to the ATM to make his transaction. For the first time he sees the blood on the floor. It's spots of drying blood that increases the closer it gets to the door. Don takes his money from the machine and wonders if he should tell B.J. about the two guys he saw running out of the bank. No, I better keep my mouth shut. "I think you can handle it from here" he says to B.J. "I need to go." They slap five and Don steps off. First to the weed spot to get three nickels. Then to the store to get wraps, brews, Newport's and candy. And then back to Lydia's house.

Meanwhile Lydia's is home steaming. She thinks, "Damn that Don. It takes him an hour to do a 15 minute thing. It's shit like this that makes me want to say fuck him. Go and grow up on your own time. I got my own life to live."

Damian is fast asleep and deep down Lydia is worried about Don. She understands that he is at that age when his manhood is constantly being tested. He is a good guy but he has his pride and will not back down easy. At least that's the side of him she knows. Then she thinks about the intelligent side of Don that could discuss almost anything with anybody. And the sensitive side that could kiss every part of her body as if he is trying to kiss all the hurt and pain away.

He can certainly make love like someone who knows her pleasures more than she knows them herself.

Just then Don knocks on the door. Although he has keys to her place he rarely uses them. Knowing his knock, Lydia opens the door prepared to let him have it. But when her eyes see the blood stains on his coat and she immediately thinks he has been hurt. "Oh my God Don what have you done?"

"What have I done?" He repeats while taking off his coat. He shows her that he is not hurt and he explains the events that took place.

"So if you saw those two guys again could you identify them?" Asks Lydia.

"Maybe!? I don't know. I didn't tell the cop about the two guys I saw running. Hopefully she will be able to I.D. those guys." Don

"And if she can't? You would be letting two attempted murderers get away. Think about what that means. You have to do something!" Lydia

"Damn Lydia. I'm the one who's suppose to be emotional. I know you feel I have to step up because no one came forth when my mother died. But you can't force me. I have to come to grips with it my own way in my own time. Please, I don't need the extra guilt trip." Feeling as if he will have a break down he says while heading for the door "I think I should go."

"Don please don't go," says Lydia in a voice that makes Don want to change his mind. He feels as if Lydia needs him. Still he twists the locks to the door and turns the knob hoping Lydia will stop him before he leaves. And she does.

"I'm sorry Don. I didn't mean to upset you. Please stay. We don't have to talk about it anymore. Fuck it we don't have to talk about anything at all," she says while grabbing his arm.

Don goes along willingly because it is really what he wants. Straight to the bedroom where Damian is asleep in his bed, Lydia quickly disrobes and still without speaking

56

commences to take his clothes off. All the while Don is checking out her lovely curves and her sensuality. Her body matches her height perfectly and without any stomach fat, hardly anyone would believe she has an offspring. She is looking so sweet with her hair in a bun. It really turns Don on when she bends down to take off his boots. By the time Lydia gets to his boxers, his private member is trying to bust out. She has to push his buddy to the side in order to get his boxers off.

After they are both disrobed, they began to kiss and embrace each other passionately. Don wants to make Lydia as horny and wet as possible before he penetrates her. Not wanting to wake his son, he picks her up and carries her to the bathroom. There he starts a hot steamy shower. He knows how she likes it from behind with the water running in between them. So they splish splash in the shower until his legs hurt. Then they wash up and prepare to continue their rendezvous in the living room.

Lydia gets out of the shower first. Don is surprised when he steps out of the bathroom to see that Lydia has pulled out the sofa bed, poured them both a glass of wine and put on an x-rated movie. She lights up a cigarette so he starts to roll a blunt.

Watching Sean Michael represent Don feels her kissing his fingers. She takes the blunt from his hand and takes two deep drags, something she does not normally do, and gives it back to him. She begins to kiss his chest and tease him with her tongue going further and further down. For the first time ever, Lydia gives Don oral intercourse. At first he wants to tell her to stop. Then it begins to feel really good and he does not want her to stop.

After a long while he wants to reciprocate the feelings she is giving him. He twists her body around so that they are in a 69 and proceeds to lick, bite and finger her womanhood. It isn't long before her grinding and pounding on his face leads her to a massive orgasm. This turns Don on so much that for the first time he reaches ejaculation from tongue and cheek.

After lying spent in each other's grasp for almost a half an hour, Lydia starts to pull on his penis again until it is once again hard like the man of steel. There they spend the next two hours exploring different positions and one another's very sensitive spots.

(Chapter 10)
IT'S ON

It's a little after midnight and Damian wakes Don up with his giggles. Apparently they had fallen asleep with the X-rated movie still playing. For some reason Damian found what he saw to be amusing because he was laughing hysterically.

Using the remote Don turns the VCR off and puts on the Cartoon Network for him. Don goes to the bathroom to take a leak and wash up. Lydia wakes up while he is dressing.

"Where are you going?" Lydia

"I have to go to rehearsal." Don

"Rehearsal? What that rap stuff!? Couldn't you have done it earlier?" Lydia

"I've been with you since earlier." Don

"A real man doesn't leave his family to go hang out." Lydia

"Please don't start with that real man shit!" Don gets angry. Noticing that Damian is observing the whole scene he calms down. "Check it Lydia, I just need to run out for a few hours because we plan on going into the studio Sunday and this will be my last chance to rehearse. Please try to understand that I'm doing this so that I will be able to provide for my family more. At the same time I'm trying to fulfill a dream of mine. Can't you understand that? I don't want to leave you. I just need to make moves, now while I can." Don

Apparently saying the right words Lydia comes back with a complete attitude change. "Well what time will you be back?"

"I should be back by 4:00 O'clock." Don

"Do you have to go to work tomorrow?" Lydia

"Yeah." Don

"What time do you have to be there?" Lydia

"Eight O'clock." Don

"Eight! When do you plan on sleeping?" Lydia

"Who can sleep when has a woman as sweet as you," Don

says to gas up her head a little. While she is still blushing he puts on his coat and prepares to leave. "Now you get some rest and listen out for me in a few hours." He says with a kiss. "Bye Damian."

"Bye Daddy," Damian says more interested in Space Ghost than his father leaving.

Once outside Don begins to breathe easier. It is as if he had to hold his breath while he was leaving. He feels that Lydia makes it hard for him to leave. She puts a guilt feeling on him every time they have to part. He knows deep down inside it is because she wants him around, but he still doesn't like it. He wishes she would express her feelings more openly. Instead he notices that she would often say the opposite of what she is feeling.

The cold air is refreshing to him. He feels free. Free to enjoy the night as it comes to him. He walks to 145th Street and St. Nicolas while enjoying the sounds of 'Sex On Fire' in his ears.

Swiping his unlimited metro card, he runs down the stairs because he hears his train coming. Taking the D train to Kingsbridge, he walks four blocks east to D.J.'s house. Feeling in good spirits he is eager to 'brainstorm something lyrical'.

"A Yo D.J.!!!" He yells about 3 times when a window 2 stories up opens.

"Yo what up D- Boogie. Here catch the keys." D.J. lets the keys fall and Don catches them perfectly. He walks up the pissy stairs to the second floor and knocks on the door. D.J. opens the door and smiles at him with a wide grin. Immediately Don sees that his friend is missing a tooth.

"Hey what happened to your tooth?"

"Man I had some beef with some niggas who didn't know. I had to let them know!" D.J.

"Word you had to represent too!" Don

"Yup, three stupid motherfuckers thought they could punk me. I had to get mid-evil on their asses!" The two burst out laughing.

60

They are interrupted by D.J.'s phone. "Aye it's these two shorties I got coming over." D.J.

"Yo I thought we were gonna practice?" Don

"We'll do a little something. But tonight I want to have fun. We're gonna freak these bitches. I got mesc tabs, haze and evil thoughts." D.J.

"Damn Nigga. All dat?!" Don

"Word. These shortys are gonna go all out." D.J. says as he picks up the phone. "Hello, who dis?...Hey baby...Yeah I've been waiting for your call...You got your friend with you?...Come out the train station and walk to Crescent Avenue. I'll meet you by the park...I'll be there in ten minutes...Peace Bye." click

"So yo where's your grandma?" asks Don

"She is not feeling well. She's in her room and won't be coming out." D.J.

"Oh," Don says not knowing what to say.

"So yo, you got some weed?" D.J.

"Most Def, Most Def." Don

"Cool cause that's all these girls do or so they will think," D.J. says with a grin. "Check these new mixes I did," he says while turning on his computer.

"I thought you had to pick those shorties up?" Don

"Yo, you gotta make em wait for a little bit." D.J.

They stay listening to his mixes for about 20 minutes. D.J. has some bad mixes. His mix of Michael Jackson to Bonita Applebaums beat is one of Don's Favorite. D.J. is an unorthodox mixologist. He mixes the usual and unordinary music. He even did a mix of a Tracy Chapman song to a Run D.M.C. beat. While listening to the music they smoke a blunt. By the time they go to pick up the girls they are buzzing.

"Hellooo Ebony," D.J. says as he grabs the slim cutie and slobs her down.

"Hey" Don says to the other one. The one who is borderline big boned to seasonally plump.

"I'm Zelda" she replies as she shakes Don's hand and

shows a beautiful set of teeth when she smiles. Still Don is kind of upset to be paired with her. She really isn't his type.

The four go to the nearest bodega and buy a six pack of Heineken, 3 fortys of olde gold and a pack of white owls. They get to D.J.'s apartment and he puts four Heinekens and two fortys in the freezer. The remainder he takes to his bedroom with his guest. The ladies sip a Heineken while Don and D.J. share a forty. They tap the bottle and twist the cap while D.J. puts on one of his mixed C.Ds. He then pulls a folding table from under his bed and goes to the kitchen to grab a few more chairs. The quartet start up a game of spades with the guys against the girls. Playing to 500 they are all finished their brews by the second hand. D.J. Takes the empty bottles to the kitchen with Don right behind him.

In the kitchen D.J. pulls 2 frosty Heinekens and one frosty forty out of the freezer. Don keeps look out while D.J. puts a mescaline tablet in each of the Heinekens. What he doesn't see is D.J. also dropping a tab in the forty. They return to D.J.'s room where each girl is rolling a blunt. By the time the girls win the game they have smoked up the weed and killed their drinks. Everyone is feeling super high as they take turns running to the bathroom.

D.J. gets the last Heinekens and forty from the kitchen while Don puts on Rumble in the Bronx. As Jackie Chan is fucking Niggaz up, Don begins to feel funny. He notices that Zelda, Ebony and D.J. have a pale and slightly greenish look to their skin. He suddenly feels as if he will burst into obscenities. It is as if he is going to regurgitate profanities. Quickly he excuses himself and goes to the bathroom. He sees the same discoloration of his face in the mirror and immediately knows what's up. D.J. has slipped him a Mickey. "Damn with friends like that, who needs enemies?"

"A yo D.J." he yells twice

"Chill nigga. You wanna wake up my grandma?" says D.J. running into the bathroom and closing the door behind him.

"You suppose to be my nigga, why you ain't tell me?"

"Yo fuck that. I didn't know." D.J.

"Oh shit," Don starts feeling hyper. "So you gonna lie about it now?!" Without thinking about it Don punches D.J. dead in the chest sending D.J. hitting the wall.

"What the Fuck!" D.J. screams, more surprised than hurt. "If it means that much to you, you can have Ebony and I'll fuck the fat bitch."

"Huh" Don replies. Feeling giggly and tickly inside. "I just wanna know..." His words become hard to get out because he keeps laughing. "Why you ain't tell me...." they laugh together. "You were gonna put a mesc tab in the forty?"

"Aye?" replies D.J. through tears of laughter. "Nigga you were...." laughing. "Right there when I dropped the tab in the bottle. I thought that was why you were dogging the damn thing."

Suddenly Don's emotions hit a 180 degree turn. He feels extremely depressed. "You my nigga! I love you like a brother! I would never hurt you." All the while Don is speaking there is someone deep inside his mind saying "Damn nigga you are blasted. You need to get a grip on yourself." That is the voice of his soul trapped from the drugs he is currently under. Without anyone having to tell him, Don knows he is wasted.

"Damn kid you're fucked up! You feel alright?" D.J.

"Feel alright?" Repeats Don not knowing how to answer because he can't describe his feelings. Suddenly he doesn't feel well. He thinks he will vomit. He gets on his knees and hugs the toilet bowl.

"Yo Don you alright? Damn kid I thought you knew." D.J. Then Don feels like his bowels are about to give. Quickly he stands up, pulls down his pants, sits on the toilet and let's loose mad diarrhea.

"A yo I better check out," says D.J. starting to exit.

"No nigga," Don whispers feeling panicky. "Don't leave me man, I'm a die!"

D.J. smacks Don across the face and says "Look nigga we drank 2 fortys, one laced with mesculine, an hallucinogenic drug and smoked nuff blunts. We are high, accept it and have fun. You're gonna be alright. You're in the bathroom, taking a shit and stinking the motherfucker up. We have two bitches in the room probably wondering what the hell we've been doing together in the bathroom so fucking long. Now get a grip, wipe your ass and put some cold water on your face so we can get this party started." D.J.

Feeling a little better Don responds with a smile, "Oh yeah, they still don't know." Feeling like D.J. just saved his life he says "Thank you fam, you my brother for life."

D.J. leaves the smelly bathroom and Don finishes his business, wipes his ass and washes his face. He takes a good look at himself in the mirror and says, "Yahweh please stand by me and guide me through the night." Instead of going directly into D.J.'s room, Don goes to the kitchen and gets himself a big glass of water, he drinks half of the glass in the kitchen which tickles his insides and seems to help the blood flow more freely through this veins. He refills the glass and walks towards the room. Almost but not quite feeling like himself Don is not prepared for what he will see upon entering the room.

If he had not had his pinky under the glass he certainly would have dropped the water. D.J. had put on his blue light so the room was dimly lit and everything was tinted blue. It takes Don's eyes a few seconds to adjust to the lack of light, so for a moment he doubts what he is seeing is true. When his eyes gain full focus he knows exactly what he is looking at, but he does not know how to react.

Zelda, Ebony and D.J. are all naked on the bed. D.J. is on his side with his back to the wall, while Ebony is on her back with her neck twisted to the side giving him brain.

Meanwhile Zelda is on her knees with her head between Ebony's legs licking away. They don't even seem to notice Don so he just stands there watching and drinking his water.

"Don can you roll a blunt?" D.J. says suddenly.

"No doubt," replies Don snapping out of his gaze.

He notices that Zelda and Ebony are not shy or embarrassed about their predicaments. He wonders what

64

kind of game D.J. spit to make them both so willing. Trying to keep his composure Don starts rolling the blunt. Even though he feels as if he can get no higher he lights it. After 4 or 5 puffs Don passes the blunt to D.J. He sees Zelda looking at him with a devilish grin. She suddenly looks very appealing.

"I have to use the bathroom," Ebony says while getting up. She is unphased by her nakedness as she walks to the bathroom.

"Are you gonna join us?" Zelda poses the question to Don. Not quite sure how to answer the questions Don says "Hmmm," as he sits on a chair and begins taking off his boots. D.J. massages and kisses Zelda's breast. She is moaning when Ebony just walks in and starts playing with Zelda's's cunt. Then, like she is a director in a porno movie she pushes D.J.'s head down to Zelda's crotch and makes Zelda lie down so that D.J.'s face is next to her vagina. Then Ebony starts rubbing D.J.'s neck and back. She slowly caresses his shoulders, his back and butt. Once again it seems that they are oblivious to Don and reveling in their own ecstasy when he sees Zelda motioning with her finger for him to come to her. Starting to get up music that is playing ends.

"Don put on the Dead Presidents sound track," asks D.J.

"And take off those clothes," says Zelda

"And pass me the blunt," demands Ebony as they all giggle.

Don does what everybody asks and by the time he gets down to his boxers D.J. is passing the blunt back to him. "The dick, pussy, ass blunt," Don thinks to himself as he takes a drag in a way that his lips do not touch the wet tip.

Once again he sees Zelda motioning for him to come closer. He walks to her and she reaches into his boxers and pulls his limp penis out of the opening. Because D.J. is still licking and biting her count Zelda closes her eyes and lets out a deep sigh of "ooohhh" as if she is coming. Starting to feel turned on Don can feel the blood beginning to pump up

65

his penis. Aware of the pulse Zelda gives his shaft a series of squeezes and pulls.

D.J. stops eating Zelda out and begins deeply french kissing Ebony with the O'Jays blasting away. Zelda turns on to her stomach and gets on her knees. She pushes Don's jimmy back into his boxers and slides his boxers down. Leading him by the dick she sits him on the side of the bed, and with her ass in the air starts giving him oral pleasure. Don closes his eyes and wonders how this is possible. For the past two to three years he had no kind of a problem getting girls, but very few was with this sucking dick shit. He wasn't really into it himself. He didn't want to be kissing on no one who had been sucking a dick. Even if it was his own dick. Besides it was embarrassing for him and it never felt all that good anyway. But now it was different. The honeys wanted to do him and it felt wonderful. It definitely seems to Don that Zelda knows what she is doing.

His eyes closed and feeling like he could burst, Zelda gives a jerk which breaks Don's concentration and makes him open his eyes. D.J. is entering Zelda from the back and although it looks as if she is in pain Don is sure she likes it. She stops giving him head and grabs the edge of the bed. She digs her nails into the bed and bites her lip. Don is thinking that D.J. must be giving it to her something awful for her to be going through these changes.

Don doesn't see Ebony walk over to him until she grabs and sucks on his dick until it is hard like granite. "How much can one dick take?" Don thinks when Ebony lays him on the bed next to Zelda and D.J. Ebony pushes Don under Zelda. The way she pushes, him Don thinks that D.J. is gonna pull out of Zelda and she will sit on his dick. He does not want to enter someone who had just had an exit when Ebony pushes his dick into Zelda's vagina.

At first Don thinks he and D.J. are in her pussy when he realizes that D.J. is giving her anal. Don could feel each thrust of D.J.'s dick. This turns him off a bit and he feels his penis going soft. D.J. however is going to town on Zelda's ass who is now slumped over Don biting into the sheets and still clawing the side of the bed.

Ebony takes his hand and places it on her vagina. He rubs the already wet clitoris and fingers her. D.J. lets out a moan, pulls out of Zelda and shoots a load on her back. Ebony gives him extra pleasure by jerking his penis off.

After a few moments Zelda's engine starts up again and she begins grinding on Don. Don knows it is only a matter of time before she explodes. This and the fact that Ebony seems to really be getting off on his fingers gets his arousal going. He can feel his penis enlarging and penetrating deeper into her wetness with every thrust. For a thick woman, Zelda is firm and tight. She pumps and shakes wildly on Don for a good 15-20 minutes before reaching a serious orgasm.

D.J. leans against the wall and closes his eyes. Zelda rolls off of Don and Ebony starts lapping up his erect middle leg. She seems to like the taste of Zelda's cum because she licks his dick clean. Then she gets on top of him and begins riding. He could feel Zelda licking and playing with his balls while he is fucking Ebony. "Damn!" Thinks Don. This is the best feeling in the world." He is enjoying himself while Zelda licks from his balls to Ebony's clitoris.

For the first time Don takes notice of the time. It is 4:30 am and he isn't nearly ready to stop. He twists on Ebony's nipples, caresses, kisses and fucks her until she cums at about 5:15. All the while he is thinking that he needs to make a phone call. He has to call Lydia and tell her he won't be in. He really doesn't want to hear her mouth but he feels he may make things worse by not calling. Now that Ebony has finished sweating all over him he wants to do three things, make a call, piss and take a shower.

Don notices that D.J. is still sitting on the bed leaning against the wall naked and snoring. "Is there anymore weed?" asks Ebony.

"Yeah sure," Don replies. "Y'all roll it up while I make a phone call."

67

"Gotta call wifey?!" Snarls Ebony.

"Word up," he says as he puts on his boxers, and gives her the last bag of weed and two dutches.

"Niggas ain't shit," he hears one of the girls say on his way to the kitchen. "That's why I do what I do, cause niggas ain't shit!"

"Fuck them," thinks Don to himself as he begins to feel nervous. Not because of what he just heard but because he knows how Lydia is going to react. He really does not want to make this call but he feels he should. His fingers tremble as he pushes the numbers and wonders what he should say.

The phone rings four times before Lydia answers with a groggy "Hello."

"Hey honey this is Don," Don

"Don? Where are you?" Lydia

"I'm still at D.J.'s house. I kind of fell out." Don

"Fell out? What time is it?" Lydia

"It's after five," Don

"After five?" She says now sounding fully awake. "It's after 5:30. What happened?"

"First, it took me a while to get here because the trains were all messed up. Then I get here and D.J. and I start practicing. I admit we were smoking and drinking but we were practicing and working up a sweat. About 2:30 we go to the burger joint to get something to eat. We get back, eat, drink, and smoke. I lean my head back for one second next thing I know it's after five." Don

Next thing you know it's after five," she repeats mockingly, "Your ass should have been on its way home the moment you left that burger joint!" She continues angrily, "A real man doesn't have to get so fucked up that he forgets his family and obligations!"

"Oh don't start that real man shit. Because a real woman doesn't bitch every time things don't go her way." Don

"My way!? You the motherfucker who said he would be back by 4 O'clock. Now it's almost six and you just calling me."

68

"I told you what happened," Don

"Am I really supposed to believe that bullshit?" Lydia

"Well fine. Don't believe me. I woke up to call you and see if you were okay. Now I'm going back to sleep because I have to get up in an hour." Don

"I just hope you feel that bitch is worth losing your family over!" Click the phone goes dead.

"What the fuck" Don says out loud. "That went really well."

He hangs up the phone and heads towards D.J.'s room. He remembers he has to piss when he hears the shower coming from the bathroom. "Damn D.J.'s grandma must be woke," thinks Don. However, when he walks in the room, D.J. is the only one there, all curled up under a blanket still against the wall. The girl's clothes are still there so they must be in the bathroom Don reasons.

"I really have to piss," he thinks. It takes him a few moments to gain enough nerve to walk into the bathroom. He doesn't knock, he just walks in.

The girls are taking a shower behind a black shower curtain and that keeps Don from seeing them. He lifts up the toilet seat and begins urinating. Just as he finishes, Ebony steps out of the shower and starts toweling off.

"You want me to leave the water on?" asks Zelda.

"That's an excellent idea," replies Don. "Let me jump in."

Before Zelda can step out of the shower Don steps in. Although her body is not as appealing as it was under the blue light, Don can see the sexiness about her. She has perfect skin tone and a healthy frame that is a whole lot of woman. It surprises Don because he mainly attracts petite women.

"You like what you see?" She inquires with a grin while passing him the soap.

"Most definitely," he replies feeling his manhood began to inflate.

Grabbing his penis she says, "I'm scared of you," as she rinses off and steps out of the shower.

Don continues to scrub himself down while the girls exit the bathroom. He rinses off and as a special treat to himself ,rubs baby oil over his body and pats himself dry. Not wanting to put on the same soiled boxers, Don wraps the towel around his waist, and vacates the bathroom. Thinking that the girls will be dressed or getting dressed he is surprised to see them both sitting on the bed just chillin. The Isleys Brothers In Between the Sheets is jammin and the ladies are puffing a blunt. D.J. is still knocked the fuck out. With complete confidence, Don squeezes in between the girls and intercepts the blunt. He is in a condition of complete bliss. Just feeling the warmth and softness of the two bodies puts him in a state of utopia.

"Somebody feels all soft and smooth," says Ebony
"You feet it to?" Zelda
"Yep. Somebody even smells like a baby," they laugh.
"What? Is it amusing to you all because a man takes care of his skin?" Don
"I like it" says Ebony grabbing his penis with one hand and the blunt with the other.
"Gimme a shot gun," says Zelda

Ebony leans over Don and gives her a shotgun. She then takes a few more drags, passes the blunt to Zelda and french kisses Don while she exhales. Don inhales most of the smoke and blows it out his nose while returning Ebonys fiery kiss. "Once again It's on," he thinks as Zelda gives his private member mouth to mouth.

Together they lay Don on his back. Zelda continues to give him head while Ebony sits on his chest. Then she moves up and puts her pussy right over his mouth. Caught off guard, he takes a lick. She moans and it doesn't seem too bad to him. He licks her more and more not minding the taste. "Is this what being a man is?" thinks Don. "Or a freak?"

He licks Ebony inside out and at her request gently nibbles at her clit. Zelda mounts his hard cock and it takes some bit of forcing for his dick to fully penetrate her. When he finally breaks into her gut she bounces her fat beautiful black ass up

70

and down on his joint hard. He knows he can't hold back his sperm much longer when Ebony starts cumin in gushes all over his face. It doesn't bother him much because he is shooting sparks deep inside of Zelda who is cringing in her own ecstasy.

All three lay spent at 6:40 in the morning. Don gets up to get his towel and wipe off his face. His jimmy is still hard and even he wonders how. Ebony sees this as an opportunity to once again get off. Before Don finishes wiping his face Ebony stands up and bends over the bed for him to hit it from behind. Just before he enters her he stops and says "Wait."

"What's wrong?" asks Ebony

"I want to change the music. Any request?" Don

"Put Kelly Roland on. I like her." Zelda screams before Ebony can answer. Don walks to the stereo feeling proud of his protruding manhood. He has performed sexually well the whole day. He feels like he has represented, is still representing and nowhere tired. He finds the music that was requested and puts it on. Zelda lies down and quickly drifts into la la Land with D.J.

Ebony however is waiting in the same position that Don left her in. Only semi-erect he fingers her and feels her wetness. Quickly he is once again hard and ready to attack. After more than twenty minutes of the upward position they lie on the rug and make love like two people who have known each other all their lives. They kiss, hug, squeeze and become one until they both climax like huge volcanic eruptions. Then they lay in each other's arms. Too exhausted to move.

(Chapter 11)
ONE MORE CHANCE

The first thing he becomes cognizant of when he opens his eyes is the time. It is a little after nine o'clock. "Damn" he thinks, "I'm stupid late." He jumps up and immediately regrets moving so quickly. He is dehydrated, still fucked up, hungry and has a headache. Everybody else in the room is fast asleep. Even Ebony is knocked out on the rug. Don pulls one of the unused blankets off the bed and puts it over Ebony's naked body. She doesn't open her eyes but she does crack a smile.

Within minutes Don is dressed and ready to leave. He wonders how he found the strength to wake up and why he isn't feeling too tired. He looks around the room and thinks about all of the unprotected sex he has been having. He thinks about the statistics and how having unprotected sex with someone is the same as having sex with everyone that person has had unprotected sex with. Snapping out of his thoughts, he knows he has to put a move on. Checking one last time to make sure he has everything. The clock says 9:28 as he heads out the door. Since D.J. has one of those automatic locks, he needn't wake anyone up on his way out.

Stepping outside to a sun that burns his eyes and makes them water, he puts on his sunglasses and embarks towards the train station. There is a chill in the air but he is warm as he puts on some classic Tupac. Don doesn't like all that east vs. west coast who's better crap. As far as he's concerned, if you're hot you're hot. No matter where you're from or where you're at. Don feels that if he got a chance to make records, he would want people to buy them all over the globe. He would try to make music damn near everybody could appreciate.

He is still deep in thought when he walks to the station towards the turnstile. His player is blasting so all he hears is Tupac rapping. Swiping his metro card he walks through.

All of a sudden three plain clothes police fly out of a small janitor's room heading towards him. Dons' heart starts beating tremendously. "What have I done now?" He thinks to himself. "I paid my fare."

The police run right past him and arrest two youths who must have hopped the train right before him. Quickly, Don keeps stepping. "Damn I've got to be far more observant," he reflects. "Anu please guide me and help me to help guide myself."

Don prays so much because his mother had emphasized it so much. She was not a religious fanatic, but she believed in a higher power. No matter what name he gives the creator, it is important that he prays coming and going. She also stressed that he should be grateful for all experiences, whether good and bad, because that is what life is made of.

The train arrives in no time. There is not much of a rush hour on Saturday so he has no problem finding a seat. "I'm in complete control of my destiny." Don repeats in an effort to regain his confidence. He gets off the train at 161st street to connect to the number 4. This train also takes no time to arrive and is fairly empty.

The train pulls into 149th street and a very attractive woman steps in. She gives Don a smile, sits down and pulls out a book. Immediately Don recognizes it as a Donald Goines books. He can't see which one it is so when no one else gets on the train at 138th street he asks "Is that Swamp Man?"

"Excuse me?" she replies

"No, I was just curious because Donald Goines is one of my favorite authors and that looks like Swamp Man." Don

"Yes it is Swamp Man," she retorts with a colgate smile.

"Do you mind if we talk about it for a moment?" Asks Don.

"Sure why not?" She answers.

"You're not a mass murderer or anything?" He asks as he sits next to her.

She laughs and responds. "No I'm not a mass murderer or

73

anything of the sort."

"So what's your name?" Don

"My name is Tyeisha. What's yours?"

"My name is Don and I am very pleased to meet you Tyeisha." Don

"Don Juan?" Tyeisha

"No actually it's Donathan."

"Donathan" she repeats "So what were you going to say about Donald Goines?" Tyeisha

"Tyeisha" he repeats because he likes the way her name sounds. They chat for a sec but 125th Street comes quickly and Don is a bit distraught when Tyeisha has to get up to leave. He doesn't even have enough time to get her number. But that's the way it is in New York. You win some, you lose some.

A rush of people pile into the train at 86th street. It's a little strange to Don but he feels more alone with all these people on the train then when the car was nearly empty. And of course the train stalls in the tunnel pushing Don back about 10 more minutes late.

He clocks in at 10:02a.m., which he thinks is good timing. The store isn't crowded but it is busy and all of the employees are working. Don goes to his section and immediately starts pulling out the bad produce. He brings fresh fruits and vegetables out of the cooler and rotates them with the ones already on display. The manager of the store is out today so he doesn't have to worry about being reprimanded for his lateness. He works steadily until noon when he gets super hungry. Not wanting to eat any dead flesh he thinks about having a fruit feast in the cooler when a customer breaks him out of his plans.

"Young man do you have any asparagus?" Sasses the elderly woman.

"Er no Mam" replies Don "They are not in season yet."

"But I just bought some from here last week," the elderly woman.

"True, that was a special. I was surprised at that myself.

74

But my supervisor has informed me that we will not be selling anymore fresh asparagus until it gets warmer. However we do have frozen asparagus in aisle 12 and canned asparagus in aisle 7." Catching an attitude, the woman walks away with a sneer.

"Yo, what's up with her?" Mike inquires walking up to Don and giving him five.

"What's up Dude. I don't know what the fuck her problem is. She just caught an attitude with me because we don't have any asparagus." Don

"Asparagus? Bitch better try a cucumber or something bigger," they laugh. "A yo, you heard about Sean?" Mike continues.

"Who Sean, the night manager?" Don

"Yeah he used to be night manager." Mike

"Say word?! What happened?" Don

"Yesterday the cops came and took him out in handcuffs."

"Handcuffs?" Don

"Indeed. Apparently he was changing figures around to make it look like the store was making less money than it was. And he was pocketing the excess." Mike

"Damn I'm sorry to hear that. Sean was a cool motherfucker." Don

"Yeah, now he's just fucked. I hear he's facing 5 to 10 for what he did." Mike

"Damn," is all Don could say as he thinks about the loneliness Sean must be experiencing? The despair and regrets he must have. The worrying Sean must be doing. It puts a sadness in Don's heart.

"Yo kid just be careful of what you do and keep it on the D.L. I gotta get back to work so I'll check you in a few." Mike

"Mike," Don calls, "Who's gonna be manager now?"

"Bobby is acting manager for now." Mike

"Bobby!? The knucklehead that's here now?" Don

"Yeah, that chicken head. So watch your back." Mike

Don goes back to work wondering how the world could

change so quickly. One moment you're at the top, and the next you're knee deep in shit. Looking to see that Bobby is busy Don heads to the cooler for a bite to eat. He devours 2 bananas, a grapefruit, a granny smith, a handful of cherries and some seedless grapes. He heads back to the department and bumps right into Bobby.

"Mr. Breyer, I've been wanting to speak to you." Bobby

"Yes," replies Don

It seems that you had some trouble getting here on time. I have no choice but to give you a verbal warning. Next time I'll have to write you up. Please understand that this company can no longer tolerate incompetency. Also I want to inform you that you will only be allowed to do overtime when it is absolutely necessary. If the schedule says for you to leave at four you leave at four. No more overtime without permission from a supervisor. Enjoy the rest of your Day. I'll be watching." Bobby walks off.

"Fuck him," thinks Don. "That asshole." Ever since Don started working his schedule has been 4 to 8 on weekdays and 8 to 4 on weekends with him having the option to stay till closing time. 95% of the time he stays till closing. Now this asshole is telling him it's going to stop.

"You look like you've had a rough night," Nicole one of his co-workers says.

"And I feel like the rough night is still going on. I must have gotten two hours of sleep maximum."

"Oh it's like that? Details please." She replies with a sly grin.

Don thinks about it for a moment and has to admit to himself that he enjoyed last night immensely. Still there is something immoral about what he has done. Something he will have to beg God's forgiveness for. "I had a nice time so I'll just leave it at that."

"Hmm" she says "Are you going to lunch now?"

"Lunch? Actually I haven't thought about it. What are you thinking about getting?" Don

"I was thinking about Mickey D's or Pizza," Nicole

"Pizza sounds good to me. Let me get my coat."

Don goes to the back of the store to get his coat. When he returns Nicole and Mike are in a heated conversation. Don catches the tail end of the discussion.

"You messed up when you told Sean lies about me" says Nicole, "You talk about keeping it on the D.L. and then you spread false rumors about me!?" She stops when she sees Don approaching then she continues. "Let's just break all of the ties that we did have. You don't say nothing to me and I won't say shit to you."

She starts to walk away when Mike screams out "Fuck you bitch. Nobody wants your stink ass pussy anyway!"

Nicole stops dead in her tracks and stares at Mike. If looks could kill, he would be put to death, brought back to life and put to death again. Walking towards Mike, she reaches in her pocket and in a flash a knife appears in her right hand. Mike starts stepping backwards and Don holds Nicole from behind, hoping he won't get cut in the process. "Please clam down Nicole, get a grip on yourself."

"What the hell is going on here," asks Bobby approaching the scene. "Oh shit!" He responds when he sees the knife. It doesn't take a genius to see that Nicole wants to do bodily harm to Mike and Don is holding her back. "Take her out of the store," Bobby orders Don. "And don't bring her back till she's calm!"

Don is able to take the knife from Nicole as soon as they leave the store. Once they step outside Nicole breaks down into some serious tears. Not knowing what to say Don puts his arm around her. She buries her face in his chest and cries like a baby. They walk three blocks in that position to a park where Nicole cries till she is all cried out.

After a while Don asks "So you wanna talk about it?"

She waits a few minutes before responding. "Mike and I almost had a lil something going on. We decided it was best we keep it a secret because we didn't want everybody in our business. Unfortunately, he told Sean that I did something which never happened. When I confronted him about it he told me to basically go fuck myself. Still I was stupid enough to keep seeing him. I even let him in my house. Ever since I let him in, I've been missing jewelry from my house which he says he never touched. Sean told me not to trust Mike because he smokes crack. But Sean was always trying to hit on me anyway so I didn't know who to believe. When I confronted Mike about it he caught an attitude so I left it alone. I guess he got jealous when he saw us talking because he started telling me how you ain't no good and all that shit."

Don is taken back. He thought Mike was his friend.

"Did Mike ever tell you about us?" She asks.

Hesitantly Don answers "No, nothing." Even though Mike had claimed she gave him oral sex in the basement.

"Are you sure?" She repeats

"I'm positive" Don replies more confidently. "Though I'm a bit more concerned about your temper."

"Huh?" Nicole

"Well you could have killed or hurt someone with that knife. Maybe you should find more constructive ways to deal with your anger."

Managing a laugh, "I don't want to hurt anybody but I'm not gonna let nobody play me out either. That nigga is plain lucky that you were there to keep me from carving his ass up."

"Did you see the look on Bobby's face? He was scared shitless." They laugh

"Speaking of Bobby I guess it's almost time to go back to work." Nicole

"Are you okay to go back?" Don

"Actually no, but I don't want to lose my job." Nicole

"Well what are you going to do about Mike?" Don

"Mike Who?" I don't know Mike. As far as I'm concerned he doesn't exist." Nicole

Nicole looks so sad to Don. Her light brown skin is a tint of red because of her crying. She is a woman with a very nice personality. She has a killer body when she wears the right clothes and her only flaw is her acne problem. She looks as if she could really use a hug so Don gives her one. During the hug he wants to kiss her but decides against it.

"I'm starting to feel hungry" she says displaying a warm smile.

"Me too. Pizza?" Asks Don

"Sure why not."

They go to the nearest Pizzeria and order two slices with extra cheese. On the way back to their job Don realizes he hasn't checked his messages since he left school, he decides to check them. The first one is from Jackie. "Hello Don, this is Jackie. I heard about you and Johnny. Please be careful. That nigga is mad and dangerous. Call me before Monday." Bleep. The next message is from Fatima, "Hello Don please call me, I'm sorry for this afternoon. I hope you will let me make it up to you. Please call me tonight." Bleep. "Hey It's Lydia. Call me when you get the chance, I feel I owe you an apology for hanging up on you. Give us a call." Don hears Damian's voice in the background before she hangs up.

"Is everything okay?" Inquires Nicole.

"As well as can be expected, but Nicole tell me something, why is it that girls seem to like guys who dog them out? And when there's a guy who treats them like queens, they treat him like shit. Why?" Don

"That's a good question. I myself seem to attract dogs more than gentlemen. I use to be a glutton for punishment and cling to those pit bulls. I guess what it boiled down to was that the ones who treated me like shit made the best love to me and the nice guys just lacked that bedroom expertise. And when a woman is not satisfied in the bedroom, she tends to get mean and evil." Nicole

"So it all boils down to sex?" Don

"Sure. If the sex is good everybody's happy, if it ain't ...you know the rest." Nicole

As the two of them enter the store they are rushed by Bobby. "Look Nicole. Mike has agreed not to say anything to you if you agree not to say anything to him. And as long as I'm making up the schedule I will try to keep you both as far apart as possible. Is that fair?" Bobby

"Yes it's fair." Nicole

"Now, I am going to need the knife." Bobby

"Why do you need the knife?" Nicole

"If Mike was to get stabbed with the knife you pulled on him the store could be liable. It's either that or I'll have to call the police." Bobby

Nicole starts going through her pockets looking for the knife. All the while Don is wondering what he should do because he still has the knife in his possession. He doesn't know if she wants him to give it up or hold out, if only Nicole would give him a sign.

"Will you give it back to me?" Nicole asks Bobby.

"No I'm afraid I can't do that and I won't be able to let you back to work until you give it to me."

"You know I'm kind of fed up with working here. So if you wanna be like that, then you are going to have to fire me cause I'm not giving up shit." Nicole

Don is dumbfounded. He wonders how and why Nicole could be so stubborn. Bobby looks as if he sees a ghost standing there with his mouth open wide. Nicole's Steve Madden boots break the silence as she turns on her heels and struts out the store.

"Nicole wait," Don runs out of the store in pursuit of Nicole. It takes him half a block before he can catch up to her. "Nicky, Nicky why did you quit?"

She stops to look at Don and smiles. "Nicky. I like that. It's been a long time since someone has called me that."

"So Nicky," repeats Don. "Are you sure you want to do this?"

"Yeah I think so. Technically I didn't quit. I was fired, which should make me eligible for unemployment, and besides I don't think I can take working around Mike anymore. It's time for me to move on?" Nicole

"Are you sure?" Don

"Positive. I'm still young, I'll be going back to college next semester and I have the rest of my life to look forward to." Nick

"And don't forget, you're also beautiful." Don

"Yes I am. You know Don maybe in another life we could have had it going on." Nicole

Shocked at her openness, "Do you think so?"

"Yeah I do. So do you mind if I give you some advice?" Nicole

"Please Do," Don

"Always follow your heart. Dogging girls out doesn't make you any more of a man than getting played out makes you less of a man. The important thing is that you treat people with respect and be happy because karma is a bitch and only you can truly make yourself happy. No one else." Nicole

"You know you are really something special. Will I ever see you again?" Asks Don

"Who knows maybe, maybe not." Nicole

"Well can I kiss you goodbye?" Don

"I would like that." Nicole

They kiss passionately for the first and last time. Then they say their goodbyes.

Don goes back to his job wondering if he too should quit. As soon as he steps in the store, Bobby is on him. "So?" Bobby asks.

"So what?" Don

"Is she coming back?" Bobby

"No you fired her." Don

"It took you all that time for you to come back and tell me that?" Bobby

"What else do you want to know?" Don

"Nothing. Just get back to work." Bobby

Don wants to say "Fuck you and stick this job up your ass," but he decides against it and quietly goes back to work. Mike passes by him a few times but doesn't say anything. Don wonders if Mike is mad at him but then concludes that he doesn't give a damn what Mike feels.

4 o'clock comes quickly. Don is not use to getting off so

early on a Saturday but what the hell. He clocks out and breaks north. On the way home his lack of sleep starts to catch up on him. He yawns every other second and feels that if he closes his eyes he will fall asleep instantly.

(Chapter 12)
NO REST FOR THE WEARY

"Sir, Sir this is the last stop. Sir, Sir!"
Don can barely hear the voice as he opens his blood shot eyes. The female conductor continues, "This is the last stop, you have to transfer to another train."
Don springs up and quickly exits the train while trying to become in tune with the world. His head starts spinning and he feels dizzy. He stumbles onto a bench like a drunken man. The past day's events have finally taken their toll.
It takes him about 15 minutes before he regains his composure. He gets on the next train leaving the Van Courtland Park station and wonders whether or not he will make it home. Luckily for him the car is empty and allows him more time to try and adjust back to normal. By the time the iron horse pulls into Dykeman Street he is almost feeling like himself. He puts on his shades and his MP3 player for the rest of the ride. Before Al Jareau can finish singing 'Susan' the 1 train is pulling into his 157th street station.
Don exits the train and immediately a migraine headache hits. He walks across the street wanting only one thing, to get home.
"A Yo!" Don hears the call but doesn't want to turn around because he fears it might be for him.
"A Yo," he turns to see Nut running towards him.
"Hey Nut, what's up Duke?" Don
"Just finished packing. I'm about to be out. What are you getting into?" Nut
"I'm beat and I'm about to knock out. Whatcha packing for?" Don
"I'm going to move to Atlanta and get my degree in Herbology. I was just headed to the weed spot to get a few bags. You wanna puff a joint?" Nut
"Nah, I'm a have to pass. Besides I don't smoke joints." Don

"Yo let me tell you about those blunts. Every time you smoke a blunt it is equal to smoking two to three joints from the weed and four to five cigarettes from the nicotine in the blunt paper. It's really the nicotine that gives you the head rush high. I prefer a mellow rice paper rolled joint." Nut

Too tired to continue the conversation, Don gives Nut a pound and says "It's all good. Take care fam," as he steps off.

"Be easy young blood and keep your head up," Don can hear Nut say as he continues down the block. Within minutes he is putting his key in the lock. His father must have just arrived home from work too because he is hanging up his coat when Don walks in.

"Hello Son." Dad

"Hey Dad." Don

"Are you okay? You look tired." Dad

"I'm fine, I just didn't get much sleep last night." Don

"Long night aye?" His father asks with a sly grin.

"Uh sure Dad," he responds feeling a bit uncomfortable at his father's sudden friendliness. His dad hasn't acted this way in years.

"Don I thought we might have lunch together. That is if you're not too tired?" Dad

"Well uh okay. Let me hang up my coat and wash up first." Don

"Franks and beans okay?" Dad

"That's fine." Don

Don goes into his room, hangs up his coat and sees that there are two messages on his phone, he hits the voice mail button.

Beep "Hey this is Jackie again please give me a call it's important bye"

Beep "Yo What up nigga. What happened last night? Gimme a call." Although he didn't say his name Don recognizes D.J.'s voice.

"So that Nigga finally woke up," Don says to himself. Not feeling like talking to anyone, he turns his ringer volume down. He goes to the bathroom to wash up and as he looks in the mirror he begins to wonder what is up with his dad.

He almost seems in a good mood. But what or why? Don knows something is up. But what is it? Then he hears something. His father is playing music. It really takes him back because his mom was the only one who used to blast music in the living room. Don opens the door and immediately recognizes the song as 'Expansions' by Lonnie Liston. "Man how she loved to dance to that song," he reminisces. He walks into the living room and his dad is doing the same dance that his mom used to do. "What's up Dad? What's going on?" Don inquires. He is puzzled because he's hardly ever seen his dad dance.

"Son do you know what today is?" Dad

"Yes it's Saturday." Don

"I know it's Saturday. But do you know the significance of today? Today has a meaning." Dad

"A special meaning?" Don repeats. "It can't be the anniversary of mom's death because she died in the summer time," Don says feeling uneasy.

"Close but completely opposite. Want to give it another try?" Dad

Angered by his dads casual manner over his mother Don blurts out, "Another try? This ain't no guessing game!"

"Okay. Calm down son. I only wanted to point out to you that today is your mother's birthday. For the past few years I've been in a depressive coma. Today however is a new day. I feel Shonna looking over us wanting us to be happy. The way she always was on her birthday. Don I don't won't to dwell in her death anymore. I want to celebrate her life and the happiness she brought me. I want to remember the love she brought to us."

Even though his dad is smiling while he is speaking, the tears still flow down his dads cheeks. Don witnesses his father crying and without warning the tears begin to roll down his cheeks also. His dad continues, "So many time's I wanted to tell your mother how much I loved her. How

85

much she gave meaning to my life. Since I wasn't much for words, I tried to show her instead. I tried to let my actions speak. I wished I would have said it more." Donald grabs his son and hugs him tight. Donathan holds him back as the tears come down in buckets. "That's why Don, I want you to know how much you mean to me. God was gracious enough to give me a son. A beautiful baby boy who is growing up to be a fine young man. I want you to know how proud I am of you. Your mother who is the better part of you loves you and watches over you and I. Don't ever forget how much I need and love you. You're everything in this world to me."

"I need and love you too dad." Don replies as they cry and hold each other till they can smell the beans burning.

Don gets up to prepare the table while his dad puts on Kool and the Gang. Together they kill a pack of turkey franks, a can of extra well done beans and for the first time they down a six pack of Budweiser together. They talk about the good times they have had with their lost loved one. They become friends once more, but more important they become family again.

Don gets up to take a piss. On the way to the bathroom he peeks in his room and sees his message light blinking. He doesn't bother to check them. Instead he uses the bathroom and returns back to the kitchen to be with his dad.

Soon after they clean the kitchen, Don begins to undergo an energy drain once more. "Dad I think I'm going to take a nap."

"Yeah, me too," replies his dad. "Oh Don, I almost forgot." Donald goes to the closest and takes out a package. "I feel kind of funny giving you this but I think your mother would have liked for you to have these." Don takes the package. His father continues, "She always said that there is nothing wrong with having nice things." Don pulls the box out the package. He sees's the logo for Nike on the box. He opens it and sees a very nice pair of expensive size 12 black and white Jordan's. Very much like the Nikes he had asked his mother for.

Don knows he should be happy, but he feels hurt. Even angry "Why doesn't dad let it rest," he thinks.

"Don are you okay?" Asks his Dad

"Yeah. It's just been a crazy day. And now you bring me the same kind of sneakers my mother died for. What is this suppose to be? Some kind of guilt trip?" Don

"No! Not at all. I only wanted you to have what your mother wanted to give you. I feel that we can finally get on with our lives and continue living." Dad

"My mother's worth more than some sneaker!" Don shouts.

"You damn right! So don't even compare her to those sneakers. Look Don, no one loved your mother more than you and me. Except her. She had a love of self that reflected a love for all. I want that. I want you to have it. I want you to be happy and really love yourself. And in return give that love back to family, friends and anyone who is deserving. I didn't buy those sneakers to make you feel culpable. Today is Shonna, your mother's birthday. I wanted to buy her something but she is no longer with us. Instead, I bought something for her son, my son. That's all Don, no strings attached."

"I'm sorry dad," Don says, "I guess I've always felt it was my fault mom died. If I never would have asked her for those sneakers..."

"Hold it right there Don. That's not true, I've asked Shonna plenty of times to pick something up for me at the store. She has asked you to go places for her. We've all asked one another for something. Your mother's death will never be justified but don't you think for one second that you were responsible, because Don I'm here to tell you that any of us could be taken out at any time. And unless it's you taking someone's life with your hands, it's not your fault." He once again embraces his son, "Your mother has raised a fine young man. She and I are very proud of you. Be happy my son."

"I love you dad."

"I love you too son."

Don goes to his room with one thing in mind, to get some sleep. He sees his message light blinking three times. He doesn't wan't to speak to anyone but he knows he should at least call Lydia back. He hits the message retrieval button and Lydia is the first voice he hears. Beep. "Hello Don, I tried to reach you at your job and they said you left already. If you are there pick up... Well call me when you remember your family!" Beep. "Hola Manuel, hola,"
must be a wrong number. Beep. "Don this is Fatima. I called yesterday and I thought you would call me back. Please give me a call. I would like to speak to you. I'll be home all day. Bye."
He looks at the time. It's a quarter to eight on a Saturday night. He decides to make a few phone calls before going to sleep.
"Hello," D.J.
"What up Zigger this is Don."
"Yo what up kid. What happened last night?" D.J.
"What happened!? You fell the fuck out, that's what happened."
"Well yo, they want you to come back over." D.J.
"What?! They're still there?" Don
"Word up!" D.J.
"Damn nigga you the motherfucking man!" Don
"Nah nigga, we all didn't wake till like 2 hours ago. I ordered some Chinese food and we've been cooling. So what time you broke out?" D.J.
"About nine-ish." Don
"I hear dat. So you comin back thru?" D.J.
"Maybe later. Right now I'm a clock me a few Z's." Don
"Alright blood, in a minute then." D.J.
"Peace." Don
"Peace." D.J. click
Don decides to make another call.
"Hello." Voice
"May I speak to Jackie please?" Don
"She's not in. May I take a message?" Voice

"Yes could you please tell her Don returned her call." Don

"Okay will do." Voice

"Thank you." click

"That was quick," thinks Don. "I might as well make another."

"Hello."

"May I speak to Fatima please?" Don

"This is Fatima."

"Hi Fatima, this is Don."

"I know. So you finally decided to call me." Fatima

"Yeah I had to work late last night and I had to go to work early today. I didn't want to call you at an indecent hour." Don

"So what are you going to do for the rest of the evening?" Fatima

"I was just going to get some rest." Don

"I thought we might go to a movie or something." Fatima

"How about tomorrow, I'm really tired and don't think I will be good company." Don

"Are you still mad at me?" Fatima

"A little, but I care about you too much to stay angry." Don

"I wish I could hold you through the night." Fatima

"That would be nice." Don

"I've been saving some money and I thought we might go to a motel. That is if you want to." Fatima

"Of course I do. When?" Don

"Tonight." Fatima

"Whoa, are you serious?" Don

"Very Serious." Fatima

"So where do you want to go?" Don

"Anywhere, you pick the place and I'll pay."

"How are you going to get out for the night?" Don

"I'll tell my parents I'm at a friend's house." Fatima

"Are you sure you want to do this?" Don

"Yes if you still want me. I'm sorry for the way I acted in the lunchroom. I just thought I smelled a woman on you." Fatima

89

"But you didn't. I haven't been with anyone in so long, I can't remember." Don lies

"Good. So how long will it take you to get ready?" Fatima

"Hmm. Give me an hour and I'll call you back." Don

"Okay. Bye honey." Fatima

"Bye baby." Don

Don sits and thinks about his predicament. He knows he ought to get some rest, yet he can feel himself getting horny just thinking about having Fatima. When it rains it pours. Then he remembers that he needs to make one more call.

"Hello." Lydia

"Hey Lydia this is Don."

"Don what's wrong with your voice?" Lydia

"I'm not feeling good at all. I think I have the flu or a bad cold." Don

"If you come over I'll take good care of you." Lydia

"I don't think I would make it, besides my grandmothers making me some chicken soup right now," Don fabricates.

"Oh, well I hope you get better. Is there anything I can do for you?" Lydia

"Nothing I can think of. Just pray for me." Don

"Okay. Call me when you get the chance." Lydia

"I will but it probably won't be till tomorrow. I'm gonna take some alka-seltzer plus and turn my phone down so I can get some rest. I'll call you when I wake." Don

"If you take a cab over, I'll pay for it." Lydia

"No, you and Damian should not be exposed to my germs. I'm going to break this cold tonight and see you all tomorrow."

"Okay," says Lydia sounding disappointed.

"Kiss Damian for me and tell him Daddy loves him." Don

"I will, but Don, do you love me too?" Lydia

"Of course I do. You mean everything to me." Don

"I hope so because I need to talk to you about a few things." Lydia

"Oh. Like what?" Don

"Not over the phone." Lydia

"But you got me curious." Don

"I was just wondering what you are going to do after you graduate?" Lydia

"Are you talking marriage again?" Don

"It's more than that." Lydia

"Well you're right. Let's discuss it tomorrow." Don

"Fine." Lydia

Don feels bad because he knows Lydia's feelings are hurt. "Look honey, if I am going to marry anyone, it will be you. Now let's talk this over sensibly, tomorrow."

"Promise?" Lydia

"Yes I promise," Don

"Okay baby, take care of yourself." Lydia

"Thank you sweetie. Have a good evening." Don

"Bye Don." Lydia

"Peace." Don   Click

Don jumps up, takes a shower and puts on some fresh clothes. He begins to feel a little energy as he wonders what the night will have in store for him. He puts on 'Love Letter' and jams as he gets dressed. While he laces up his new kicks, he calls Fatima up and arranges to meet her on 125th and Lenox. "It's gonna be good night," he declares as he puts on his leather bomber and prepares to exit his place of residence.

(Chapter 13)
PROTECTED

Fatima is the first one to make it to 125th street. She is nervous and excited. She has only been with one other guy and he left her for someone else right after he took her virginity. She has always felt he left because she was a bad lay. She is determined not to let that happen to her again. She is going to whip something on Don that he will never forget.

As usual Don is late. Fatima wants to be mad at him but the dozen roses he hands her is enough to bring a smile to her face. She can't remember anyone giving her roses before.

"You're looking good." He says as he gives her a juicy kiss.

"Thank you," She blushes.

The two walk hand and hand do the New Orleans motel. Although Don has been there a few times already, he acts as if it is his first time there. The room is tiny with a twin bed, a black and white television and few furnishings.

"Is anything wrong?" Asks Don.

"I just expected a nicer room." Fatima

"Well all the nice rooms are in midtown and run between 150 to 250 dollars. I didn't want you to spend all of that money. Besides I'm sure we can still have a nice time. Want to go get some Chinese food?" Don

"That sounds good to me." Fatima

Since there is a Chinese store on every other block, they have no problem finding some shrimp egg foo yung, shrimp rolls and chicken wings.

"Fatima would you like to get something to drink?" Don questions.

"Sure, why not." Fatima responds.

They cross the street to the liquor store and purchase a large cold Alize. "Anything else?" asks Don

"Do you have any condoms?" Fatima
"No I don't." Don
"Maybe you should get one." Fatima
"One! I'm gonna get a whole box!" He says making Fatima
laugh. They stop at a store to buy condoms and then head
back to the motel.
"Don I want to apologize again for flipping on you in the
lunchroom. I don't know what came over me. After I
thought about it I asked myself if you smelled like it when I
saw you after third period and you didn't. I must have been
bugging because I'm afraid you will leave me." Fatima
"Leave you!? I would never do that. And I would like to
apologize for the way I came off on you too. We should
have a better understanding of each other. We should be
able to talk things out." Don
"You speak so sensibly Don. That's one of the main
reasons I love you. You always make sense to me." Fatima
"There is something you don't know about me," Don says
as they enter back into their room for the night.
"What?" Asks Fatima eagerly
"I enjoy a certain pastime." Don
"Huh." Fatima
"I indulge in a vice of life." Don
"I don't understand." Fatima
"I smoke." Don
"You smoke what?" Fatima
"I smoke cannabis sativa." Don
"Is that like a Newport or something?" Fatima
"No!" Don
"Is it like crack?" Fatima
"No, No, No. It's seis, budha, chocolate tye, choke, hydro,
chronic, marijuana, blunts." Don
"Oh you mean weed." Fatima
"Yeah weed. Are you disappointed?" Don
"No not really, just surprised. You don't seem like the sort
of person who would do drugs." Fatima
"So weed is a drug to you. What about Alize?" Don

93

"Alize is a legal drug." Fatima

"Weed is purely natural. You grow it and smoke it just like tobacco." Don

"Yeah but tobacco is legal." Fatima

"Haven't you ever wondered what it is like to smoke some herb?" Don

"No not really." Fatima

"Do you mind me smoking or is that something you would rather I didn't do?" Don

"I would rather you didn't." Fatima

"I like smoking weed and don't see myself stopping anytime soon." Don

"It means that much to you?" Fatima

"Yeah it does." Don

"Well just don't do it around me." Fatima

"That's not fair. If were gonna be together you have to be ready to except all of me. Even the parts you don't like. I could be real good to you if you let me." Don takes her hand gets down on one knee and screams, "I got nuttin but luv 4 ya baby!" Fatima laughs.

They devour their food straight out the container because they don't have plates. They get their fingers and lips all greasy from the chicken wings and shrimp rolls because they don't have napkins. And they get tipsy off the Alize straight from the bottle because they forgot to get cups.

When they are done he gets up, wets a wash cloth with hot water and wipes Fatima's face and fingers off. He knows she likes the hot washcloth treatment because of the look on her face. Feeling too full to start making love Don asks,

"Remember what you said to me on the phone?"

"I said a lot of things on the phone." Fatima

"You said you wanted to hold me through the night." Don

"I said I wish I could hold you through the night. And I do." Fatima

"We can get in the bed, hold each other and watch T.V." Don

"So let's get to holding." Fatima

94

They undress and put their clothes on the only chair in the room. Down to her bra and panties Fatima grabs her overnight bag and goes into the bathroom. He continues to take off his clothes until he is as naked as one can get. He does 40 pushups, stretches and jumps into the bed before Fatima can exit the bathroom. She comes out in a black teddy tip toeing towards the bed. She tries her best to cover the parts that are bulging out but to no avail.

"What are you, shy or something?" Don says as he holds up his hand, stops Fatima from getting into the bed.

"Let me in." Fatima pleads

"No you can't come in yet." Don

"Why not?" Fatima

"Because you haven't turned on the T.V. yet and there's no remote." Don

As she walks to the T.V. Don gets a good view of her from the back. She has a wonderfully athletic but thick body.

"What is that Victoria Secret?" Don

"No I got it from the pink pussy cat boutique." Fatima

"I like it. Model for me." Don

"I don't know how and I can't get any of the channels to work. Come help me." Fatima

"I rather watch you keep trying." Don says feeling extremely lucky. He feels blessed to be in the company of such a beautiful woman. As he gets out of bed, Fatima catches sight of his manhood and can't take her eyes off of it. It seems to swing like a pendulum. Don also has a difficult time finding a working channel. But, after a few tries he is able to adjust the T.V.'s antennae to pick up the channel five news. While he is messing with the boob tube, Fatima slips in the bed and is checking him out. She likes what she sees and feels excitement running through her solar plexus.

He gets back into bed and to his surprise Fatima is totally naked. Her body is soft and warm as he gives her a big hug and sloppy kiss. He holds her tight and squeezes her till she can't breathe. And even though she can't breathe, she loves every second of the affection. "Don't ever let me go," she manages to whisper in his ear.

They are caressing each other's bodies when the news of the city cuts into their foreplay concentration. "There's been another brutal slaying in Manhattan," the newscaster goes on to say. "It is the fourth slaying this month where a black female victim has been robbed and shot in front of an ATM. There has only been one survivor who is in critical condition at Presbyterian. So far the police have no leads and stress that all women should try to use the automated tellers during the daylight hours only. These killers rob and shoot without any mercy. Back to you Bob."

"Thanks Bill, and up next, what do the Knicks need for a winning season? Does racism really exist in the congress and what the FDA doesn't want you to know about beef. After these messages."

"Gosh Don. Sometimes its so scary living in this city." Fatima

"It's scary living anywhere. You're just as much of a statistic here as anywhere else." Don

"What do you mean?" Fatima

"If you move to a smaller town you have less of a chance of becoming a victim because there are less people. Here you have a chance of being a victim but because there are more people here there's less of chance that the victim will be you. It kind of all balances out." Don

"But why do they have to shoot anyway. I mean they rob you. But why do they have to shoot you too?" Fatima

"I don't know. There's an evil out there that manifests itself in so many ways. But I also believe that there is a thin line between good and bad. Like have you ever seen this movie called The Prophesy with Christopher Walken?" Don

"No I don't think so." Fatima

Well the movie took a lot of things from the Bible. It talked about Angels and how God would send them to earth to do his dirty work. And how they are mad at God for giving humans souls. Now a devil is a fallen Angel. Someone who has lost their faith in God. In themselves.

Since Lucifer supposedly took 1/3 of the Angels with him when he was cast to the earth. I think it's only fair to say 1/3 of the people of earth are evil."

"So you honestly believe that 1 out of every 3 people are devils?" Fatima

"Yes. But it goes much deeper than that. You really can't go around labeling people good or evil because there are different degrees of both in each and every one of us. People are constantly transforming. You can be a good guy and still do bad things. Although those good deeds do not cancel out the bad things, the bad ones don't cancel out the good ones either. None of us can really judge the other. We must leave that to the supreme Judge.

"Who? God?" Fatima

"Exactly!" Don

"I'm not God but I know that robbing someone is wrong. Robbing them and shooting them for no reason is evil. I can judge that easily!" Fatima

"I'm not gonna argue with you there, but I want you to know that in your own right you are God." Don

"What are you talking about?" Fatima

"It's too deep and I don't want to go there now. But there is something I would really like you to do for me." Don

"What?" Fatima

"I could really use a nice back massage." He grabs her and kisses her breath away for a few moments before turning on his stomach to let her do her finger magic. She has rubbed his back in the lunchroom once or twice before. But this is clearly different. As he relaxes, he drifts off into another plane when she brings him back this world.

"I heard you had a fight with Johnny. What was that about?"

"Just some jealousy shit." Don

"Why is he jealous?"

"He's jealous because your man is so handsome. I don't know. Maybe because I beat him in twenty-one. Oh yeah right there on my neck." Says Don

97

"Yes you are tense." Fatima

Easily Don drifts back into that state of weightlessness in which all burdens are laid to the side. Within minutes he is at rest. Unaware that Fatima has stopped massaging him and is sipping the last of the Alize. "Shit, I feel so horny," she thinks, looking at Don and enjoying the expression he wears for his dreams. She leaves him alone for a good twenty minutes when she starts to thinking about how she had to do a lot to get Don here. And she spent her money. She isn't sure whether she should leave him alone or not. Massaging him some more, he purrs in his sleep. She gets him to turn on his back and she massages his chest. Soon she is pulling up and down on his piper until it is hard. He half way wakes up. Not so much because she is gently caressing him, but because he has to take a mean piss.

Without opening his eyes, Don puts his arm around her and pulls her close enough to feel her heartbeat. He rubs her over her body and gets even harder with her moans. He does a circular motion on her clit with his finger until she is nice and wet. "I have to use the bathroom," he says.

"Not if I get there first." Fatima says jumping up and running, giggling to the bathroom.

He is right behind her running as she makes it to the toilet first. Even if Don had of made it first, he would not have been able to piss with his dick pointing straight up in the air. Fatima finishes quickly and Don pats her on her butt as she exits the bathroom. Hardly able to wait, he has to push his penis downward in order to urinate. He relieves himself and wishes he could roll a blunt. He decides against it because he does not want to mess up the mood.

He walks out of the bathroom to see Fatima under the covers engrossed in 'Tales From The Crypt'. He slides in the bed next to her and she smiles when he puts his arm around her. To Don, this is the best part. There is something about holding a soft, attractive, warm body that makes him feel life is worth living.

He rubs her hips and commences to squeezing her tight

when she throws him a curve ball. "So what did the Dean want with you yesterday?"

Caught by surprise Don hesitates "He wanted to talk to me about my lateness."

"I heard he called Jackie into his office around the same time." Fatima

"Yeah he called a whole bunch of students into his office." Don

"Really? Like who else?" Fatima

"A few people I didn't recognize." Don

"You didn't recognize any of them?" Fatima

"Uh..Nope." Don

"Jackie is the only one you recognized?" Fatima

"Yeah." Don

"Don, you don't have to lie to me." Fatima

Don thinks about it. He really wants to tell her the truth. But the truth is hard to tell. He can't possibly describe his desire for sexual conquest and expect her to understand.

"Who says I'm lying?"

"Look, I'm not here to debate with you. If you don't want to be honest then don't." Fatima

"Okay, fine. The truth is Jackie filled out late slips for me a couple of times and we got caught." Don

"Huh?" Fatima

"I cut school a few times and asked her to fill out late slips for me. So when my home room teacher would mark me absent, the late slip would nullify the absence and the school secretary would mark me late." Don

"So what happened?" Fatima

"I don't know, somehow we got caught." Don

"Is that why you and Johnny were fighting?" Fatima

"Yeah but I'm not sure why he's so vexed at me." Don

"Maybe he thinks there is something more to you and Jackie." Fatima

"That's possible. But he sure wasn't trying to talk things out." Don

"Is there something going on between you and Jackie?"

Fatima

Don wants to say "Ya damn skippy and her head is da bomb." But instead he says "No our relationship is strictly platonic."

"Just remember Don, you don't have to lie to me." Fatima

He wonders if she could handle the truth. Still he knows this is neither the time nor place to chance it. "I'm sorry for not coming clean sooner. I should have known better. I just didn't want you to get the wrong idea."

Again they cuddle as another episode of 'Tales From The Crypt' comes on. But they don't watch if for long as they become engrossed in some heavy body friction. This time Don is strapped with the jimmy hat.

It is not long before he reaches his peak and very soon after is fast asleep. While Fatima lays awake satisfied but wanting more, she decides to leave him alone and let him sleep. Soon she is also wandering in dreamland and having nice dreams.

Don on the other hand is having awful nightmares. His heart rate is beating at an accelerated pace and he is grinding his teeth. His dreams, most of which he won't remember is about an unseen force of wind that keeps pushing him back.

In one dream, he and a group of associates rob a bank. It is a successful robbery where he and his crew exit the bank one by one. Don is the last to leave. He runs out the door and the police sirens can be heard very close by. He goes to turn a corner and make his getaway when a wind pushes him back. He frantically tries to keep running, but the unseen force doesn't let him get far. He can't move because the wind is too powerful. He wakes up just when the sirens are right behind him and he is about to get caught.

He has another dream where is playing ball by himself in the park, suddenly a pack of vicious dogs approach. He takes off and the dogs chase him. He is out running them until he turns a corner. Then that unseen force returns and he can't go any further. He wakes just when the dogs are about to attack. This unseen force stays with Don, causing him to slip in and out of dream scenarios throughout the night.

(Chapter 14)
UNPROTECTED

Fatima is the first one to wake up. The first thing she notices is how damp the sheets are. She feels Don and realizes that he is the cause of all the wetness. He is hot and sweating like mad. She slides out of bed, quickly brushes her teeth and grabs a dry towel. She pulls the covers off of Don to his waist and towels off his neck and chest. As she is wiping under his arms he breaks into a wide grin. Not wanting to open his mouth because he knows his breath is woofen, he lets her continue to dry his torso. When she is done, Don opens his eyes, gives her a big hug and points at the bathroom then to himself.

He gets out of bed and is surprised to see he still has his prophylactic on. He grabs the top of it, so it won't fall off, smiles at Fatima and walks to the bathroom. Inside the bathroom he lets the used condom drop in the toilet. He proceeds to start pissing which really stings. He starts thinking about Lydia and Damian. He could feel himself missing them. He feels guilty, knowing he should not be playing with Fatima's emotions like he's doing. Thank God I wore a jimmy hat he thinks while brushing his teeth.

Don walks out of the bathroom and starts looking for his underwear. He glances at Fatima who is still under the covers giving him that come on look. Just then there is a knock at the door. Don walks over to it, "Who is it?"

"Housekeeping. It's check out time."

"Okay we're motivating now." Don

"That'll be fine."

"Well Fatima, I think you should start getting dressed."
Don

Fatima slides from under the covers and walks seductively and totally naked towards Don. She stops about six inches away from him and asks, "Do you see something you like?"

"Yeah I see that you need to get your ass dressed so that we can get up on out of here!" Replies Don in a much meaner tone than he even expected to have.

Fatima looks as if her whole world is crushed. Something inside her appears to die. Her eyes get all glossy and red but not a teardrop falls as she and Don gets dressed in silence.

All the while Don is feeling like a prude. He wants to apologize for his rudeness but at the same time he wants to see how far he can go with Fatima. When they are fully clothed and ready to exit the premises, Don takes a good look around and retorts, "You got everything?"

Without looking around Fatima nods her head in a gesture of yes.

It is a sunny but cool Sunday morning when they hit the streets of Harlem. They walk towards the subway and Don asks, "Are you headed uptown?"

"Yes." Fatima responds. Then silence.

"Well I'm headed downtown." Then silence.

They stop on the corner of 125th and Lenox. Don kisses her goodbye thinking he is not even going to walk Fatima downstairs to the turnstile. He is wondering how that will make her feel when she turns, walks to the street and quickly hails a cab. In a flash she is gone. Don knows he just played himself. Here he is trying to be a player and he just got played.

He decides to walk west on 125th and catch the one train on Broadway. While strolling he thinks about the last 48 hours and he knows he needs help. He reflects upon how much of his life is built on lies, illusions, drugs, and lust. He knows he isn't living right, and that life has taught him two lessons. You don't get what you pay for, you pay for what you get. And what goes around comes back around. Everything else is up in the air. "Father of Adam, please watch over me," he says out loud as he bops past the state office building.

Don makes it home a bit before noon. On his bed he finds a note that reads:

Don, your father and I went to church. We tried to wait for

you. Maybe next Sunday, Love Grandma.

"What," thinks Don "Dad went to church!? Times really are changing." He pushes the message retrieval button on his phone and the recorded messages commence. Beep. "Don...Don this is Jackie call me back as soon as you get this message." Jackie says in an earnest voice. Don is sure it has something to do with Johnny. Beep. "A yo Don diggy, yo diggy you in dere?" It's D.J. yo! The shorty's are leaving. If you ain't coming by nigga let me know something." Beep.

"Yeah this is Butler asking Don to hit me on the hip at 9179152026. Don wonders what Butler wants and it makes him feel a bit uneasy. Beep. "Don... Don... Don call me I'm home." It is Jackie again. Beep. "Gosh that is a long beep. I guess you haven't woke up yet. Call me when you wake up,"says Lydia. Don can hear music blasting in the background. He decides to call Jackie first to see what the fuss is.

"Hello."

"Yes, may I speak to Jackie?" Don

"This is Jackie."

"What's up Jackie it's Don."

"Oh hey how ya doing." Jackie

"Chillin. What's up you been calling me like mad." Don

"True, True," Jackie says and then silence.

"So what's up!" Don asks getting tired of Jackie's evasiveness.

"Ah,... I really can't talk now, can I call you back?" Jackie Don pauses for a moment not knowing what to say. "No problem" he finally says. They hang up and he decides to call Lydia.

"Hello."

"Hey It's Don." He can hear music blasting in the background.

"Hey. Are you feeling any better?" Lydia

"100 percent." Don

"I called a little while ago. Where were you?" Lydia

"I was in the shower." Don

"You had a long beep when I called." Lydia

"Yeah...D.J. called right before you and played some of his new mixes into the phone. He gets pretty excited. So what are you doing? Having a party?" Don

"No, just cleaning house." Lydia

"So when do you think you'll be finished cleaning house?" Don

"I don't know. Why?" Lydia

"Well," Don thinks as he glances at a newspaper. "I want to take Damian to a movie."

"A movie? I think Damian would really like that." Lydia

"So..." Don

"So what are you taking him to see?" Lydia

"I was thinking about..." Don quickly turns to the movie section.

"What were you thinking about?" she repeats

"I was thinking about whatever is playing at the IMAX." Don

"That should be fun." Lydia

"Yeah It's supposed to good effects." Don

"So what time are you going?" Lydia

"I thought we'd try to catch the 4:00 show." Don

"I guess I could get Damian ready." Lydia

"What about you?" Don

"What about me?" Lydia

"Are you going to get ready too?" Don

"Are you inviting me too?" Lydia

"Yeah. Why not?" Don

"I thought you had some type of male bonding going on with your son." Lydia

"If you rather not then... "Don

"No it's just that I have a few more things left to do around here." Lydia

"Would you rather catch the 6 O'clock show?" Don

"Hmm. No the 4 O'clock sounds better. Are you coming to get us?" Lydia

"Yeah, I will be there in about an hour. Can you put on the

True Religion jean suit I bought Damian."

"Fine, anymore request?" Lydia

"No, but if I think of anything else, I'll be sure to write it down." They laugh and hang up.

It suddenly dawns on Don that he is suppose to go to the studio with D.J. today. He decides to call him.

"Hello." D.J.

"Yo, what's up nigga?" Don

"Chillin. What happened Don? The freaks waited for a while."

"Sorry Duke but my jimmy been going for 2 grand a pound and the demands been high."

"Huh?" D.J.

"I was somewhere else knocking boots." Don

"Damn Nigga. I thought I was da man." D.J.

"So whatcha was doing?" Don

"Just puffin some lye. Checking out In Da Hood Videos. I got their number. I'm a call them up so we can get some shine." D.J.

"Word!" Hold on let me throw it on too." Don turns on his tel-lie-vision. "Yeah, that video is the bomb. So what's up with the studio today?"

"We straight." D.J.

"You still wanna go? We ain't even get to practice." Don

"You could come over and we could throw together a quick routine." D.J.

"See. That's what I don't want to do. I don't want to do nothing in a hurry. I want us to be able to take our time and put together some phat shit. We should cancel for today and practice some more." Don

"Well you call the studio and tell Chuck. You know how he be flipping when people cancel on him." D.J.

"Yeah he be bugging sometimes." Don

"Na Mean!" D.J.

Don hears two beeps in his ear. "Hold on D.J. he says as he clicks over to his other line to see who is calling him.

"Hello."

"Don, how you feeling?"

"Oh what's up Jackie. Can I call you back?" Don

"It's really important." Jackie

"Okay I'll call you right back." Don

"Hurry up!" Jackie

Don clicks back over to D.J. "So what he say?" Asks D.J.

"Who?" Don

"Who you think? Chuck Nigga! Who were you talking to?" D.J.

"Some bitch." Don

"Oh I thought you called Chuck." D.J.

"Nah but let's call him now. You know what though D.J.?" Don

"What?" Don

"That's the last time I'm a call a woman the B-word." Don

"What the fuck are you talking about?" D.J.

"Alright check it. As I say these words I am deleting them out of my vocabulary. This is the last time I am going to refer to my beautiful sisters as bitches, hoes, sluts and butts. We got to start representing them more." Don

"Shut up nigga and call Chuck." D.J.

"Hold on." Don clicks over, dials Chucks number and clicks back to D.J. connecting his two way line.

"Studio."

"Yo what up Chuck this is Don Diggy."

"Word. What's going on?" Chuck

"Just wondering what was up for today."

"Yeah. I'm in a session. Probably go to six, six-thirty." Chuck

"That's kind of late. I have something to do at eight. We will check with you later for next Sunday." Don

"Cool." Chuck

"Peace." Don. Click

"So watcha gonna do now?" D.J.

"I'm a go chill with my little seed." Don

"True dat, get up with you later." D.J.

"Peace." Click

107

Don immediately dials Jackie number
"Hello."
"What's going on Jackie, this is Don."
"Don... I - I -I know I have to tell you this, but I don't know how. All I can say is that you need to go get yourself checked out."
"What do you mean? I have to leave town? I don't understand!" Don
"No! No! No!... You need to see a doctor."
"A doctor? Why?" Don
"I had a check up Friday after school. Just a routine check up and the doctor told me I have Chlamydia," Jackie
"Chlamydiwho?" Don
"Chlamydia, it's a venereal disease?" Jackie
Silence.
"Look Don for all I know you gave it to me. I'm only telling you this because you were the last one I've been with. Please don't be upset." Jackie
"Upset? What am I suppose to be happy?" Don
"Of course not. I'm sorry. It's my fault. I just got caught up in the moment. I never meant to hurt anybody," she rambles almost in tears.
"O.k... Is it curable?" Don
"Yes it is. I have a list of clinics you can go to." Jackie says through sobs.
He writes down the addresses of several clinics that Jackie gives him. All the while he feels a nausea in the pit of his stomach. He hangs up the phone thinking some horrible thoughts of himself. He feels dirty. Then it hits him hard and he feels really bad. He remembers that he has had unprotected sex with Lydia after he had sex with Jackie. He really does feel sick now and doesn't want to go anywhere.
He can tell that he is about to break out in a cold sore because his lip is beginning to itch.
He lays there in a daze not even hearing his Dad and Grandmother come in the front door. He doesn't even realize they are in the apartment until his grandma taps him

on his leg. "Boy I hope you still alive. Your breathing and your eyes are open."

"Grandma?!" Don sits up, surprised at how deep in thought he was.

"Are you okay?" She puts her hand on his forehead, "You feel a bit hot. Let me take your temperature." She quickly gets a thermometer and places it in his mouth. "You missed a good sermon" she continues, "With some good singing. I thought I would catch the Holy Ghost myself. You really should go to church with us next Sunday." After a few minutes she pulls the thermometer out. It reads between 99 and 100 degrees. "You have a slight fever. You should try to get some rest."

"I can't rest mom. Someone is taking me to the movies," he half lies.

"Well eat some fruit before you go. Don't have me worrying about you." Grandma

Dons Dad enters the room. Clean shaven with a shirt and tie on. Don wants to grab hold of his dad but he is afraid he will burst into tears like a little child. Which is really what he wants to do. Instead he gives his Dad a firm handshake. Unfortunately for Don his Dad wants to hug his son whom he takes into his arms. Don embraces his father and immediately the tears began to fall.

Donald senses something is wrong with his son. He tries to pull Don away to find out what's wrong. Don holds on tight and doesn't budge. So Donald hugs his son firmly, tells him to "Let it all out and everything is going to be alright."

Don gives a good cry before he is able to pull himself together. All the while he is thinking about how he should come clean to his Dad and Grandma about Damian, his problems at school and maybe even tell them about the woman he saved.

He goes into the bathroom to blow his nose, wash his face and tries to pull himself together. All of his thoughts are interrupted when he attempts to take a piss. Pain shoots through his penis, up his ass and out his spine. Because he has started pissing he can't stop and it is an agonizing few minutes of pain which he has never felt the likes of before.

This time his eyes are wet for a different reason and he doesn't have to think too hard as to what the problem is. It is then that he notices the yellow puss stains in his underwear. I'm gonna be the first one at the clinic he tells himself while trying to find the right facade to put on for his guardians. He rinses his face, puts Vizine in his eyes and rubs lotion on his skin. Just before he is ready to exit, his grandma knocks on the door, "Is everything alright?"

Don opens the door, "Yes everything is good. I didn't mean to fall apart like that, it's just, it's just that ..."

"Don't worry. Your father told me all about it. I understand your sadness so I'm going to let you grieve. It's healthy. Just don't forget that you have a family that loves, needs and supports you."

"Thank you grandma."

"And have a nice time at the movies."

Don is out the door in less than five minutes. He hasn't had anything to drink yet he still feels intoxicated. He is thinking about the fact that he needs to stop his drug habit and try to clean up his act. He is feeling like a cat on his ninth life. He not sure how he will pull through all of this, but he knows he has to. Before he is ready he finds himself on Lydia's block.

How the fuck do you tell someone you gave them a venereal disease. He knows one thing for sure, he will let her know today. Don knocks on the door and tries his best to look normal. He gives Lydia a light peck on the lips and a cheap hug. He picks Damian up, gives him a squeeze and asks, "Is everybody ready to go?"

"Go? Are you kidding? The movie starts at four and it's only two. You still don't look well. Is everything alright? Are you sure you feel like going out?" Lydia

"Yeah It's cool. Actually I'm feeling kind of hungry, so I thought we might stop by Wendy's before going to the movies."

"Oh, so the day is getting better and better." Lydia

"True and it will probably get even better," Don says in a sarcastic tone that is meant more for himself than Lydia.

By 2:15 they are out the door heading towards the train station. Don feels anxious and fidgety because he knows Lydia will be furious when he breaks the bad news to her. At the same time he wants to have a really good time with his family. Especially since he is not sure if he will ever be given the opportunity to enjoy time with them again. The train doesn't take long, they are at Wendy's by a quarter to three. Feeling his appetite returning Don eats two chicken burgers, chili fries, apple pie and no soda. Lydia has the same minus one burger plus a soda. And Damian is not too far behind her because the boy can eat.

After they devour their meal, and they walk to the movie theater. Inside the theater Don's stomach begins to bother him and he can't seem to concentrate on the movie. He has so much on his mind that he feels he needs to start rebuilding immediately.

"Don what's wrong?" asks Lydia

"Nothing. Why?" Don

"You seem so distant. It seems you have a lot on your mind. Do you want to talk about it?" Lydia

"No. Not yet. I just don't feel fully myself. I think I still have a slight fever. How are you feeling?" Don

"Pretty good. I'm happy to be out with my two favorite fellows." Lydia

"If you only knew," thinks Don as he puts his arm around her. The movie is over before he is ready to leave. He knows the time is approaching when he will have to tell this woman what has happened. They take a cab back to Lydia's house and Don feels like a bundle of nerves.

"Don your lip is breaking out." Lydia

"A fever blister. Right?" Don

"That's what it looks like." Lydia

"I could feel it coming up since this morning." Don

"You should put some baby oil on it. It will help dry it out." Lydia

111

"I will give it a try." Don says as he excuses himself to the bathroom. The closer he gets to the bathroom the more he feels like he has to take a serious crap. He sits on the toilet but produces no movement. He feels no better when he has to do number one. It feels as if he is shooting fire from his dick. He does not want to live through the pain, unfortunately he does.

Don wipes his eyes and then wipes his ass when the idea hits him. He reaches in his back pocket for a pen and begins writing on the toilet paper. His first few attempts wind up in the toilet but finally he is able to leave the proper message.

Dear Lydia,
I'm sure this will mean the end of our relationship. Just remember that Damian and I need each other. But I may have given you a venereal disease. Hopefully one day you can forgive me.
Very Truly Sorry
Don

He walks out of the bathroom and tells her that he is not feeling well. She tries to get him to stay, but he doesn't want to be around when she finds the message. As he is leaving he can only hold back the tears for so long. Lydia sees one fall but doesn't know what to say. She is not even sure what is troubling him. Soon she will be glad he left.

Don feels lonely on a crowded street. He digs his hand in his pocket and is surprised to find Mary, his one true companion. "Ra please look over me," he says to himself as he struts down the block towards the park.

(Chapter 15)
KARMA

Don stops at a bodega and buys a dutchmaster. He walks to the park and picks a secluded spot in the shade. He dumps the weed into the dutch and rolls it. He lights it and starts puffing. He is feeling his lowest and dirtiest. He convinces himself to smoke the whole blunt because it is suppose to be his last.

Meanwhile, Damian who has recently learned to use the toilet on his own steps into the bathroom to do his thing. He is oblivious to the writing on the tissue which gets wiped up his butt and flushed down the toilet. Lydia never gets the message.

Don puffs on his blunt and wonders how his life has become such a mess. He didn't want to hurt anyone. All he wanted was to love and be loved. After the blunt is done, Don starts stepping. By the time he gets in front of his building, he isn't ready to go home so he keeps walking. Soon he looks up and finds himself in front of Prebertyrian hospital. He decides to inquire about the health of Ms. Shahard the woman he saved.

He finds out that she is still in serious but improving condition in room 308 north. He goes to her room and is surprised to find that she is not alone. A young teenager is seated next to the bed.

"Can I help you?!" Says the young man in a tone that is meant to protect his mother from any more possible danger.

"Yes, I just wanted to check on Ms. Shahard and see if there is anything I can do for her." Don

"I don't know you. Who are you?" Interrogates the teen.

"Donathan Breyer," says Ms. Shahard with a faraway look in her eyes. "He is the man who saved my life. Don this is Basheem my son. My pride and joy."

"It's nice to meet you Basheem." Don says while shaking his hand. "I'm glad to see you looking after your mother."

"So I guess Officer Butler told you I wanted to see you. The way the doctor's explained it to me, your quick response saved my life. I want to thank you. You are truly an angel."
Ms. Shahard.

Don stays with the woman and her son for over an hour. For a person who is in serious condition she can clearly talk a lot. Don learns that Basheem has been practically taking care of himself since she has been in the hospital. Don also finds that he and Basheem share a lot in common.

By the time Don is leaving, he is looking at Basheem like the little brother he never had. He truly wants the best for this family, and hopes Basheem won't make the same mistakes that he has made. Don hopes that somehow he can redeem himself and start over fresh. But now he feels corrupted and corroded. "Oh Heavenly One please stand by me," he says to himself as he begins his trek towards home.

Don arrives at his building feeling dehydrated. He has a thirst that he is afraid to quench. He doesn't want to go through the pain of urinating again. He walks into his apartment, says "Hello" to his grandma and heads towards his room. He is a bit relieved to see his Dad's room shut. He steps into his own room, undresses and hits the shower. The water is steaming hot but his body is numb to the heat. He scrubs himself thoroughly but still he feels unclean.

As he is toweling off, drops of discharge hits his foot and he really feels dirty. "The clap on my dick, a fever blister on my lip and a big ass pimple on my nose, I'm ready for the big time," he jokes while looking in the mirror.

Don slips on an old pair of underwear and puts wads of tissue in it to absorb the puss. He then puts the stained underwear he had on before his shower in a plastic bag and throws them away. He clicks on Tracey Chapman's 'Crossroad' CD, turns the light out and slides into bed. He reaches over and sets the alarm clock for 6:30.

When he finally relaxes, all of his muscles seem to ache. It isn't so much a pain type of aching but more like an over worked body that's spluttering to an idle state. Soon Tracey

Chapman takes away all the feelings and thoughts he may have had. He becomes lost in her melodies, lyrics, rhythms and music. He has always felt that Tracey made music especially for him, but of course he never told anyone that.

Tracey is telling Don about all the bridges he is burning when the phone rings. It rings five times before he picks it up. He puts the receiver to his ear feeling nervous about whom it may be, "Hello."

"Hello Don, It's me Jackie."

"Yeah what do you want?" Don

"I just wanted to call...because I needed someone to talk to." Jackie

"Talk about what?" Don

"I feel nasty and unclean." Jackie

"How do you think I feel?" Don

"I'm thinking about taking an Aids test."

"Huh?" Don

"You should take one too." Jackie

"Damn! Shit! What are you trying to say?"

"Nothing I just want to know I don't have it so I can go on with my life." Jackie

"Jackie why did you drag me into this shit?" Don

"I never meant to drag you anywhere. Everything happened spontaneously. I never for one moment thought I would catch a venereal disease. Not me. That happens to other people." Jackie

"So what did you tell Johnny?" Don

"I blame Johnny and yes I told him. I told him off real good. And he hit me in the eye," she begins to cry "That motherfucker hit me!"

"Say word! Are you okay?" Don asks but she continues crying "It's lonely ain't it?"

"What do you mean?" She manages to asks between sniffles.

"Tracy Chapman has a line in her song where she says 'One day you'll find you walking lonely.' That's the way I feel, lonely and walking nowhere." Don

115

"Yeah that's how, sniff, I feel, sniff. I can live with losing that no good motherfucker I called a boyfriend but I don't want to lose a good friend."

Not knowing who she is talking about Don asks "Who?"

"You Don. I don't want to lose your friendship." Jackie

"Look Jackie if you're looking for forgiveness, its much too soon. I mean I want to forgive you but every time I go to piss I can't forget. It's like trying to pee acid. I've been afraid to drink anything all day because it hurts so much."

Don

Jackie doesn't have much to say anymore he hangs up. Don feels sorry for her but he is in no mood to try and ease her conscious. His life is screwed up because of her. "The nerve of her," he thinks when he hears Tracey Chapman tell him to be careful of her heart. Then Fatima flashes in his mind. He decides to call her.

"Hello."

"Fatima?" Don

"Yes." Fatima

"This is Don."

"Oh hi." Fatima

"Can you talk? Are you busy?" Don

"No." Fatima

"I just wanted to thank you for a wonderful night." Don

"I had a nice time too." Fatima

"I would like to apologize for being grumpy this morning. It's just that I have a lot on my mind." Don

"Anything to do with the fight you had?"

"Yeah, and now the principle wants me to bring a parent to school. I don't know what to do." Don

"Don there's been a few times when I felt like I was at the end of my rope and you had some positive uplifting things to say. I remember you once told me life is a lesson or blessing. That really meant a lot to me. All I can say is hand all of your burdens over to God. Ask him to help you find the answers. In time he will."

It feels funny to Don, hearing his own quotes being thrown

back at him. "I guess I need to do like Barry White and practice what I preach."

They laugh, talk a little more and hang up with Fatima feeling good and Don fronting like she made everything better. He puts on some Miles Davis and wants to call Lydia but he does not dare. His grandmother comes in to say goodnight and commends him on hitting the bed early. She leaves and Don lies there thinking of what it would be like to have his own apartment. That is one of the main reasons he has stayed in school. He wants to be able to get his own crib. He definitely doesn't want to move into someone else's house. He wants to be his own man. Why live in one person's house just to move into another person's house. Get your own he reasons.

He thinks about how he should tell his father and Grandmother that he has a son that they may never see. He also should tell them about his fight at school and that one of them has to come in to speak to the principal. Maybe even tell them about how he saved Ms. Shahard. And maybe not tell them about how he caught V.D. "The ish is about to hit the fan," he says out loud as he grabs a piece of paper and a pen. The room is too dark so he pulls the shades up to let the moonlight fill the room.

Dear Dad and Grandma

There are a lot of things going on in my life. Things I am not proud or happy to tell you. But things you should know. First of all, Dad you are a grandfather and grandma you are a great-grandmother. Have been for over two years now. Hopefully one day you will get to meet Damian. Secondly, I had a fight at school on Friday, so someone has to come to speak to the principal. And lastly, I saved a woman's life. I was walking to the bank, saw she was hurt and rushed her to the hospital. I'm sorry for all the pain I have caused you.

Sincerely Don

He folds the letter twice and sticks it in his side knapsack

117

pocket. He feels somewhat relieved after writing it. It is as if a big burden is lifted off his chest. 'The Man With The Horn' comes on and although Don has never seen Miles Davis perform he can visualize Miles turning his horn into any instrument he wants. Sometimes it sounds like a guitar or violin and even a singer. Miles horn sings songs that Don hears and feels. It's a music thing, if you can't feel it you won't understand. He is lost in Miles message when the phone rings.

"Hello."

"Hey Don this is Lydia."

"Hi Lydia."

"Are you okay? Were you sleeping with the music on?" Lydia

"Yeah kind of," says Don feeling nervous because he thinks Lydia is waiting to let him have it. "So what's up?"

"I'm just calling to see how you are doing. Why are you acting so snotty? Are you alone?" Lydia

"Of course I'm alone. My grandma wouldn't let me have no one in here like that." Don

"Like what?" Lydia

"Like how you mean." Don

"Is there something you want to tell me?" Lydia

"No but I bet you want to tell me something." Don

"What are you talking about?" Lydia

"Have you been to the bathroom?" Don

"What?" Lydia

"Have you been in the bathroom?" Don

"So many times I lost count!" Lydia

"Since I left, have you been to the bathroom?" Don

"Yes I have. Why?!" Lydia

"You didn't see?" Don

"See what?" Lydia

"Is Damian using the toilet on his own?"

"Yeah, I thought you knew." Lydia

"He wipes himself, flushes the toilet and everything?" Don

"As best as he can, why?" Lydia

118

Don's mind begins clicking. "I'm just so proud of him that's all."

"Oh..." Lydia

"But I haven't been feeling good at all. I've been having these pains. Tell me have you slept with someone else? You must tell me the truth. It could mean life or death." Don

Lydia is taken back by Dons question and his seriousness. She goes silent because she is not sure how to answer. Don elaborates, "Did you give my pussy away!?"

Lydia is broken. "Yes," she mumbles "I had sex with someone else."

"Well you better stop it because I have a feeling that he gave you something you really didn't want. And you may have given it to me." Don

"What do you mean?

"I only did it once and we used a condom." Lydia

"I don't give a fuck if you used a garbage bag! Condoms aren't 100 percent safe. And you too stupid to realize that niggas with germs want to spread them. He could have put holes in the condom on purpose. Did you buy the condom?!" Don

"No." She bows head in shame, sniffling and breathing hard.

"Now I'm going to the doctor tomorrow to see what's up. I know I haven't been with nobody but you so if it's what I think it is you better get your ass to a doctor quick cause you're burning like a hot wheel!" Don says regretting his last line.

What more can Lydia say? Deep down she knows Don is a player. But she admitted to having an affair and he didn't. She will have to bare the blame for this one. After a while she will actually think it is her fault. She will believe that she gave Don some horrible disease and that this is her punishment for sleeping around.

When they hang up, Don really wonders about himself. He is becoming a very deceitful man? He knows he now has the upper hand on Lydia, but he also knows that his predicament is nothing to be proud of. He is just glad to have been given another chance to keep his family together. Now that he can blame Lydia, which he will never throw in her face, he does feel a little bit better. Don decides to do something he has not done in a while, he gets on his knees and prays. He asks the Lord for forgiveness of all of his sins and thanks God for his life. He asks to be made strong to overcome all obstacles that are put in his path. He asks God for continued blessings and guidance. He concludes with asking God to maintain the good health of his family and his family's friends and his friends and friend's families.

He gets back into bed, closes his eyes but cannot fall asleep. For over an hour he lays there unable to reach slumber. When he finally does fall asleep, the nightmares begin.

He dreams that he has just awakened from a good night's sleep. He yawns, stretches and groggily gets out of bed. He looks at himself in the mirror and sees a tired looking face starring back at him. He starts brushing his teeth vigorously when he feels a tooth become loose. He goes to touch the tooth and it falls onto his tongue. He spits the tooth into the sink, rinses his mouth, he grins in the mirror to see how the missing tooth looks. The tooth next to it is leaning so he tries to straighten it out and it too falls into his mouth.

He begins to panic because teeth are falling out left and right. He runs out of the bathroom and suddenly he is in a boxing ring. He looks to the other side of the square and there is a 7 foot 300 pound red eyed Answar glaring down on him. Don is about to jump over the ropes when he takes a look at the seated crowd. His whole high school, teachers, staff, family, friends, everyone Don ever knew and doesn't know is in the crowd. They are watching and expecting to see a fight. He turns and Answar hits him with an uppercut to the chin. Don is literally lifted up in the air and flies a few feet backward. The crowd is laughing at him. He starts to plead with Answar to stop. Answar hits him again and knocks out any remaining teeth. Don gets angry. He punches the huge Answar in the stomach and Answar smiles. Don hits him again and again and again. Answar doesn't seem to be hurting but he's being kept busy trying to block Don's punches. Don keeps swinging on Answar and yelling, "You're not a man. You're not a man!" He feels like he's been throwing punches forever while Answar hides behind his gigantic muscular arms.

Don keeps swinging till his arms get tired. Especially his left one. Soon his left arm drops limp. He can't pick it up and it feels completely numb. He is still swinging with his right when Answar peeks from the cover of his biceps and gives Don a menacing look. Again he smashes Don across the jaw. Don feels his jaw snap. He hits Answar with his right but his left arm is still down. The crowd is roaring with laughter and Dons heartbeat is going a mile a minute. He is just about to be hit with a fatal blow when he wakes up in a cold sweat.

Even awake, the nightmare is not over. His left arm really won't move. It is locked in the above his head position that he fell asleep in. Apparently the blood couldn't flow properly through his arm and the arm went to sleep. The cut off circulation made it unusable. Don uses his good arm to lift up his bad one and place it by his side. It feels like needles are pricking his arm while the blood begins to circulate through his arm, but he is relieved when he can move his fingers.

He then gets up to check his teeth and thank goodness they are all still there. He wants to use the bathroom but he doesn't dare. He gets back in bed at 3 a.m. feeling as if he hasn't slept at all. This time sleep comes quick, but so does the nightmares.

Once again it starts with him getting up in the morning. He stretches, walks to the bathroom and starts the shower. He gets in and proceeds to get wet. He scrubs his body and lather's his hair. He starts to rinse off and puts his head under the water to be rinsed. He is startled when clumps of hair hits the tub and heads for the drain. The more he rinses the more hair falls out. He scratches his head and a fingernail becomes loose. He touches it and the entire nail attached to his finger falls off. The inside of his finger looks pussy yellow, red and gooey. Every nail he tests for strength afterward falls off.

Throughout all of this he glances at his penis which looks like a piece of soap shaped like a dick. He puts it under the water and it begins to melt like if it is made of comet or flour. Don is horrified but he can't seem to take his joint from under the water until it has almost disappeared.

The steam from the shower fills the room. He frantically turns the knobs but the water won't stop. He steps out of the shower and tries to open the bathroom door. The door won't budge. He can feel the oxygen in the room decreasing. Then a red light above the door begins to flash and an alarm starts to ring. This only panics Don more as he pounds on the door screaming. Unable to breath he falls to the floor.

His last thought is that he is going to die as the light continues flashing and the alarms volume becomes deafening to his ears.

(Chapter 16)
COME CLEAN

Somehow Don wakes up and realizes that the alarm in his dream is his own alarm clock which has been going off for the past fifteen minutes. He shuts the clock off but he has trouble getting up because he feels like he has not slept at all. He thinks about his johnson and decides he better get up.

Sitting up, he thinks back to when he had sex with Ebony and Zelda. He did not use anything as far as protection. Don wonders if he should tell D.J. who probably hit it some more after he left. "Shit," he says while getting dressed and deciding not to call his boy yet. Don feels nervous because he knows anything can happen at any time.

He looks in the mirror and thanks the Supreme Being that all of his teeth are still there. His hair and nails are also present but he can feel the disease inside him. His mind is putrefying from the drugs, his body is infected with deadly germs, and his soul is haunted by his conscience. A conscience that tells him he needs to come clean and tell the truth.

As he brushes his teeth, he plans his next few moves. He will leave the letter in the living room before going to the train station. Then he is going to the clinic on 23rd street because he wants to go far away from where he lives. He does not want anyone to recognize him.

As he prepares to leave, his mind wonders about what the day will bring. Once again he kneels down to pray. Then he grabs his music player and knapsack as he makes his exit.

"You're up early," says his grandma sipping tea in the living room.

"I'm trying to get an early start." Don

"Good. Good. Want something to eat?" Grandma

"No I have to run. But I will take an apple. Love you grandma," he kisses her goodbye. It isn't till he gets to the station that he remembers he forgot to leave the letter for his

Dad and grandma somewhere they could find it.

He arrives at the 23rd street station quickly, however when he gets to the front of the clinic there is already a line. Don gets on the back and counts about 18 people in front of him. He puts on his shades and tries his best to blend it.

There are all kinds of people on the line, mainly men. Some look like bums. One guy has on a three piece suit. There are a handful of females, some of whom look like prostitutes. Don wonders how he fits in.

By the time they start letting the infected into the clinic, there are about twenty to twenty-five people behind him. The chaos begins when the people at the front of the line cram into an elevator while the ones who can't fit in the elevator run up the stairs in an effort to beat the ones in the elevator to the third floor. Don hits the stairs and follows the crowd to the third floor when the elevator opens up and the rush intensifies. He manages to maintain his previous position on line.

All of a sudden the place gets quiet and a man's squeaky voice is heard saying "Excuse me but I was here first." "Fuck you," says another voice and then silence. Within seconds the murmur of voices is back in sync and the line starts moving. Everyone has to take a number, fill out a form and have a seat. Don gets a blue ticket marked number 19 (women get pink tickets) and finds a seat in the back rows. One row up to his left Don sees someone sit down. At first Don thinks it is an attractive woman but when he does a double take he senses that something isn't quite kosher.

Soon they start calling numbers. Don can see an adam's apple on the woman when they call her number. He wonders if the doctor will be surprised to find out that the woman is really a man. Nevertheless it is less than a half an hour before Dons number is called.

He is asked to roll up his shirt and wait in a small room. About ten minutes later a nurse who looks like an older version of Lil Kim walks in. She takes his heart rate, his blood pressure and some blood. She asks him if he wants to

124

take an Aids test and he declines. She puts a check in a box on his form.

"Pull down your pants and sit on the table," she orders. Don is embarrassed when he pulls down his underwear and a wad of tissue is stuck to his tool.

As if she sees that all the time, the nurse calmly produces a plastic baggie. Don peels the tissue off and drops it in the bag which she wraps up and discards. Then she pulls out the longest Q-tip Don has ever seen. She rubs the cotton swab on the tip of his penis to soak up some discharge. She then rubs the discharge on the left side of a slide. She gets another jumbo Q-tip and without warning sticks it up his penis shaft. He is paralyzed with pain, but before he can react, she pulls it out. It has puss mixed with blood on it. She rubs the disease on the right side of the slide, covers it and tells him to get dressed.

"That's it?!" Asks Don

"For now, they will call your name to see the doctor." Nurse

"The doctor?! There's more." He screams angrily.

"Do you want to be cured!?" She snaps back.

Don quietly gathers his belongings. He is feeling small and defeated knowing he can't win with negativity. "I'm sorry for getting uppity. This has just been an experience I could have done without."

Her eyes soften to his tone. "It's okay sweetie. Now you just wait for your name to be called so the doctor can give you your medicine."

"Thank you," Don says about to leave.

"Just remember honey, condoms save you a whole mess of trouble." Nurse

"True, true," he says trying to leave.

"You look like such a nice young man. I'm going to pull a few strings and get you out of here as quickly as possible. But I don't ever want to see you here again. Is that a deal?" Nurse

"Yes, absolutely. Thank you. Really thanks. And God

Bless" he finally exits. He takes a seat and wonders what kind of strings she can pull. Within twenty minutes they call his name and he is once again escorted to a small room.

A doctor who looks like Flava Flav with a West Indian accent walks in and introduces himself as Dr. Chissmor. He opens up Don's file and says, "You have been diagnosed with Gonorrhea. It is commonly called syphilis or the clap. Do you have any idea who you may have contacted this disease from?"

"Yes, the young lady who told me I was infected did it." Don

"Is she seeking help?" Chissmor

"Yes she is." Don

"It says here you don't want to take an Aids test. Is there a reason why?" Chissmor

"I'm just not ready to know if I only have a short time to live."

"Are you currently taking any medication or are you allergic to penicillin?" Chissmor

"No and No." Don

"Please pull down your undergarments," the Dr. says while putting on some rubber gloves. Don does what Dr. Chissmor asks but becomes terrified when the Dr. reveals a 12 inch long needle.

"Please tell me you are going to put me to sleep first." Don

"Ha ha, no. This will only take a second. Please turn around and bend over." Chissmor

He is relieved to find that the good Doctor isn't going to stick the needle in his penis. But the pain is quite devastating when the doctor sticks it in his right butt cheek. Within seconds it is over and the Doctor is giving him a prescription to fill. As he walks out of the cubicle, his right leg and hip become increasingly numb with each step he takes.

He drags himself up to the pharmacy and the lady behind the counter takes his prescription. Within minutes she returns with two bottles of pills. "Are you currently

126

employed?" She inquires.

"Yes I am." Don

She writes something on his form, "How much do you make?"

"Before or after taxes?" Don

"Before."

"About $320.00 a week. Why?" Don

She writes it down and pulls out a calculator. "I need to calculate your rate of payment."

"Payment? I thought this was a free clinic."

"Only if you're unemployed. It will cost you eight dollars to fill your prescription."

Don digs in his pocket and pulls out a ten dollar bill.

"I'm sorry but we don't give change. Please read the sign."

The sign says Exact Amount Only.

"I'm glad I didn't only have a dub." Don

"Next time you'll know."

"There won't be no next time." Don

"Do you want to go change this?" She says holding the ten up in the air.

"No keep it for a tip." Don says taking his prescription and limping out of the clinic. Out of the blue he gets the bright idea to ask Butler if he could pose as his uncle and speak to the principal on his parent's behalf. He takes out his phone and hits Butler up.

"Hello." Butler   "Butler?" Don

"Yep."

"This is Don. Donathan Breyer. We met at the hospital Saturday"

"Yeah, I remember. I left a message on your service." Butler

"True, True." Don

"I wanted to let you know that Ms, Shahard wants to see you and thank you."

"Yes as a matter of fact I went to see her yesterday." Don

"Word?!" Butler

"Yeah I even met her son and all that."

"That's wonderful. So what's up with you?" Butler

"Well I'm not too great." Don

"Nah? What's up?" Butler

"Well, yo...this honey at school threw the trim at me so I tagged it. Her man got mad. We fought and now I have to bring a parent to school. To top it off, she burned me." Don

"Oh shit! Nooooo." Butler

"It's true. I just left the clinic." Don

Damn kid, haven't you ever heard that 'Wu-Tang' Aids kills joint? You got to respect it. Jimmy's have to be fully strapped."

"I know. It all felt so innocent. I wore one the first time..." Don

"You gotta wear a Jimmy hat every time. There are so many things that can happen."

"True, true." Don

"So you headed to school now?" Butler

"Yeah and I need a favor from you." Don

"A-ight, watcha need." Butler

"I figured I could help you out if you help me out." Don

"Okay, what's on your mind?" Butler

"I need you to come to my school, and say you're my uncle, and tell the principle that I will stay out of trouble for the rest of the year." Don

"And what's in it for me?" Butler

"I may be able to help identify the ATM killers." Don

"Well as of last night we have someone in custody who has confessed to the crimes."

"It was two of them." Don

"Are you sure?" Butler

"Yes." Don

"Can you identify them?" Butler

"I believe so." Don

"Okay. I'll pose as your uncle if you come down after school to see if we have at least one of the right culprits. Deal?" Butler

"Deal." Don

128

"Where should I meet you?" Butler

"Could you meet me on 110th and Pleasant in about 45 minutes?" Don

"I'll be there." Butler

Don hangs up and his stomach begins to bubble. He feels like he won't be able to hold it so he runs back into the clinic. He takes a big dump and a painful piss. He looks in the mirror and sees an exhausted looking face staring back at him. "I have to get something to drink," Don thinks feeling extremely dehydrated. On the way to the train station he buys a cranberry/apple juice and chug-a-lugs. It feels like he hasn't drunk anything in days. He has to get another. The train takes longer than its usual lateness so by the time Don gets to his destination he is twenty minutes late.

"I was wondering if I was at the right place." Butler says while slapping Don five.

"The trains Duke, my fault. Damn you look like a true hood without your uniform." Don

"This is how I am most comfortable. So what's the plan?" Butler

"Okay, the principal's name is Ms. Castilla. You are my Uncle, here to support me on my Dads behalf because he has to work. Stress the fact that I only have a few more months left to go and it's crucial that I graduate." Don

"What about your moms?" Butler asked feeling a bit guilty because he already did his research and knows what happened to Don's mother.

"My mother passed away a few years ago."

"I'm sorry to hear that." Butler

"I will do most of the talking," Don says as they head into the school. The first person they bump into is the dean.

"What do we have here," the Dean sneers. "Donathan Breyer trying to sneak one of his home boys in."

"Actually this is my uncle and we're going to see the principal."

"Oh really," he says in a I don't believe you tone. Looking at Butler he asks "Do you have any I.D.?"

129

Don watches Butler pull out his badge and show the dean his I.D. But he doesn't see Butler flash his gun at the dean.

"Fine" the dean says and hurries away.

"I'm starting to think he's a real bitch as nigga," says Don. "Ms. Castilla's office is this way."

They knock on the door. "Enter" they hear. As they walk into the office filled with awards, degrees and plaques, Don feels his hands getting sweaty. Butler on the other hand is only taken back by the radiance of the principal.

"Hello Ms. Castilla, how are you?" Don

"I'm fine thank you. And how are you?" She asks never really taking her eyes off of Butler.

"I'm okay. This is my Uncle Butler." Don

"Without sounding rash" Butler jumps in, "I would like to iterate that you are the most stunning principal I have ever seen," he finishes by bowing and kissing her hand.

"I appreciate that very," she manages to reply after a few moments of blushing. Don thinks Butler sounds corny but he likes the affects.

"Unfortunately" Ms. Castilla continues, "This is not a pleasant visit. Your nephew had a fight and seriously injured another student. We have rules against such acts."

"But Ms. Castilla, It was purely self defense. I was in the pool when he came after me. He was trying to drown me!" Don

"He claims that you attacked him for no reason at all." Ms. Castilla

"May I add" Butler drops in, "Don only has a few more months left and this time is crucial to what he could be doing for the rest of his life."

"Also," Don jumps in. "I can prove that Johnny came after me. I was playing twenty-one with Drew, Tony and Gary when Johnny came after me the first time. He missed me and busted Gary's lip! Ask Gary. Then I left and went to the pool. Ask them and they'll tell you. I left and he came after me. All I want to do is finish school and move on with my life."

130

"Well you can't get on with it if you're spending it in the custodians bathroom!" Ms Castilla. Both Don and Butler are dumbfounded by her curve ball.

"I really had to go Ms, Castilla and you know none of the boy's bathroom stalls have doors. I couldn't be comfortable. It was either that or use the girls bathroom. They have stalls." Don

"And how do you know that?" Ms. Castilla

"A girl told me." Don

Ms. Castilla goes silent. She looks as if she is seriously pondering the situation.

"I guess I will have to look further into the matter. But you stay away from Johnny."

"I will, I promise." Don

"So I understand you have a job," she says to Don.

"Yes for almost two years now." Don

"I'm proud of you for that. Make me even more proud of you by graduating without any more trouble." Ms Castilla

"Thank you Ms. Castilla." Don

"Yes thank you Ms Castilla," Butler says once again grabbing her hand. "And hopefully next time we meet it can be over lunch."

"Sounds nice," Butler and Don are surprised to hear.

"May I walk my Uncle to his car?" Don

"Make it quick," Ms Castilla.

As they exit Butler leaves her with a "Ta Ta."

Once outside Don replies "Ta Ta?" What's a Ta Ta?" They laugh and Don continues. "Thanks a lot B.J. I really mean it. I owe you big time."

"It seems like you would have done fine without me." Butler

"Nah I couldn't have done it without you. Word up!" Don

"No problem. But I still need you to come downtown and see if you can identify this guy. Just tell me something, how come you didn't tell me about the two guys from the beginning?" Butler

"At first I couldn't see myself helping brothers go to jail."

Don

"So what's changed?" Butler

Don takes a moment to seriously think about the question, "I've changed and I actually wish someone could have done it for me when my mother was killed."

"I hear that." Butler says as he opens the door to his Acura, "I'll see you in a minute." They slap five, Butler gets in his car and Don heads back into the school.

Don is feeling on the road to recovery. He feels as if there is a ray of hope left. He is even feeling lucky. A little too lucky. He hates this feeling because something always happens to fuck up everything.

Just before he gets to the school doors, Johnny comes bustin out and looking wild with a bandage taped to his nose. Johnny stands stationary starring Don down. Don feels nervous at first. Then he decides that he will fight if he has to. So he stares back. Then Johnny does the unexpected, he pulls out a very long and skinny knife from his inside coat pocket. Without warning he lounges at Don with the blade. Don turns to run. He takes a couple of steps when he feels a hot flame go through his lower back. He turns around swinging wildly. One blow catches Johnny in the nose and blood spatters out from under the bandages. Johnny starts running away and Don kicks him right in the butt. The kick hurts Don as much as it does Johnny because Don feels like he broke his foot. Johnny keeps running while Don feels the pain of the kick and the pain of the knife stuck in his back.

Butler is looking for his Kay Slay CD when Johnny goes dipping past his car. He doesn't think much about it until he makes a u-turn. He looks in his rear view and sees someone crawling on the ground. "It can't be," he panics and hits the car in front of him. Jumping out of his vehicle Butler sees Johnny about a half a block away still running. He wants to give chase but goes to the guy who is crawling instead hoping it is not Don. "Nooo!!" He screams when he realizes it is. Butler kneels down and grabs hold of Don. "Help! Help!" He begins to yell. Some students look out a window.

"Tell your teacher to call an ambulance!" He screams.
"Hold on Don help is on the way," Butler says sitting on the pavement with Don cradled in his arms. "It's gonna be alright Don. Just stay with me man. Don't let go little brother."
"Yeah" Don says in a far away voice. "There's a letter...My bag... for my Dad. Please give it..."
"Nah man you can give it to him yourself. You ain't going nowhere!" Butler is alarmed at how much blood Don is losing. He wants to cover the wound but the knife is protruding out of Dons back. He is afraid to injure Don more by pulling the object out.

Butler barely notices the crowd forming. Students are coming out of every exit. Fatima runs out screaming and crying. Her grief starts a chain reaction and more girls start boo hooing. Jackie comes out and gets all hysterical, screaming, carrying on and setting off more teary eyed spectators. When the principal comes out and damn near breaks fool it makes everyone watching cry. Butler looks up and can't believe it. He has never seen this much mourning at funerals. Then he concludes that this is a funeral. All these people are crying for Don because he is dying.
"Nooooo" he screams and cries with everyone else until the ambulance takes Don away.

THE END
(of Act I)

"Dedicated to all of my adversaries
I spit upon you..."

Not Just Sex (Act II)

Formerly known as "PUBLIC ACCESS"

Contents

(Chapter 1)
Run Nigga Run

Johnny runs. He runs so fast that he is a blur to most people. The world is moving quickly, but his mind is moving slow. He can clearly see it all. He knows his time is near. He has overstepped his boundaries. He has killed somebody and nobody can help him now.

Johnny really doesn't understand why he is so mad at Don. He is sure that Jackie was the one to press up on Don. She is fine as hell and very flirtatious. Still he has a rep to protect. After Don bussed his ass on the basketball court and fought him back so hard, he had to do something. The people would start talking and nobody was going to call him soft. So he stabbed Don. He wanted to shoot him but he couldn't get the burner into the school. He actually didn't even expect to see Don again so soon.

Johnny has a temper. A temper that has got him into plenty of trouble. He has talent in athletic areas, but he cannot stay out of trouble long enough to really accomplish anything. One must understand that Johnny comes from a good loving home. He has siblings that are positive and very well behaved young adults. Yet he is different.

Some people simply enjoy being mean and doing mean things. Johnny is one of those people. He is condescending to anyone who will put up with it. Even adults. He is quick to test what a person is made of. He is like a dog that can smell fear. Now he is running to find solace and ease from the only one he knows who has a nastier temper than him. His cousin Killa.

Killa is in hiding. His partner in crime, Atom, has recently been arrested. Together they are known as the ATM Killas. They rob women at ATM machines and shoot for the hell of it. Johnny was going to be down with them but curfews and other things always got in his way. Besides, Atom doesn't like him anyway.

Johnny bee lines straight to Webster projects where Killa is hiding in a friend's second floor apartment. He knocks the secret knock and becomes increasingly nervous when no one answers. Finally he hears a badly impersonated female voice say AWho is it?"

"It's me, Jay. Open up quick!" Johnny cries out. The door opens, he steps in and slams it shut. The first thing he sees is Snoop, a mean looking pit bull mixed with Great Dane. Then he notices Killa, standing in the shadows with a loaded gun in his hand. "Man I hope you ain't bring no attention with you, with all that noise you been making. Is you crazy? You know I'm not trying to get hemmed up because of your bullshit."

"Chill man. I just need some heat. 5-0 is after me and I ain't going out like no punk. I already caught one body so it's a done deal."

"For real?" Killa asks.

"For real. I shanked him real good." Johnny said. Killa can tell Johnny is dead serious. He wipes off the gun in his hand and gives it to him. It is the same gun that was used in his ATM murders, but he doesn't care. Maybe if Johnny gets caught, the police will think he did those crimes. "Here you go. Just remember if you get busted, my name should never come up."

"A yo, thanks man." They give each other pounds and Johnny steps outside the door.

Johnny moves so fast that everyone who sees him takes notice and is able to point his direction out to the cops. The police get right on his trail. He hears the sirens approaching as he runs through a playground with a few preschoolers playing tag. For a second Johnny wonders what has happened to his childhood. It seems to have come and gone so fast that he can hardly remember it. "Freeze!" He hears as he spins to point the gun into the direction of whoever is speaking to him.

He is about to squeeze off his trigger when he notices it is just a little kid with a toy gun. The child saw Johnny with his gun and thought it would be fun to yell freeze. When the kids mother realizes that her son is about to get shot for real she yells her son's name and flys to his aid. Johnny takes off running, and the little boys mother vows to never let her son play with guns again.

"Put the gun down," Johnny hears. This time it really is the cops.

He turns around to face two officers with their weapons drawn. He shoots and hits one of the officers in the leg. The cop goes down and the other officer starts shooting . Johnny shoots back. In all, the two exchange at least five bullets apiece and no one else gets hit. Then the officer who got shot starts firing. Johnny uses up all of his bullets and is sure he is going to get hit when Killa comes from out of nowhere blasting his gun. Shots hit both officers and Killa yells to Johnny, "Follow me, quick."

The duo run around the building and cut down a ramp into the maintenance entrance. The police think they ran past the building and kept running because so many people are scattering all over the place after hearing the gunshots. Killa and Johnny take refuge right back in the apartment Killa has been hiding in.

They remain quiet in the apartment for hours. They can hear 5-O knocking on doors asking for information. When the cops knock on their door, Johnny feels like his heart will jump out of his chest. Killa on the other hand has a smirk on his face like he is enjoying the intense moment. His dick is hard and he has his tool cocked and ready blast off.

Snoop sits right in front of Johnny, so as a friendly gesture he begins to pet the big dog. The dog does not bark nor does he bite. He used to be a very loud dog until he choked on a bone. Killa had to cut open his throat to remove the bone. He saved the dog's life, but Snoop lost his bark. Johnny finds comfort in petting the canine.

After the police go away, Killa and Johnny begin to move around the empty apartment. But they are careful to keep quiet and stay away from the windows. "Damn Killa," Johnny says in a hushed excited voice. "That was some crazy shit. You came through like out of no where and just started blazing. That was some real movie type shit."

Killa smiles. He is proud of himself. Even more, he is happy they got away.

Then they both hear the secret knock on the door. Killa goes next to the door and answers in a female voice "Who is it?"

"It's Haywire." He is the owner of the apartment. He steps quickly in, "Yo it is mad hot on the streets. Po Po is everywhere. I got stopped by police at the entrance of the projects. They are frisking everybody. Two cops got shot and they want the person who did it. They know Jay here was a part of it, but they don't know who his accomplice is. They have reporters, television vans, cameras, and all type of shit. I think you are on the news now."

138

"What, we made the news?!" Johnny says excitedly. He is a little too excited. Killa has to tell him to keep his voice down. There is a big floor model television in the living room but it does not work. They flick on a small colorless T.V. that is on top of a broken VCR that is also on top of the big set. Being only a quarter after four, there is no news on at the time, but a preview of the news mentions, "Two cops wounded in the Bronx, story at six."

In the meantime, Killa gives Haywire a list so he can venture back out and get them some groceries. While Killa takes a nap, Johnny is left to think about his situation and Jackie keeps coming into his mind.

Why did she even mess with him? He was mean and rude to her. He disrespects her and even hit her. More than once. The truth is, she intimidates him.

She is more woman than he ever deserved. Whenever they had sex, he came mad fast. She just made him cum. Sometimes he would stick it in one time and just buss off. Then he would feel real bad. So bad that he would get mad. He would get mad at her for making him cum too quick. Then he would treat her mean.

As he thinks about it he realizes what a cruel cycle he had created. None of it was her fault, except that she kept being with him. Sure he would have kicked her ass if she tried to leave him, but she was going to get her ass kicked anyway. All she really had to do was stand her ground, or tell somebody with some real authority.

Jackie is not the only one. He knows a couple of girls who gravitate towards his mean streak. Some women just love bad boys. And Johnny is bad, but Jackie is different from other girls. She is the type of girl you marry. Picturing himself getting married brings a smile to his face.

139

Man how he wishes he could have Jackie with him now. He definitely would not be mean to her. Not even in front of his boys. He would hold her tight. Then he thinks about his family. His mom and dad will be very upset. Not just upset, furious. They will probably disown him. There really is no turning back. His name is out there already. The only thing left to do is get caught or die in a blaze of glory. Johnny prefers the latter.

For now however, there is a more pressing concern for him as he stares toward the bathroom. He has to urinate, but he dreads pissing because it stings like a scorpion. He should have gone to the doctor last week. The puss dripping from his penis contains strands of blood, and the odor has become unbearable.

He tiptoes past the room where Killa is sleeping, steps into the bathroom but does not turn on the light. He doesn't like the way his penis looks and it hurts more when he looks at it. In an effort to decrease the levels of agony, Johnny shuts his eyes tightly and tenses up his whole body. He pushes hard on his pee button but waste is not easily let out.

By the time the infected urine finally reaches the outside world, he wants to scream like a bitch in pain. After a few seconds, he stops. He really isn't finished, but he refuses to continue. Any urination left will have to wait until next time.

Before he can pull up his pants, the bathroom door is pushed open and snoop gallops in. He goes straight to the toilet and starts drinking. "Wait Snoop I didn't flush the toilet yet." He flushes but Snoop continues to drink until he has had his fill.

Time creeps by very slowly for Johnny. He constantly looks at the phone. In fact he has been staring at the phone for a good hour before he can muster up enough courage to use it. He presses * 67 and then calls Jackie.

"Hello." Jackie

"Remember me?" Johnny

"You got a lot of nerve calling me."

"You got a lot of nerve playing me out like you did."

"You were never good to me."

"So what's supposed to change now?"

"I can't believe you. You called me just to disrespect me? You ain't nice to no one unless you can get something out of it. That is the beginning of your problems right there."

"Who the fuck are you to tell me what my problem is?"

"See, that's why I'm about to hang up on your ass right now?"

"Okay, please don't hang up. I really need to talk to somebody. I need to talk to you."

"About what?"

"About us."

"There is no us."

"What the hell you talking about there is no us. There is always going to be an us." Johnny sounds more threatening than he means to. He often comes across as intimidating when he does not intend to.

"It is definitely hang up time," she is about to hang up the phone.

"Wait. I'm sorry."

Needless to say, Jackie is shocked. Johnny never says sorry for anything. He never appears to show remorse for any wrong he does. He is one of those cats that just don't give a fuck. His predatory bad boy way of life was an initial turn on for Jackie, but it quickly became problematic and degrading. Now here he is showing a vulnerability that she has never witnessed, by using two simple words. Quickly she tests his new found remorse, "You're sorry and you should be. You need Jesus."

"Bitch! Don't tell me what I need."

"There it is. Let the real you shine through."

"You need Jesus because you are the reason Don is dead."

Jackie starts laughing.

"You think I'm a joke?"

"You really are stupid. Don ain't dead. But you soon will be. You're a dead man talking. Bad boy bad boy, what you gonna do when they come for you," she teases.

"You really are an evil bitch. You fucked him didn't you?"

"Fucked him? I sucked him and rode him. Maybe I'll go to the hospital and blow him."

"Yeah and maybe I'll go to Harlem Hospital and pay him a visit too."

"Damn you>re dumb. He's not at Harlem Hospital, he's at Metropolitan."

Johnny is about to tell Jackie how much of a knucklehead she is when he hears the secret knock at the door. Quietly he hangs up the telephone and deletes her number from redial.

Jackie realizes that she gave out way too much information and tries to change it. "Not Metropolitan Hospital, I meant to say Lincoln Hospital." But her words fall on a dead line.

(Chapter 2)
Rude Awakening

Don watches himself walking the downtown streets of New York City looking good. The air is crisp, and he feels a euphoric high as he ditty bops to Swiss Beats playing from a parked SUV. The driver of the loud vehicle nods to him in acknowledgment of his presence. He walks to a corner store and buys a Guinness Stout. The clerk opens his beer and he walks out of the store sipping the icy cold lager through a straw. He passes by police officers who clearly see him drinking, yet they greet him in a friendly manner and then go about their way.

Don gets to the next corner and there are guys shooting dice and smoking weed. He stops to say what's up and everyone embraces him warmly. Like he is somebody special. And he does feel special. A big jamaican fanta leaf spliff is passed to him and he accepts it whole heartedly. Life is good. Don steps on and there is an excitement in the air. Everybody he passes, white, black, spanish, men, and women, look at him and smile. He is in tune with the world. As he walks on, two extremely beautiful women jump right in step with him and grab his hands from both sides. They are happy, radiant, very sophisticated and in perfect synchronicity. Their minds are on a collective consciousness.

No words need to be spoken, they all know the plan. To the club they go. They don't have to stand in line. They don't have to pay, and they don't have to go through the metal detectors. The trio walks past everyone and nobody gets upset when Don and his honeys are let in ahead of them and are given such presidential treatment. He is not a celebrity or professional athlete but, everyone is feeling his vibe. He's not recognized, but they recognize.

Don and his ladies get three incredible hulks, for free of course, and head to the dance floor. The drinks go straight to their heads and the music is on the money as he and the girls get down together. The whole club is jumping but Don and his crew are the center of attention. Their dancing gets intense and the song ends with some spectacular shit. One girl sitting backwards on his shoulders, her legs are wrapped around his face. And the other girl is under him looking up with her face between his legs.

The crowd claps at the end of their routine. Don and the girls are hot and sweating. They get three waters and leave the club. A yellow cab pulls up and they jump in. "City Island," Don tells the cab driver, and those are the only words spoken all night. As the car for hire glides along the streets and highways of the city, Don and his girls are in the back seat feeling each other up, french kissing and really warming up to one another. The cab has a bar, one of the ladies has weed and Anthony Hamilton is playing on the stereo. Within minutes the cab is pulling up at one of the smaller seafood restaurants on City Island. They get out the cab and Don tries to pay the driver but the cab driver shakes his head no, and refuses to take any money.

The crew head into the dimly lit, rather crowded restaurant, and are taken straight to their seats which seems to have been reserved just for them. In a matter of seconds, a large seafood salad is brought to them. Just one big salad with chunks of seafood for them all to share. They happily feed each other. Before they can finish their salad and raw clams, the biggest shrimp Don has ever seen is placed in front of them. Not a bunch of jumbo shrimp, just one big pot roast sized shrimp. Don literally has to carve it with a knife. Super King Crab legs and fried salmon are also served. All the food is delicious and the champagne is icy cold.

Don and his people devour all of their sea food and get up to leave. They don't have to pay and the waiter is ecstatic that they had such a good time. They step outside and the same cab that took them to City Island is still waiting for them. One by one they get into the very roomy backseat and the car takes off.

The taxi pulls up to the Econo Lodge Motel in the Bronx and the trio get out. Don walks to the check in area and the clerk gives him his key. Room 116, his birthday. The room is bigger than Don usually gets, and the refrigerator is stocked extra well, especially for a sleazy motel. The girls waste no time getting comfortable.

The two females strip down to nothing and begin to give each other oral pleasures. Don is watching and hefeels his erection growing. The girls are perfect in every sense. Not one ounce of extra fat and no stretch marks. They are moaning and enjoying one another while Don is taking off his clothes and feeling his jimmy trying to bust out his pants. He gets down to his underwear and the girls are about to climax. They start cumin in convulsions and he is so turned on that when he takes his underwear off, he starts cumin too. Then everything changes.

The expression on the girls faces change. They are angry at him. He was not supposed to bust off yet. Everything was going perfect until he shot his load. The two woman stand up and now they are much

145

more muscular than they appeared earlier.

Beginning to look really creepy, their nipples turn into pointy needles and they keep trying to hug Don. To be squeezed by one of them will mean getting impaled.

Their persistence to hurt him becomes more intense. Don finds himself swinging hay makers at them and making some good connections. Still they keep coming at him, infuriated because he ejaculated.

He begins to really duke it out with one when the other grabs him from behind and pushes her pointy titty into his back. The pain is explosive and he feels it all through his body as he tries to break free, but her grip is too tight and she just will not let go.

The more he struggles, the weaker he becomes. And the other girl is about give him his fatal hug, with a spike to his heart.

Suddenly Don hears his name being called, and his penis starts to have feeling. "Yes," he believes his hard penis will save the day. These girls won't be mad anymore once he get his erection back. But the ladies keep fighting him. Even with his fully erect johnson sticking up, they are too angry to stop. Don hears his name being called again. He is about to take a tit to the heart, when he hears, "Don, wake up baby, you're dreaming!"

He opens his eyes and looks upon the concerned face of his grandmother as she places a pillow on his stomach. He is happy to see her because the nightmare felt so real. So real that his back is still hurting. As he looks around he realizes he is not home. Then he sees his Dad, Lydia, and Damian. He tries to sit up but his back really does hurt. And most embarrassingly, he becomes aware that he has a hard on under the pillow. That's why his grandma put the pillow on him.

"Having a bad dream son?" His Dad asks trying to be funny and break the tension.

"Er, something like that. Hi Damian, come give your stinky breath daddy a hug." This is the first time Don has had his son, dad and grandmother in the same room. It also dawns on Don that he is in the hospital. Then it clicks as to why he is here. He also remembers what he did to Lydia. And he remembers that he never told his Dad or his Grandmother about Lydia and Damian. What a tangled web we weave. "I assume you have met Damian and Lydia," Don says to his Dad and Grandmother while hugging his son.

"Daddee hurt?" Damian sobs.

"Only for a minute," Don replies. ASo what is my prognosis?"

"You are going to be fine, until you get out of here. Then you will have to deal with me." Grandma says assuredly. "You know you really should have told us about this a long time ago."

"Mom, I thought we were going to wait until he got out of the hospital" Dad says.

"I know, I just can't believe I am a great grandmother." She reaches her arms out to her great grandson Damian, and he rushes into her grasp. It is obvious that they have taken a liking to each other. "And there is a lot I don't understand. Like why would anyone want to hurt you?" She pauses to let her words sink in. "What about Lydia and Damian? If this never happened, would I have ever known about them?"

"Mom maybe we should wait until he has more strength" Dad states.

"Grandma I did want you to know. I even wrote you and Dad a letter explaining everything."

"We got it." Dad chimes in.

"But would we have gotten it if you were not on your death bed?"

"I thought you said I was going to be okay."

"You are and you know what I mean. You knew something was going to happen to you."

"How was I supposed to know?"

"You knew. That is why you wrote the letter in the first place."

If only Don could tell her the whole truth of why he put the pen to the paper. "I wrote you and Dad the letter because I had a heavy conscience. You needed to know. I kept it from you for too long and I'm sorry."

Grandma begins to feel a bit guilty about grilling her grandson so hard. "Don't get me wrong, I'm very proud of you. You saved a lady's life. The lord has blessed you for that."

Don had forgotten. Sometimes he does good things... sometimes. "Thanks Mom."

The fire burns in Grandma's eyes once again as he will not be forgiven so easily. "I'm still very angry Donathan! How could this happen?"

The hurt in the question his grandmother poses, gives him the strength to sit all the way up. If there is pain in his movement, he does not feel it. He is lost thinking about why someone tried to kill him. How could someone be so angry at him that they would want to eliminate him? And even more outlandish, why was he still alive? A bunch of questions filled his mind.

"Who is the boy that did this to you?" Grandma breaks into Don's thoughts.

"They say his name is Johnny" Dad answers for him. "They are still looking for him."

"Still looking?"

"Yes. What does he have against you?" Grandma demanded to know.

Maybe, just maybe if Lydia were not standing there, Don could tell the truth. That he got involved in some pussy that he should never have touched. He got duped. But that still is no excuse for his stupidity. "I waxed his butt in a basketball game and he has been hating on me ever since."

"Is that what this is all about? A basketball game?"

"People have been hurt for less" Dad replies.

"He has issues with lots of people. I think I just really got his goat."

"Are there any females involved?" Lydia speaks for the first time. Everybody waits for Dons answer. Her question was on everybody's mind but Lydia was the only one who had the guts to ask.

"No there are no females involved," Don lies with a double negative.

"Well I'm glad you are okay. And I will feel much better when they catch that Johnny." Grandma

"You and me both." Don is relieved when a nurse walks in to check all of his vital signs. Her name tag says Linton, RN. She is a proud, no nonsense woman of Jamaican descent. She is quick at her job and ready to see about the next patient. Don is not quite ready for her to go. "How am I doing?" he asks of her.

Nurse Linton looks around the room at his concerned family. "You will be fine under my care. You will be even better if you listen to your family, trust in God and stay out of trouble." She exits with an amen and a hallelujah.

Grandma looks at her son and Lydia, "May I talk to Don alone for a moment please?"

Don's dad is hesitant for fear that his mom may

break fool on Don. "Okay mom, but take it easy on him. He still needs time to recuperate." Dad leaves the two alone to talk.

"Don you have to decide what you are going to do with your life."

"I know you are worried about me. I'm worried about me." Don wants to tell her that he is willing to consider all options set before him. He is glad to be alive and wants to keep it that way.

"I'm more than worried about you, I'm terrified. And it's not so much your life that concerns me, it's your death. I couldn't take it if something happened to you. I would just die. I felt like I was going to die when I first heard the news that you were hurt. It's time you thought of an alternate route."

"I know you want me to go to college."

"It doesn't have to be college. You should consider the army, or the Peace Corps. Anything that could get you away from here."

"I guess I really disappoint you."

"I am disappointed, but don't get me wrong, I'm very proud of you. You have come a long way. Especially since your mother's passing. That devastated all of us. And you have had that job for over a year. You are proving yourself to be a responsible young man, with lots of potential. How could you have a child? Why would you keep it away from me for so long? Am I expected to come to grips with being a great grandma so easily? I'm too young to be a great grandmother." She breaks a smile from her own flattery. But the tears still begin to fill her eyes."That is precisely why I can't go anywhere. I have to be here for you, dad and Damian." "It's so violent here. It won't do us any good if we lose you." Grandma begins to cry. "You could be dead right now."

(Chapter 3)
In Da Hood

About a half an hour after Don's family leaves, his friend DJ comes to visit him. "My man D Boogie what up nigga"?

"Hey DJ my favorite DJ. How's it hanging?"

"Swinging my brother swinging. I brought this for you," DJ hands him a bottle of Hennessy.

"Damn kid, some Hen Dog in the hospital?"

"What you wanted me to bring you, some flowers and a card?"

"Nah this is some real cool shit. I need to come to the hospital more often."

"Get real man, you's a star now. And if you ain't a star I'm going to make you a star," DJ says with a smile.

"What'cha talking bout D?"

"In Da Hood Videos is here. They want to do an exclusive on you and they are outside waiting for the word."

"Say word."

"Word. And Ebony and Zelda have been asking about you."

"Bang, bang baby" Don says with a smile. "Tell me DJ, have you heard anything about Johnny? What happened to him?"

"That nigga is on the run, he shot at some cops. Man I wish I was there when it went down. You know I would of had your back," DJ states very seriously.

"Yeah you would have had my back, way back there," Don replies kidding.

"Yo, don't even worry about that chicken mcnugget. The cops are on his ass and they probably have him in custody as we speak." DJ can see the concern on Dons face. "Fuck that punk ass, stab a nigga in the back bitch. What he do, sneak up behind you and jig?" He does a stabbing motion with his hand.

"Nah kid, I was running from that motherfucker." They laugh it off.

"So is In Da Hood in or what?" DJ asked.

"Hell yeah. What I got to do?" Don questioned.

"Just chill, I am going to run downstairs and bring them up". As DJ is leaving, Fatima walks in.

Fatima looks at Don and burst into tears. "Oh Don," she cries as she flies into his arms. "I thought you were dead. I didn't know what I was going to do. I love you so much." She kisses him passionately.

Nurse Linton walks in to write something down on his chart. She looks at Fatima and immediately does not like her. She knows Don's family and son's mother was just there a few minutes ago. She assumes Fatima is a home wrecker. The truth is Fatima knows nothing about Don's other woman or his son. The nurse is barely out of the room before Don and Fatima continue their conversation.

"Hi baby, I was thinking about you," he lies. "Stop all those tears. I ain't going nowhere."

"You'd better not," she puts her hands on his shoulders, "I've got plans for you."

"I can read your mind and you have dirty thoughts" Don chuckles.

"Yes I do." They flirt back and forth until the In Da Hood crew step in.

"Hey Don, I'm Rich Fanatic and this is Sunny Boeno. We are here with your permission of course, to set up a few small cameras that will be filming for the next 48 hours. It will be like a reality show. A showed based on the people who come to see you in the hospital. So of course when everything is said and done, anybody shown on the actual show will have to fill out consent forms, blah, blah ,blah...."

Don hears Fanatic talking but he is lost in his own world. 50 Cent got famous by getting shot, and he is going to get famous by getting stabbed. That is alright with him.

"So Don, any questions?" Sunny Boeno inquires after they plant three small cameras around the room.

"No, everything is greasy. I just need to act normal and forget the cameras are there."

"Exactly. And we out of here." In Da Hood exits. DJ walks to one of the cameras and starts cursing and giving shout outs. Then he remembers there is a female in the room. He turns his attention toward her because he is cool like that. "Hello," he says.

"Hello, my name is Fatima. And you are?"

"DJ Extra Ordinaire. The D stands for dashing, dubious, and down for what ever."

"Don't forget dummy," Don chimes in.

"Don't hate the playa, playa." DJ starts to eye Fatima up and down like he is trying to find something. "I'm looking for the fuse baby, because you are the bomb."

Fatima laughs, "You got game."

"Like Kobe, Shaq, and Jordan. I got everything, except your arms to hold me tight."

Don doesn't take offense to DJ, but he still doesn't like him hitting on his girl like that. He is not so surprised though, because DJ will hit on your great grandmother if allowed to. "That's my baby now DJ, be easy."

"Yeah, she is a diamond," he gestures toward Fatima. "And I'm blinded by her radiant glow."

"You can't be serious, using those corny ass pick up lines. Get real."

Fatima likes the compliments and the attention. "I think he is cute and sweet." She eggs him on, "With the gift of gab."

"I got a million of them. Let me lay some on you," DJ continues. "I'm not very religious, but you are the answer to my prayers." Fatima blushes, DJ goes on. "Now that you're here, I can make my other two wishes." Fatima chuckles.

Don acts like he is about to barf, "I wish you would stop. You are upsetting my stomach."

DJ ignores him and continues to butter up Fatima. "You really need to stop taking those pretty pills, you are becoming way too beautiful."

"DJ, do you do mixed tapes?"

Now DJ is the one who is flattered by his recognition. "Yes I do. I am DJ Extra Ordinaire, the one and only."

"I have a few of your CDs. I really like the RnB blends CD. That shit is off the chain."

"It is so wonderful to meet a woman who can appreciate good music. We must dine out sometime, so we can discuss matters of the utmost importance."

"Oh really? Important matters?"

"Yes, like why did God allow you to come down and grace us with your presence?"

She giggles as she guzzles up all the gas.

"No seriously." DJ gets real serious and declares, "Should you ever discover yourself in a dark red place, do not be afraid, for you are in my heart."

"And if you find my size twelve in your ass, be afraid because you'll be shitting nikes for the rest of the week," Don states.

"I'm a lover, not a fighter. I don't thug, I hug."

154

He gives all of his attention to Fatima, "You might have to pick me up, because I'm falling for you."

"Do you do this often?" Fatima asks.

"Never. This is the first time I have ever been this close to a goddess. Can I interest you in a foot massage?"

"A who?"

"A foot massage. I give the best."

"That sounds nice." She looks at Don and can tell he does not like the idea. But she likes the thought of being able to make him jealous. "Well my feet do hurt," she lies.

Don can feel what she is thinking. "Don't do it DJ. Her feet are deadly." He edges her on.

"Excuse me. I have very nice feet."

"Nobody has nice feet," Don retorts.

"Why don't you let me be the judge of that?" DJ likes to touch female feet. He is a toe sucker.

"My feet are nice. You just never noticed," she shows off her pedicure.

"They look like feet that could be in a foot commercial." DJ likes what he sees. "Why don't you have a seat." She sits down. He puts her foot in his hand and gives each toe a meticulous rub down. Fatima becomes so relaxed that she feels like she can fall asleep before DJ starts on her other foot.

Nurse Linton enters the room again and witnesses DJ giving Fatima a foot massage. In her mind Fatima is a hoe. First she was kissing and hugging up on Don, now she is letting another man touch on her body. Nurse Linton thinks the young women of today are way to loose. She cuts her eyes at Fatima.

Fatima sees how the nurse looks at her. In her mind the nurse is just an evil jealous bitch who can't get a man. She probably never had someone give her a foot rub. Fatima leans her head back to emphasize to the nurse how much she is enjoying her massage.

Nurse Linton tends to Don's stab wound by rubbing on some kind of ointment. She gives him some pills and a glass of water. "This is codeine, it's for the pain. It may make you feel very relaxed, but I'm sure that is nothing new to you." The sarcasm in her voice is quite clear.

Don wants to bite his tongue, but he just has to know why this lady is so bitter. "What is that supposed to mean?"

Nurse Linton is happy to vent. "Your generation is hell bent on getting high and destruction. You know nothing about hard work and do nothing but complain. You have no concept of what it is to struggle or work. Everything for you is plug in, automated and instant. You have no appreciation for life. It is worthless to you. You probably don't care whether you live or die. And you probably will be dead soon."

Don is stunned. He wants to come back with some witty shit to say to the nurse, but he is dumbfounded. For some reason when ever anybody says something about him, he has to think it over and decide if it is true or not. Don stays quiet and takes his medicine. Luckily, DJ has something to say.

"Hey lady, we don't all do crime and hurt people."

"But you don't do anything constructive. She is probably the only one thinking about going to college. Then she'll become a stripper to pay her tuition and get lost to drugs."

"Are you serious? You don't know me. How the hell are you going to judge me and tell me my future like you some know it all?" Fatima says in an angry voice.

"I've seen it a thousands times. Crack babies who were never spanked."

"Crack babies? Now hold up, my parents never did crack. They are respectable professionals. I don't do drugs and I know the value of hard work. You are an unhappy individual who wants to find fault with everybody else. For all your troubles miss, I suggest you look within."

Nurse Linton walks out with a huff. "I guess you told her," DJ says as they all laugh.

"The nerve of her, pre judging us like that."

Fatima breaks the laughter.

"You must admit, she does have a point," Don replies.

"What? You can't believe that shit!" DJ takes a stance and also rubs Fatima's foot against his aroused private.

"I mean, most of us, especially males, will not go to college. Or even want to go. There are more of us in jail than higher learning facilities. All of us want to be entertainers or ballers. We are a generation of wanna bees. And what is messed up is society makes it seem that we have to live up to certain standards. Wear the latest gear. Drive the coolest ride. Drink the beverage that is in the hottest rap video. Hard work like our parents did doesn't mean anything anymore. We want it now and are willing to kill or step on anybody to get it."

"I don't know man, there are a lot of exceptions to the rule," DJ points out.

"You see that's the problem, because that is the rule. We're all expected to have the newest Jordans, smoke the best weed, and sing, dance, ball, rap, or act. What are the alternatives, minimum wage?"

"That is not my reality. I know that being a success in this world takes hard work. I don't have a problem working at Mickey D's until I can get something better." Fatima takes her feet back and gets deeper into the subject.

"I think our generation is a group of entrepreneurs. We don't want to settle for the typical nine to five. We'd rather go into business for ourselves," DJ adds.

"You think selling bootleg CD's is entrepreneurship? Anybody could do that."

"Hold up, you know I take that personal because it is what I do. I am in the process of starting my own company. I ain't looking to work for somebody else for the rest of my life while they make all of the profit," DJ barks.

"You know I'm mad proud of you, but what you do is illegal. It's ingenious, but if the cops or record companies decided they did not like what you were doing you could get arrested."

"That is true but let me tell you something about the music industry. Record sales have gone up every year, despite the bootlegging that I do. Actually I help to promote their hot artist. And as such I should be getting paid for all my hard work."

"True, I just feel like the nurse gave us something to think about."

"Well I need to raise up. Fatima, my contact number is on every mixed tape I put out. If you ever need me or just want to talk, please call me."

"Yeah. Yeah." Don yawns.

DJ leaves and there is an awkward moment between Don and Fatima. Fatima liked the chance of being able to make her man jealous, but she doesn't want to push him away. She wonders if she went to far by letting DJ rub her feet.

As if reading her mind Don responds, "You know in that movie Pulp Fiction a character was killed for

158

touching the feet of another man's woman."

"Does that mean that you are going to murder DJ Extra Ordinary?"

"You're not funny."

"Maybe if I tickle you, you will think I'm hilarious." She grabs Don and makes him laugh. "I didn't know you were so ticklish."

"There's a lot you don't know about me." Don wishes he did not make that comment because it changes the whole mood.

"You are absolutely right. There is much I do not know about you. Like why are you even here?"

"I'm here because Johnny tried to kill me. I just hope he doesn't want to finish the job."

"Do you think he will try again? Is it safe here? Does it have anything to do with Jackie?"

Don wishes she didn't asks such questions. He honestly hates to lie. Still, he lies about each one. "No, I don't think he will try again. Yes it is safe here. No it had nothing to do with Jackie."

"I feel so much better to hear you say that. Besides I don't like that girl. She thinks she is hot shit. Is she attractive to you?"

"You mean is she pretty or something?" Don asks to buy time as he looks for an appropriate answer to her question.

"You know what mean?"

"She's alright, but she's not real. You are a real person. A real lady. I wouldn't trade her for you on any day."

"Well I don't trust her, and don't forget, she is Johnny's girl. You don't know what she would do for him. She could send one of her friends to come here and hurt you." Fatima puts a Listerine strip in her mouth. "Oh Don I'm so scared." She holds him, squeezes him tight, and is very overly

159

dramatic. "I can't have anything happen to you."
She gives Don fresh breath passionate kisses. He
returns her spark, but his flame quickly burns dim as
his medication kicks in. It is not long before he
drifts into a semi sleep with Fatima's tongue still
roaming his mouth.

(Chapter 4)
Cat Fight

Fatima walks in the bathroom, as Lydia strolls into the room. They do not see each other. The codeine 4 that Don was given has taken effect and he is feeling so drowsy that he does not realize that Lydia is there. She gives Don a big sloppy kiss. He returns her fiery kiss and his hands instinctively begin to roam all over her booty. Then he notices something different about the kiss. "Yuck," he says aloud without really meaning to.

Lydia is a little offended, but she knows that she just chain smoked four Newport's, and had a Heineken before she came to visit Don. "What, you don't like my breath? You trying to hurt my feelings?" Lydia playfully puts her hands around Don's neck and pretends to choke him.

Fatima opens the bathroom door. At first she can't believe her eyes. Is Don being attacked? Is this a nurse checking his vital signs? What the fuck is going on? Without thinking about it Fatima yanks Lydia off of Don and nearly flings her across the room. Lydia does not know what is going on, or who is attacking her. She tries to maintain her balance, but she knocks over medical equipment in the process.

"Don't fight," Don murmurs as loud as he can. But it is too late. The cat fight is on and he does not have the strength to stop it.

Hospital items begin to fly in Fatima's direction. Lydia is quite good at throwing stuff, because every item either hits the target or comes incredibly close.

An ice water pitcher knocks Fatima dead in the head. She sees stars, and stumbles backwards, but she does not fall. The blast to her noggin only makes her angry.

Lydia hesitates while looking for more things to throw in a second attack. Unfortunately she leaves enough time for Fatima to rush her and slam her against the counter. With the wind blown out of Lydia, Fatima proceeds to pick up an aerosol disinfectant spray can and aim it at Lydia's face. Lydia has to keep her mouth and eyes shut tight, as Fatima sprays the cleaning solution in her face. Fatima wishes she had a light so she could set the bitch on fire.

Taking complete advantage of the situation, Fatima proceeds to slam Lydia's head against the counter. Lydia's searching hands manages to grab hold of a large petroleum tube. She squeezes until the Vaseline is oozing out. Then she smacks Fatima across the face with the tube. Fatima has to let Lydia loose in order to keep the grease from getting into her eyes.

Before Fatima can finish wiping her face, Lydia begins to bang her nugget against a hard surface. Fatima tries to break free, but Lydia has a strong hold on her long shiny braids. Luckily her flailing hands connect to Lydia's nose and sends her tripping backwards and sliding on her butt. Unluckily, Lydia still has clunks of Fatima's hair in her hands.

Fatima at once realizes the error in her ways. She has started a fight with someone she knows nothing about. Now she wants to talk and find out the nature of the relationship between her and Don. But, it is too late. Lydia has already picked up a needle and is coming for her. Fatima is frozen scared. Lydia brings the needle up and goes straight for her forehead.

Something stops her. Is it God? An act of

compassion? A show of wisdom? Nurse Linton screaming at the door? Her son watching everything? Lydia is able to stop her hand less than a quarter inch from Fatima's dome.

"Daddy sleep?" Damian inquires

Daddy? Fatima's mind starts to race as things become clearer. She almost got herself killed over someone else's man. She is so wrong. Fatima stares at the little boy for what feels like an eternity. There is no doubt that it is his son. He is the spitting image of Don.

With nothing to do but admit defeat and raise up, Fatima slowly gathers her things, and silently walks out with tears in her eyes. Having seen the whole thing Damian asks, "Mommy made a mess?"

Lydia looks around at the disarray, and then looks at Don, who is sleeping peacefully. "No, your father made a mess, and he's going to have to clean it up."

(Chapter 5)
Boys To Men

A few days ago, Don stumbled onto a woman who was wounded by the ATM Killas. He rushed her to the hospital and was crucial to saving her life. He befriended the lady's son Basheem and B.J., the cop who wrote up the report. When they step into the room Don is pleasantly surprised to see them.

"What's up my brother. I am glad to see you." B.J. says.

"I am glad to see you too. And very happy to still be here." There is silence as the two reflect on the scene that lead to Don winding up in the hospital. B.J. thought Don was a goner. And he was right. "I see you brought your bodyguard with you. What's the deal little man? Give me a pound."

"I went to check on his mom and he asked to come check on you."

"Man, that is some cool heart warming shit. Pass me a Kleenex." They laugh. "Nah really, you think about a lot of things when your life flashes before your eyes. Man I don't know how you deal with it in your line of work everyday."

"I'm happy to see someone recognizes the perils of being a police officer. The job becomes even more difficult when you are a black man" B.J. says sadly.

"I wanted to ask you about that. You don't look like the typical cop. I can tell you still have a lot of hood in you. Doesn't that make you feel like an outcast among your peers? And how do you arrest someone who looks just like you?"

"What is this Oprah? For real though, I judge a person by their deeds and actions, not by how they look. I don't care if you are black, white, or red. If you do the crime, you should do the time."

"And if the glove doesn't fit you must acquit. Seriously, don't you take into account the lack of positive role models and activities in our community?"

"Are you asking me if there should be a set of laws for white people and a different more lenient set of laws for disadvantage people of color? Hell no! But we all know there is. And it's not in our favor."

"It's almost like you are working for the man against your own people. I mean the word officer comes from the word overseer used during slavery times."

"That may be true, but never forget that the American slave trade could never have flourished had it not been for the help of other Africans. Brothers sold their own brothers into slavery. I don't listen to all that talk about what whitey did. The worst devil is a black devil. I have to judge each person by their deeds, not the color of their skin. Let me make one more point. We, you and I, would be slaves today if it were not for the help of plenty of white people who sacrificed their lives for the American Negro."

"The white man is the evil one. He has been the cause of every major war on this planet." Basheem breaks into the conversation and throws Don completely off balance.

"Whoa little man. Easy on the hate. You can love yourself without hating others. Besides, that is a very untrue statement. People of color had fought and won many wars, before the Europeans ever crossed the ocean," B.J. states.

"I'm talking about Vietnam, the Iraqi war, world war one, two, and you know they'll be responsible for world war three." Basheem replies with a conviction that is rarely seen in such a young individual.

B.J. looks at Don, who has his mouth wide open with nothing coming out. He is still dumb struck at Basheem's rhetoric. "We've been going at it like this for hours. He has some good points. I just want him to understand that there are always exceptions to the rule. And especially that all white people are not bad, the devil, or out to get the black man."

"He is right. Both your mother and I are in the hospital and there were no white people involved in making that happen. Only knuckle headed black folk. There is more black on black crime than anything else."

"Brothers are angry, and rightly so. Life is very hard for most people of color here in America. But let's face it, it is better here than anywhere else on this planet. Do you think you would have it any better if you lived in Africa, South America, Asia, or Europe? Where on this earth can a black man be freer to express himself, or have more opportunity? Where else can you start from the bottom and make mad money while riding to the top? You can disrespect America all you want, but it's the only country that will tolerate your criticism. Go to China and talk about their president ain't shit and see what happens to you. America is the only place that allows you to get away with that kind of freedom of speech. I say God bless America." B.J.

"True dat, but if I could just change the subject a little bit, I believe rap music is one of the greatest art forms to come out of America. It has influenced many cultures around the world. Now you have Japanese, Africans, Germans, and South Americans trying to be like us." Don adds.

"They are not trying to be like us. They are trying

to be like the images that are being portrayed in the videos. Most of us will never have all that bling, or all those fine girls pouring champagne all over their voluptuous behinds and supple breast." B.J. makes everyone laugh.

"Hey Basheem, who do you like in music?" Don asks because most people have someone they like that makes music.

Basheem cracks one of his few smiles. For a young boy, he is very serious. "I like the so called conscious rappers like Common, Dead Prez, and Lupe Fiasco. But I think all of G-Unit spit hot flows, and Ludacris makes hits. Still Lil Wayne is the man."

"All I know is the best rappers are old school. Nobody's messing with Rakim, KRS-One, or Kool G Rap. That's when cats had real skills in the game. I used to do a little rapping myself." Butler makes everybody laugh.

"Let me hear something then."

"Oh you want me to buss a rhyme?"

"Yeah show us what you got."

"Okay. Check it, check it. Innovator, fast rhyme inventor. Perpetrators, know you all wenta, my pad and took notes, then you tallied your votes and voted me as the best, because the rhymes that I wrote."

"Hold up B.J. I don't think so. That's a Kool Moe Dee Rhyme."

"Oh is that who that was?" B.J. acts like he didn't know he bit somebody's rhyme and they all laugh.

The trio talks about everything from God to Women. They continue to chat about fun stuff and discuss sensitive issues. When it is time for them to depart, Don does not want them to leave.

167

(Chapter 6)
Killa Cooking

Haywire knocks the secret knock and Killa eagerly opens the door. Haywire walks in with two bags filled with groceries. "I hope you got everything on the list." Killa immediately starts taking the food out the bags.

"I hope your boy wasn't using the phone." Haywire says.

Killa stops what he is doing and looks Johnny straight in the face. "Did you make a telephone call?"

Johnny can feel the apprehension of the moment and the sweat trickling down his back. "Nah son, I wouldn't go out like that. Besides who the fuck am I going to call anyway?"

Killa stares at him for a few seconds, as if he is trying to detect the truth. He really doesn't want to deal with this shit. He wants to dive into one of the few pleasures he gets out of life. "Good enough for me, I'm ready to cook." The young thug is in a joyful mood because he is about to do something he likes to do and is quite good at. Besides robbing ladies at the ATM, it's his favorite thing to do.

Haywire isn't so convinced. He is sure he heard someone talking on the phone while he was outside the door. He stays quiet but his abrupt exit speaks volumes.

After taking everything out the grocery bags, Killa becomes upset. With a knife in his hand, he storms out of the kitchen to confront Haywire. "What happened to my fresh garlic? You know I need to have fresh garlic steamed with my broccoli!"

Snoop feels the tension in the air and starts running around in circles.

Haywire is still ticked off about the phone incident, so he does not appreciate the way Killa is stepping to him. "I told you before, there is garlic in the bottom of the refrigerator!"

Johnny is bewildered at the confrontation in front of him. "Are two gangsters going to kill each other over garlic?" he thinks to himself. At school he is the bully, the one to be feared. In this place, he is the lowest man on the totem pole. These cats make him nervous.

Killa steps back acknowledging he is in the wrong. "My bag. I hope you are hungry." He retreats into the kitchen as if nothing happened. "By the way, thanks for not forgetting the Adobo," he yells backwards.

Johnny hangs out with Killa as he puts salmon, lamb, and pork chops into pots of cold water and vinegar. "What's up with that?" he inquires.

"I always soak my meats in vinegar and water to kill off bacteria before I start cooking."

"Isn't the food going to taste funny?"

"No, I use very little vinegar and a lot of water. You'll never be able to tell."

"Man I can't boil a mother fucking egg."

"Well I can. Cooking is my first love. My passion."

"You kind of remind me of Steven Segal when he was in this movie where he was a cook and he was still cracking heads."

"Yeah I remember that movie, he was a chef on some boat. That nigga still couldn't fuck with me in the kitchen."

"That's what's up. What are you cooking anyway?"

"I'm hooking up some stuffed lamb, salmon in lemon garlic sauce, and fried pork chops. Baked potatoes with butter and sour cream, and steamed broccoli with fresh garlic."

"Steamed broccoli with fresh garlic. That sounds real good." Johnny sucks up to Killa.

"Ya damn skippy." Killa rinses off three large red potatoes and wraps them in aluminum foil. "I put these in the oven first because they will take the longest to cook." He rinses off the boneless breast of lamb and expertly carves a hole through the center. He seasons the lamb and stuffs it with chopped asparagus and crabmeat. "I love culinary arts," he declares as he slices off pieces of the lamb to cork the holes.

"What the hell is that?"

"It's the art of cooking. Using food as a form of self expression. But basically it's a fancy name for a chef." Killa throws Snoop a few slices of raw meat.

"Damn nigga I never knew you were down with the food game like that."

"It's nothing I can really go bragging about. Niggas will definitely try to clown a brother. Until they taste my cooking, then they can't say shit." He sets the lamb aside. "You know food can be used as a deadly tool. Many people have died from eating the wrong foods."

Johnny does not like hearing him talk about deadly foods while cooking a meal. "So what is your favorite thing to cook?"

Before Killa can respond, they are interrupted by Haywire, who is famished and still upset. He walks passed Killa and Johnny, straight to the telephone. He presses the redial button, hoping to catch Johnny in a lie. The redial comes up empty. Haywire knows it has been erased because his last call should have dialed. He looks at his so called comrades and decides against saying anything. He believes Johnny is guilty and the cops will probably beat down their door any minute now. He gives them both the evil eye as he leaves the kitchen.

Killa goes on with the conversation as if Haywire never walked in and walked out. "My favorite foods to cook are chinese and spanish foods."

"You burn those too?" Johnny is antsy because he knows Haywire is still out to get him. But he is slightly reassured to believe Killa is on his side, and he wants to keep it that way.

"Hell yeah. I could put all of these so called chinese food stores out of business. Besides we don't get real chinese food in the hood anyway."

"What?"

"They don't cook fried chicken, cheeseburgers, and spare ribs in authentic chinese restaurants. You can't get that shit in China town. What we get in the hood is the chinese version of soul food."

"How about the spanish food?"

"Is it the real thing? Yes it is. Spanish people know what they want. They don't go to a spanish restaurant looking for american food. They go to eat traditional spanish grub." While Killa is talking, he is preparing his lemon garlic sauce and seasoning the pork. Enjoying the spot light Killa goes on to say, "The difference is the demand. How many times have you seen other Asian people go into a chinese joint in the hood and order some food?"

Johnny shrugs his shoulders. He has never seen it happen.

"Even the people who work at these rinky dink restaurants don't eat the food on their own menus. That's the main difference right there." Killa heats up the olive oil to fry his marinating pork chops. "Spanish people patronize their own establishments.

171

They go to their own restaurants and demand the real thing."

"You sure know a lot about cooking, I mean the culinary arts."

"It's something I really like doing. I'm fanatical about it. I know how to cook foods called aphrodisiacs."

"I think I heard of that."

"Those are the foods that make you horny. Cook the right meal for a shorty, and you are guaranteed some good pussy."

"Say word."

"I'm serious. But my favorites are the psychedelic foods. And foods that kill. I can have a nigga literally eat himself to death."

"Damn, that's cold."

"I cold grind up some glass real good. If you do it right, you could have some one eat a bowl of soup with the glass in it. They won't even know it's there, until they start shitting out their insides."

"That's awful."

"I'm into stuff like that. There is this woman named Dorothea Puente. She was an old woman who murdered people. Everyone said she was such an excellent cook. She never killed anyone with her food but she is remembered most for her cooking. I know you heard of Jeffrey Dahmer. He was a cannibal. He cooked mother fuckers and ate them. I know I could cook up a nigga real good. I could make nigga stew, or a fucking puerto rican pate. I could probably feed you some dead bitch, and you would say that it taste like some good chicken. Shit you never know what the fuck you are eating anyway. Especially when you eat hot dogs and cheese burgers."

"You trying to make me lose my appetite?"

"No just making conversation. I could tell you about Albert Fentress. He shot somebody, cut him up and ate him. The cat he feasted on was about your size."

They stare at each other with Killa holding a big kitchen knife in his hand. "Yo dog, you making me nervous." Johnny says.

Killa ignores his comment and goes on talking. "You ever heard of the date rape drug GHB gamma hydroxyl butyrate or ketamine? Those are tastes less, colorless drugs you can put into food that could paralyze a person. Easily."

"You are fanatic about food."

"Yeah I wish I could have gone to school for it."

"You? School?"

"What the fuck? You think a nigga stupid or something?" Killa points a big turning fork at Johnny.

"Nah. Never that."

"You fucked up. You should not be here. You got talent and you had a chance."

Johnny has an idea but he is not exactly sure what Killa is talking about. He plays dumb, "Huh?"

"You my cousin right? You think I don't know about your basketball skills? You suppose to go college, maybe pro. All jokes aside, why you want to be a thug?"

That is the last kind of question Johnny expects to hear coming from Killa, the ultimate thug. "I can't have nobody trying to play me out."

Killa puts the pork chops in the hot grease. The aroma of the cooking swine quickly fills the air. He rinses off the salmon and prepares it for seasoning. "Sazon is the number one seasoning if you are not going to do it botch. It brings the meaty flavor out of the fish. Vegetable seasoning gives it a unique not too salty taste. Garlic powder and red pepper intensifies the explosive flavor. A pinch of black pepper adds character and lets the taste linger in your mouth longer." He turns his pork chops, heats up another pan for the salmon and puts the oven on broil. "Timing is of the essence but heat is the most important thing when it comes to cooking. Different foods require different amounts of heat," he says as he puts the lamb in the broiler.

Killa goes on about the proper way to cook and then causally switches the subject. "So you're worried about a rep? That's the main difference between me and you, I hurt people for financial freedom, you hurt mother fuckers for pride. Or a lack there of."

It takes Killa a little bit less than an hour to hook up a scrumptious meal. The three fellows eat like pigs and Snoop greedily chows down on the scraps.

They throw table manners and etiquette out the window. With elbows on the table, they use their fingers, burp, and fart without saying excuse me. When it seems that Haywire will win the burping contest, the news comes on. Quickly Killa pushes record on the vcr.

"Good evening, I'm the newscaster and tonight's top story is...The punk who shot two officers after stabbing another kid on the eastside of manhattan has been identified as nineteen year old Johnny Stinger. Known among his peers as an imitation bad boy, here's what his classmates had to say..." Johnny see's Jackie on the screen, "He has a little penis and tries to compensate by hurting other people." Then he see's Answar, "Don put a whopping on his ass and that's why he stabbed him." Then he see's his mother, "Please baby turn yourself in." Then it's back to the newscaster, "The police are offering a five hundred dollar reward for any information leading to his arrest."

The news man goes on but Johnny's anger doesn't allow him to hear another word. The story was a blatant disrespect to his character. "They called me a punk," he says to no one in particular.

"Plus you got your ass taxed." Haywire laughed.

"And you got a little dick." Killa says as he and Haywire began to laugh at him.

Johnny jumps up like he is going to get bad. Haywire pulls out a gun and points it at him. "Nigga don't give me a reason to shoot you when it is what I really want to do anyway."

Before he can respond, Killa gets some duct tape, and starts to tape Johnny's hands behind his back.

"What's the deal?" he inquires.

"Just buying some time while we decide what to do."

"Do about what?"

"Do about you." Killa goes into the kitchen and quickly returns. He has one hand holding his nose and his other hand holds a damp rag. "Lights out," Killa places the wet washcloth over Johnny's face. "Breathe mother fucker."

Even with his hands bound Johnny puts up a good resistance. He refuses to breathe in the fumes from the liquid, which he has concluded is not water. Haywire steps up to Johnny and punches him right in the gut. With the wind blown out of him, Johnny has to gasp for air. He gets weaker with every breath, and he goes unconscious while hearing his so called friends laughing at him.

(Chapter 7)
Double Jeopardy (two2tangle)

*Don dreams about all kinds of food. He is at a
table filled with an assortment of fruits and
vegetables all laid out for him to taste. The scent
fills the room with a fruity, wholesome smell. His
stomach growls as he reaches for a large juicy
purple grape, and plucks it into his mouth. Don
bites down and samples the sweet juice, while at the
same time feeling the pain of tiny needles sticking
into his teeth, tongue, and gums.*

*He spits the grape out and sees the cactus shaped
seed at the core. "What kind of a grape is this?"
He thinks to himself. "Must be a fluke." He
cautiously tries another and the pointy spine sticks
into his lip. He spits blood.*

*Instinctively, he picks up a banana and peels it.
The fruit under the skin looks perfect and delicious.
Still not convinced of its safety, he breaks the
banana in half and almost cuts his finger off from
the razor blade core in the middle of the banana.
"What's going on?" His stomach growls while he
dreams, and gazes at the strawberries. He wonders
about the dangers they hold inside.*

*He eyes a juicy orange and quickly decides against
peeling it, because the citrus could really be
burning acid. Instead he carefully handles a jet
black plum. It is shiny and perfect in form and
shape. Don speaks out in name of the fruit
"Ebony."*

"Your eyes are closed yet you say my name."
Don retreats out of slumber to find Ebony smiling
before him. She is a jump off that DJ set up for
them both to hit. Although it didn't quite go out as

176

planned, Don royally knocked the boots. While she does have a pleasant face, Don shudders to think what would happen if Lydia found her here. "Hi, what are you doing here?"

"I'm so glad you remember my name. DJ told us you were here. He said we should come by and pay you a visit. He said you wanted some company."

"We?"

"Me and Zelda. She is in the bathroom smoking a cigarette. We have been here a little while, trying to wake you up. I think visiting hours are over."

Ebony stares at Don in a moment of mental connection. She likes him. Without saying a word it is quite clear. "Let me check on her," she says in order to move from him and hopefully stop the hot flashes that she feels.

Within seconds after Ebony steps into the bathroom, nurse Linton walks into the room to take vitals and talk shit. "I can't believe you are visitor free," she says sarcastically. Convinced they are the only two there, she goes on to say, "No hoochie mama drama thrashing the room over some sick dangling manhood."

"Excuse me?"

"No, excuse me. You think woman are something to be conquered. A game that is played. They mean nothing to you. Just another notch on your belt."

"How do you know?"

"I know you don't respect woman, and you don't respect yourself."

"How dare she?" Thinks Don. But words are hard to find as he evaluates her comments. Could she be right? Is he that bad? Most of the times, females come on to him, and he has a hard time saying no.

"You don't know me."

"I do know that the stab wound on your back is not

the only thing you're being treated for." She gives him two pills and some water as she lets her words sink in. "You need to become friends with these if you care about yourself and other people." She drops a pack of condoms on his bed as she makes her exit. "Goodnight Mr. Breyer, safe dreams." Nurse Linton turns out the light and closes the door.

Don lay in the semi darkness contemplating his character. He does not set out to hurt people. He genuinely likes meeting new girls and finding out about them. Talking, laughing, eating. He enjoys the company of beautiful women. He just has a problem with commitment, or they have a problem with his lack of commitment. The thing is he likes them all equally, he just likes a variety. Everyone wants more than one friend. Is there anything wrong with that? Why does it have to be such a terrible thing?

Then Don remembers that he has company. He sits up and mentally prepares to head to the potty. No he does not have to use the restroom. There are two hot mamas in there, and it doesn't take a rocket scientist to realize the possibilities. It's a short distance, yet a long walk to the bathroom. He opens the door hoping to see some freaky shit going on. He'll just watch and won't participate because he is trying to get his mind right. No more sexual activities until he gets himself together. He needs abstinence right now.

Instead he opens the bathroom door and sees nobody. The cubicle can't be much more than a 12 by 12. Where can they be? Don begins to wonder if he has imagined the whole thing. He is about to shut the door and go back to bed when he decides to look behind the door. There is hardly any room, but sure enough the two women are behind the door against the wall, trying to make their selves as flat as possible.

He is a bit relieved to see them because he thought for a second that he might be bugging out. "Hey ladies," he steps into the john. The girls are excited to be in his presence and greet him warmly with hugs and kisses. They have been looking forward to seeing him again. Especially Ebony. They are all so excited that they just laugh and giggle as if they just got away with robbing a bank. The knock on the door halts their laughter.

"Who is it?"

"Is everything alright Mr. Breyer?" Nurse Linton asked.

"Yes, thank you."

"Are you alone Mr. Breyer?"

Don cracks open the door slightly, "Of course I'm alone. Can't a brother have any privacy?"

Nurse Linton stomps off with a huff. Don shuts the door and the three of them begin to laugh again, only at a much lower volume. A towel is put on the floor under the door, and a blunt is lit. In hushed voices they converse.

"Blow the smoke into the ventilator," Zelda says after taking two tokes and passing.

Don wants to protest just for G.P., but he has been wanting a puff all day. He happily takes the weed and inhales deeply.

"So what happened to you anyway?" Ebony wants to know.

Don tries to process the question asked of him. He is in the hospital for being stabbed. But what brought the blade upon him? What has he done to deserve this fate? He knows the answer, still he feels that getting stabbed is more of the symptom than the problem. "I was stabbed."

179

"I've never seen anybody so sad about getting cut. Usually they get angry." Zelda sighed.

"I guess you are an expert on how somebody acts after getting shanked," Ebony comes to his defense.

He likes what he hears and replies, "You sound like you have done some psychological studying Ebony."

She smiles. "Well it is one of my favorite subjects."

"Mine too." Don looks deep into Ebony's eyes as they make another mental connection.

Zelda can tell what is going on. "You two make me sick with all that lovey dovey crap. I told you before Ebony that you better not try to fuck him in this hospital. You really shouldn't fuck him at all."

"Who said anything about fucking?"

"Don't act stupid. I know you."

Don is assessing his situation. He is in the hospital with a possibility of getting laid. On one hand, sex is good. It is great, and it feels wonderful. On the other hand, there is more to it than just the physical part. There is a mental aspect that he can't keep overlooking. He poses a question that he mostly asks for himself, "What about love?"

"Love? That's the flip side of hate. They are both on the same coin," Ebony states. "It's just a matter of probability."

"Love is a probability?" Don questions.

"Love is taking care of you. If you can't love yourself, you can't love anyone else." Zelda replies.

"Love is something I can't fuck with. Love makes too many mistakes and hurts too many people. I care, I have concerns and I pray for others, but I don't love. Incidentally I don't hate either. I just accept life as it is," Ebony speaks.

"Sounds like somebody who has had a very good

life. Or an extremely rough one." Don feels the weed taking hold.

"Things have not been easy. Even though I may have had a difficult life, and I know it could have been better, I also know it could have been worse," she locks eyes with Zelda. "No matter how hard I had it, somebody else went through more."

"Perception is a mother fucker. Everybody goes through the experience of life. It's all a matter of how you perceive the situations you go through. I was recently reading about how there really is no victim. Whether it's a car crash, a rape, or a broken heart. It is all a part of life." Don expounds.

"So fuck it. Let's all just go around and kill everybody we don't like. It's only life," Zelda says smartly.

"No, that's not at all what this philosophy was saying. There is a karma to life. You should strive to be a good person and treat others fair, with dignity and respect. But there are certain things that will happen to you in life that you will not have any control over. Bad things happen to good people, and vice versa." The weed puts Don in an analytical zone. He goes on, "When someone kills, the killer and the victim's family share a common bond."

"I thought there were no victims," Zelda states.

"Don't interrupt him. He's deep." Ebony looks at Don like the words coming from his mouth are law.

"I only used the word victim because I had no other way to describe the players in the game of life and death. So if someone murders your son, you refer to him as my son's murderer. He becomes almost like a part of the family."

"What a crock of shit."

"How rude Zelda! He has a very valid point. And he sounds like he knows what he is talking about."

Ebony has admiration in her voice for Don.
"I don't mind. It's all a matter of point of view and personal observation."
"Point of fucking view?" Zelda screams and the reality of just how angry the conversation has been making her becomes known. "You stand there and talk about there is no victim. How the little girl who is being abused is not a victim. How being made to eat food that causes you throw up, and then being made to eat the throw up because you wasted food by throwing up in the first place is victimless. How freaking dare you."
"Girl you don't have to go there." Ebony tries to console her friend. Don understands how personal this has gotten for Zelda. She is upset. He says nothing, knowing she needs to vent and let it out.
"No I want to go there. It's people like him, who never have to go through shit, that want to justify their position. You are not the victim here because you deserve what you got. You probably did some grimy shit and paid the consequences for it." Zelda let her words sink in. She feels a little better already and hopes Don has something to say. But when he doesn't, she continues to speak.
"There were times when I was made to drink with my mother because she did not want to drink alone." Zelda tries to keep it serious. Don bursts out laughing. He doesn't want to laugh but he can't help it. "Are you laughing at me?"
"No it's just that having a drink does not sound so bad." His comment sort of lightens the mood. Even Zelda cracks a smile. "I definitely, don't want to make mockery of your tribulations." Don continues, "I acknowledge them as being real and unjust. From my position in life I can only give thanks to the Creator for allowing me to be here

today, in my right mind. I know I don't have control over others, so for that I must take heed to the forces of negativity, and recognize the imperfections of man. Yet I cannot judge anyone. And I definitely cannot cast the first stone. Many people would possibly say that my trials have not been hard. Does that make me less caring or less of a real person?

You might hear my story one day and decide I did have a trying time in life. That I tried to do good in a bad world. It really doesn't matter because I know I have been blessed. Regardless of what people may say and feel about me, I know that God has my back whatever I do." He waits for Zelda's rebuttal, but she is speechless. He goes on.

"Let me ask you something," Don inquires. "You brought up Ebony fucking me a little while ago. Now I didn't ask for it, I have been here in this place tending to my wounds. You and Ebony come in here with your fine asses. Looking good, smelling good. Regardless of my status, wouldn't I be a fool or called gay to tell either of you no, if sex was offered to me? If I was to decline and told my story to someone else, what is the likelihood that they would agree with what I did? What would you think of a man who told you no?"

Ebony is clearly turned on by Don's speech. She moves close enough for him to smell her J-Lo perfume. "I would not like it one little bit."

Zelda also loosens up, "You got mad game son."

"That's not all I got," Don remembers the Hennessy DJ brought him. "I got some Hen Dog under my pillow. Let me slide out there to get it."

He leaves to get the cognac.

Don is just about to pull the alcohol from under the pillow and tip toe back to the bathroom when the room door opens. Nurse Linton peers in, "Where are you going?"

"I'm getting in bed," He replies while sliding the Yac back under the pillow.

"Are you okay?" She walks into the room.

"Don't you ever go home?" He gets in the bed.

She tucks the covers over him, "My job is never done." She sniffs the air. "Have you been smoking ganja in here?"

"Me? Of course not." He is not very convincing.

The Registered Nurse leaves and Don waits a few minutes before going back to his company. Briefly he contemplates taking the condoms Nurse Linton gave him into the bathroom. But how would that look if he walked in there with liquor and rubbers. Like he was so confident that he would get some ass. That is a sure fire way to not get some ass. He decides to leave them on the bed where he could easily reach them if he needed to.

He strolls into the lavatory, holding the bottle behind his back. "Do you know what the penalty is for hiding out in a hospital?" Don asks like they are in trouble.

"Do you know what the penalty is for harboring someone hiding out in a hospital?" Zelda gets funky too.

"The penalty is one shot," Don holds up the Hen Dog. He pours some into a small paper cup. Zelda gets the first shot. Since Ebony already seems down to get freaky he knows he has to get Zelda feeling good. They'll be no cock blocking up in here.

Four shots a piece and a blunt later, the mood in Dons hospital bathroom has had a complete metamorphous. Ebony is rubbing on his exposed penis, while Zelda looks on, sipping her fifth shot. Don sits on the toilet, peter standing at attention.

184

Ebony slowly takes off her apple bottoms, does a shake in her panties, and then takes those off. She stands in front of him and her supple breast look him right in the face. Don licks and sucks them while massaging every part of her body his fingers could reach. He saves touching her womanhood for last. By the time he does finger her sweet honey pot, she is wet with anticipation.

Her clitoris sticks out and begs for some love. He obligingly puts her right leg on his shoulders and buries his face into her pulsating vagina. As he gives her oral pleasure, he bears witness to the peace that can be found in giving her pleasure. He could actually get lost in eating her out. He feels like he could lick her forever. She has other plans.

Ebony turns around, ass facing Don. She is about to squat down on his erect cutter when he stops her and says, "Maybe we should protect ourselves." Ebony looks at him like she might get mad and walk out.

Instead, "I was thinking the same thing," is what she says. She goes into her tiny knapsack/purse and pulls out a condom. Easily she opens the Trojan and slides it on to his waiting manhood. Within seconds she is gliding up and down on his shaft, trying not to scream too loud. Riding like she has a purpose.

Don holds on to her breast, closes his eyes and leans back to enjoy the ride. Soon he finds a nipple pressing on his lips. Since Ebony is still playing hide the penis, who can it be? It is Zelda, joining in on the action. Her breasts are tasty also. He gets so caught up in them that he barely notices Ebony getting off and Zelda taking her place.

She smacks down wet and heavy on to his hard cock. So hard they he hopes she won't break the seat. As she reaches one of her many climaxes, she claws at his back. Her long nails scratch at his stitches, pulling many out, and opening up his wound. Lost in the sex, weed, and alcohol, he is oblivious to the damage being done.

The three of them go at it for hours. They try every position they could think of in the tiny room. Some work, some don't. But none of them have ever laughed so much while having sex and trying crazy shit. By the time Don blows his second load, he is exhausted. He falls out on the floor. The other two quickly follow suit.

Don is awakened by a knock on the door and a call of his name. He opens his eyes to find himself all cramped up, wrapped in a sheet along with his two friends, still in the bathroom. One of them must have gone to get the sheet off the bed.

Knock, knock. "Mr. Breyer is everything okay?" "Is that still you Ms. Linton? You're back early." "That's Mrs. Linton or Nurse Linton to you." She walks off in a huff.

Don lays there for five minutes. It takes the females another twenty minutes to get ready. Don hopes to sneak the girls out quietly, but when he opens the door, Nurse Linton is right there waiting.

"I can't believe this shit. This ain't no hotel!" Nurse Linton sees the girls. "Smells like fucking." She sees the empty bottle, "And drinking. You're all going to hell." Mrs. Linton personally chases the two young ladies out the building. Cursing and spewing Bible excerpts. Don goes to his bed and falls out.

(Chapter 8)
No Honor Among Thieves

Johnny regains consciousness to find himself on the floor of the kitchen still tied up. Pain in his stomach from being hit, he is angry at the world. He wonders what the hell is going on and what plans Killa and Haywire have for him. He can hear them discussing his fate in the next room.

"You can't walk in the precinct with little John and ask for the reward because you are a known felon. You are going to need identification to collect your check. And if they run a check on you, we will never get paid." Haywire is heard talking.

"You think I'm stupid. You will probably take the loot and go down south. I know that's where you want to go. And that would be just the amount of money you would need to make it happen." Killa replies angrily.

Johnny can't believe his ears. They are actually talking about turning him into the police. First they risk their lives to harbor him, now they are discussing how to get their hands on the reward money when they turn him in. Grimey mother fuckers.

He looks around the room to check out his environment when he suddenly hears someone coming in his direction. He closes his eyes and remains motionless. Killa walks into the kitchen and steps over Johnny like he is a mere inconvenience.

Killa tries to open the refrigerator and has to move Johnny over to get it fully open. He uses his foot and is not nice about it. Johnny does not appreciate being kicked. He wants to jump up and let Killa know how he feels, but that is impossible with his hands tied behind his back.

Killa pulls out a can of Del Monte fruit cocktail, rum raisin ice cream, whipped cream, a banana, unsalted cashews, and a mystery powder. He adds all of the ingredients into two bowls in a very meticulous manner. Ice cream first, he cuts up the bananas next. Then he does the whipped cream, and tops it off with the cashews and fruit cocktail. The single difference is that he only sprinkles the mystery powder on one of the desserts.

He picks up the knife he uses to slice the banana and bends down towards his apprehended cousin. He turns Johnny on his back and forces open one of his eyelids. Killa holds the knife in front of Johnny's face to check for a response. Johnny lays still and doesn't move his eyeball. Killa is satisfied that Johnny is still knocked out, so he walks back out to Haywire with their treats in his hands.

Killa passes the bowl with the extra powder to Haywire as he starts to devour the other. "Are you sure you don't want to turn me and Johnny in?"

"What are you talking about?"

"You probably want to keep the reward money for both of us."

"I didn't hear about any reward money for you," Haywire replies while eating his delicious dessert.

"I'm just trying to stay one step ahead of you."

"We have been boys since juvee. What, you suddenly don't trust me no more?"

"I have trust issues. I don't trust nobody."

"That's some cold shit. If I wanted to turn you in, I could have done it a long time ago." Haywire begins to feel a bit peculiar. He feels his body growing numb, and he starts to lose the sensation in his arms and legs. He looks at Killa knowingly, "You put something in the ice cream."

"Yes I did. I told you I have trust issues, and I don't trust you."

Killa watches while Haywire's jaw becomes stiff and he loses the ability to be verbal. Meanwhile Johnny has somehow gotten hold of the very blade that Killa used to cut the fruit and make the delicious dessert. It is very difficult and he believes he will get caught, but he commences to slice at the ties that bind him.

"I can't move," Haywire drawls with lots of spit and extreme difficulty.

"Yes, just like Johnny boy, you will become immobile. The only difference is he is completely unconscious, like he is sleeping. You will stay conscious and probably aware of everything that happens to you." Killa pulls out a small briefcase. He opens it to reveal a sparkling set of stainless steel knives as he talks to himself. "The problem with getting rid of a body is leaving evidence behind. Especially blood. Blood leaves stains behind that could be picked up by a blue light years later."

Haywire sits completely still, staring straight ahead. He can't talk or move, and should somebody tap him, he would simply fall over, unable to hold himself up. Still he is cognizant of everything around him. He can see and hear everything Killa is doing and saying, but he is unable to respond or prevent anything from happening to himself.

Johnny slides on his belly and peeks around the corner to see Killa standing over Haywire with shiny carving knives, ready to dig in. "Hold on, I forgot something". Killa turns to go in the kitchen where Johnny is supposed to be laying.

Johnny quickly slips back into his previous position with his hands and the knife behind his back, away from view. Killa strolls past him and grabs a roll of paper towels and a cutting board. Johnny peeks at him out the corner of his eye. He wants to jump up and get Killa, but his arms are still bound together. And Killa is carrying two knives with other items as he steps over Johnny to rejoin Haywire.

Johnny lies still trying to think of a plan. He doesn't hear Killa creep up on him until the wet handkerchief is placed over his nose and mouth. Johnny holds his breath for as long as he can, but he still inhales enough to get knocked out.

He wakes up shortly because he didn't breathe in as many fumes as his captive intended. He also is awoken from the loud sound of the meat grinder going to work. Johnny looks up to a frightening scene. Killa is grinding up what appears to be an arm. Deeply involved in his task, he isn't paying any attention to Johnny.

Johnny's first thought is not to scream. His second thought is to check to make sure he has both of his arms. Surprisingly he has both of his arms, and even more surprisingly, he still has the knife in his hands. Within minutes Killa grinds the arm down to chopped meat. He pours the excess blood down the drain, then pulls out various seasoning and a small spray bottle. He grabs a few paper towels, sprays them with the spray bottle until they are soaked, and without warning, puts them over Johnny's face.

Johnny gets knocked out, yet again.

Arms aching from being behind his back for so long, Johnny opens his eyes and nose to what smells like spaghetti simmering. His stomach rumbles at the scent of the herbs and spices. He wonders if he dreamed about the horrific scene of the arm in the meat grinder when he hears Killas voice in the next

room, "Haywire I wish you could taste this."
Johnny tries to stretch his limbs and almost cuts
himself with the knife he forgot he had in his
possession. Meticulously moving the blade up and
down, he finally frees himself. He spots the bottle
of knock out liquid and rags on the counter.
He stands up and feels a bit disoriented. He takes
the liquid and drenches the towels with it. The
fumes alone are strong and make him feel dizzy. He
hears Killa coming and almost panics. Quickly he
decides to lay back down in his previous position.
Killa steps over him and begins washing dishes.
In the middle of cleaning his first plate, Killa
senses something is awry. He sees the knife on the
counter. It was not there before. It was, but then it
disappeared, only to reappear. Killa can not
contemplate the situation any longer because
Johnny has placed the saturated rags over his face.
Johnny applies the pressure to Killas face with
both of his hands, but Killa won't go down easily.
He picks up the knife and stabs Johnny in one of his
hands. He pulls the knife out and goes to stab the
other hand. Johnny moves his hand just in the nick
of time and Killa stabs himself in his gums through
his cheek.
Yanking the blade out of his jaw, Killas blood
squirts over the stove and counter. He is more
irritated by the mess being made than he is by his
wound. He wants to hurt Johnny bad as he starts to
get woozy.
With all the strength he has left, Killa spins around
to face Johnny and stabs him in the thigh. He
wanted to shank him higher but his arm became so
heavy from the anesthesia that he hits him much
lower than planned.
Johnny screams but still manages to place the rag,

dripping with blood and good night fluid back over Killa's face. No longer able to stand, Killa becomes like putty and falls in slow motion to the ground, head hitting the floor with a heavy thud.

(Chapter 9)
Androgynous Answar

Don wakes up to the smiles of Answar, a fellow schoolmate. It takes him a few moments to adjust to his presence. Don prefers for him not to be around. Answar has always been cool, but recently he has changed. To put it plainly, his female side has started to emerge.

"Hey, que basa man? What a surprise to see you." Don says while wondering what kind of security they have in the hospital. They seem to let just about anybody in.

"Bueno diaz Don." Answar gives him an unexpected hug. As if reading Don's mind, Answar goes on to say, "I almost couldn't get in this morning. Visiting hours haven't even started yet. Luckily I got a few connections. You know I've been here quite a few times. I got the hook up. Isn't that great?"

"Yeah, that's what's up." Don replies, while thinking Answar sounds extremely gay.

"Dude you are the talk of the school. Well you and Johnny."

"Johnny?" Don says nervously.

"For sure. He had a wild shoot out with the cops. Three cops got shot."

"What! So is Johnny dead or in jail?"

"He escaped."

Answar could see the look of worry on Don's face. "Don't worry he'll get caught. They have so many police officers looking for him that he will never be able to get anywhere near you." While Answar is talking he sits on the bed next to Don and holds Dons hand. "Besides I'll be here to protect you."

Pulling his hand away, Don exclaims, "Answar

this scene is way too gay for me. Are you a homosexual?"

Taken back by Don's sudden hostility Answar finds it hard to respond, "I...I don't know."

"You don't know? How could you not know if you like boys or girls?"

"It's not so simple Don. You know my story and it's not so black and white."

"You're right. I do know your story and it is complicated. It's just that I have always seen you as a guy. You've always been my homeboy, not homegirl. Have you ever even tried to make out with a girl?"

"Of course not. I can't get hard. My dick does not work. You know I was born without any fully developed sex organs. I can't do nothing for no woman." Answar begins to cry.

Don is quiet as he thinks about Aswar's dilemma. It's not his fault that he could never penetrate a woman and know the pleasure of ejaculation. Then Don wondered what Answar would look like as a girl. What kind of satisfaction would he receive from sodomy? Probably the only pleasure he could receive would be in giving pleasure to his partner. He could give oral and anal, and hopefully find some comfort in that.

Don knows that Answar needs a friend. He doesn't want to go as far as Answar would like him to go, yet he doesn't want to turn his back completely on him. He puts his arm around him as a friendly gesture. "You know Answar, I have tried to pride myself as being a person who tries to understand everybody. I have heard that God's Angels have both sexes. I understand that Adam's son Cain went to the land of Nod to find a wife. And that the land of Nod was a place where any sexual desire could be fulfilled. The word Nod itself has been said to mean nudity. From what I have learned, from the limited knowledge that I have, God has destroyed cities because of man's appetite for sexual perversions. What I am trying to say is that I believe homosexuality has been present since day one."

"Yes," Answar stops crying and responds, "But my plight is quite unique. I look at homosexuals as being put into three categories. First there is the born homosexual. They are the ones who know they are gay since day one. You have seen them on Oprah and Montel talking about 'I knew I was gay since I was two years old.' To me that is the most natural way of all.

Secondly, there is the forced homosexual. Those are the ones who have been raped at an early age, in jail or anytime for that matter. Those are the ones who relive their trauma over and over. And if those individuals were going to be gay to begin with, that kind of trauma could have very complicated implications.

Lastly, there are those who discover late in life, or stumble upon the pleasures of man on man or woman on woman. These people are just experimenting and enjoying what they discover. Most of them would be considered bisexual because they will also engage in sex with the opposite sex. I don't see much wrong with that. It's kind of natural.

Then there is me. I don't fit into any of those categories. I am more of a mistake. I was already born when my parents had to make a decision about me. A very quick or I would die decision of whether they wanted a boy or a girl. They were expecting a girl, but when my father was given a choice, he chose a boy. A boy who he could play ball with and take fishing. A boy he could teach all the things a man should learn. Unfortunately he did not stick around long enough to show me what it is like to become a man. He broke out and let somebody else raise me. Now my step dad is a good man, but he is always working. I believe he understood the complications of raising another man's child and chose to keep his distance.

I guess I'm the exception to the rule. When I think about it, I have no choice but to be gay. I can't please a woman. And I've had too many operations to turn back now. If I try to reverse the process now things could get really messy. And I could possibly lose my life. All I can do is try to give pleasure to the man I love."

"I'm not so sure you would make a good looking girl anyway." They look at each other and crack up from Don's comment. "On the real though Answar, I'm not gay. I really love females. I love wet coochies and pointy nipples. I get turned on by the scent of fresh pussy." Don gets a bit carried away, "I adore bottoms. All types of booties, hips and thighs. I live for woman. To have sweaty, smelly sex with them."

"Don," Answar grabs his hand. "I was hoping we could do some experimenting."

Don pulls his hand away, "I really don think so Answar. You're asking me to do something I sincerely don't believe in."

"But I could be your first," Answar insists. "You could be my first. I have never been with anyone and I could never be a threat to your manhood."

"You can't be serious," Don replies. "Answar you are a good friend and I value our friendship, but we could never be lovers."

"Yes and because you are my friend I want you to see something." Answar pulls down his pants and reveals his sex. It is deformed beyond belief. It doesn't look much like a penis or vagina. It looks like a beat up swollen clit with testicle sacks minus the testicles. It is a frightening sight and Don feels like he is in some kind of crazy twilight zone. He is dumbfounded.

"It's ugly isn't it?"

"Well it's..." Don doesn't know what to say.

"It's disgusting and no one will ever want me."

"I'm sure there is someone for you out there somewhere."

"I want that someone to be you. I thought we were close, and I was certain you felt the same way."

"You thought I was a homo?"

"Of course not. I just thought we had feelings for each other."

"We do have feelings for each other, but it's on a level of friendship. It's a brotherly type of bond that we have. Now please fix your pants before someone comes in here."

"A brotherly thing?" Instead of zipping up his pants, Answar rips open his shirt. ADo brothers have breast like these?" Answar reveals his breasts which are much bigger than Don could ever have imagined. In fact, out of Answar's whole body, his breasts are the most perfectly formed. Maybe Answar should have been a girl. If he was female he would have nice tits. But he is a guy and Don is disturbed at the thought of finding Answar's breast even remotely attractive. AFeel them," Answar continues while stepping closer to Don, almost putting them in Don's face. AThey are very real."

"What are you doing?" Don goes to push Answar back and touches his breast in the process. They are rather firm and ripe. For a split second Don imagines that if they were in the dark, he would not be able to tell Answar's breast from any typical female. They feel very supple and very much real. But only for a mini second. Don cannot forget that Answar is a dude. "Answar I don't care how nice your tits are, you are still a male. I see you as a male so it can never happen between us."

Answar's eyes turn red and get watery. He is about to cry. Don sees this, feels sorry for him and wants to comfort him, but does not know how. "Look my good friend, there is someone out there for you. You just have to have faith and patience. Someday you will meet your significant other." The tears begin to flow down Answar's cheeks and Don feels so bad that he opens his arms to embrace him. Answar hugs Don and immediately tries to take it to the next level by kissing him on the neck. "No Answar!" Don yells and tries to push Answar away. But Answar wont let go and Don feels like he is about to have an anxiety attack.

(Chapter 10)
Is Gay Okay

Donald walks in just in time to see his son struggling with Answar. "What is going on here?"

Answar looks up and in the moment of his distraction, Don decks him in the face. From the force and sound of the blow it is likely that he has cracked a few teeth in Answar's mouth. The blow throws Don off balance and he begins falling off the bed. Donald runs to catch his son before he hits the floor. Answar calmly fixes his clothes and spits a wad of blood on the floor. He turns around and serenely walks out the hospital door.

There is a silence between them as dad helps his son back to a comfortable position on the bed. After more silence, Donald looks hard at his son and raises an eyebrow. Without saying a word Don knows his father wants answers.

"No means no," Don begins. "And I can respect that now more than ever."

Donald doesn't know what to think. He doesn't even want to think. Is his son gay? Was that somebody trying to molest his son? "What happened? Was that boy trying to rape you?"

"No. Maybe. Not exactly. He wanted some affection that I did not feel comfortable giving."

"Whoa I think I'd better sit down."

"Dad I'm not trying to speak up for him, but he has a lot of issues he has to deal with."

"Don are you gay, or bi-sexual?"

"No Dad. I just know what Answar has been going through. We go to the same school. And let me reiterate, I am not gay or bi-sexual."

"You know I would still love you the same even if you were."

"Thanks a bunch Dad, I really appreciate that, but I am not gay."

"Good, glad to hear it. But you know that there is nothing wrong with homosexuality. I mean there is, but I'm willing to except you any way you are."

Don can feel his blood began to boil. "Dad I am going to say it for the last time. I am not a homosexual. I have never been, and I never will be. Frankly, I am real surprised that you would ever even consider your son being gay. It just won't happen. And that is final!"

Donald gives his son an I'm not so sure I believe you look. "I ever tell you about my gay uncle?"

"No Dad you have not and I am not."

"Well my uncle Larry was my favorite uncle. He was almost like a dad to me. He was a strong man who did not seem to possess any feminine qualities. It was not until he passed away that I found out about his alternative lifestyle. Some of the family tried to speak ill of him, but I remember the kindness he had shown me. I remember him helping me with my multiplication tables until I knew them by heart. He often encouraged me to pursue my dreams and believe in myself. He gave me the courage to ask your mother out."

"And your point is?"

"All I'm saying is it's okay to be gay."

"Pop, for the very last time, I'm not gay."

"There have been plenty of famous people who shaped history that were gay. James Baldwin, Elton John, DNA, Holiday Heart, and Benjamin Franklin are just a few."

"You're kidding me right? I am not a homosexual! And for the record they say Benjamin Franklin was a pedophile, not a homosexual."

"Yes but he liked boys. They were young boys,

but he liked them."

"That's even worst. Why would you try to even put me in a category with him. I'm insulted."

"I'm not trying to insult you. I just want you to feel comfortable enough to tell me the truth."

"The truth? What the hell do you mean the truth? I am telling you the truth."

"Don't use that tone of voice with me. I am your father."

"I respect that Dad, but you keep implying that I am queer and I simply am not."

"You know there is an old funny saying that if you do it once then you are not gay, you're just experimenting, but if you do it more than once..."

"How about if you do the sticking only. You know be the one on top and treat your partner like a real woman. Are you still gay then?"

"Is that what you did?"

"No Dad, end of discussion please."

"Okay, but let me say this one last thing. I have read that approximately fifteen percent of all species exhibit gay tendencies. From insects to mammals. Homosexuality can be said to go along with the natural order of things."

"Enough Dad."

"There is a story in the Bible. I think the mans name was Lot. Or was it Job? Anyway he was the only honest man in the whole city, so with the exception of him and his family, God sent Angels down to destroy the wicked city. The town's men knew the Angels were in this man's house and they wanted to know the Angels. This righteous man offered his two virgin daughters to the angry mob, but they didn't want the women. They wanted to have sex with the Angels. Homosexual sex!"

"For real pop, I wish you would get off the subject

of homosexuality. Still since you brought it up, my understanding of Angels is that they had both male and female genitalia. They supposedly even had breast. Is it possible that those men wanted the female parts of the angels?"

"Are you kidding me? All of the angels are male. That is why they all have masculine names. They wanted the men."

"Dad, throughout history women have not been considered equal to men, and it is reflected in books like the bible. And if all Angels are male, how do they reproduce? Men can't make babies by themselves."

"True, but with God on your side, anything is possible. If God so wills male Angels to have babies, he could make it happen."

"You're bugging. There are no babies in heaven. I have never heard any mention of children being born in heaven. If Angels had kids where are they?"

"Bugging?! Please stop trying to disrespect me with your street slang. I am not one of your homies!"

"No disrespect, but bugging is in the dictionary. It's there with ain't, fittin, and wanksta."

"Wanksta?"

"Yeah, a want to be gangster."

Their conversation is stopped short by the entrance of nurse Linton. She is the same nurse who tended to Don yesterday for a double shift. She considers him to be trouble, and says nothing to him. Rolling her eyes at him, she checks the medical equipment, and his vital numbers, and fluids. After giving him his medications she goes to look at his knife wound, sees the bloody gauze, removes it and makes a gasping sound. "Someone has been messing with your stitches."

"Huh?" Don plays dumb.

She also notices the scratch marks on Dons back and remembers the two young ladies sneaking out his room in the wee hours of the morning, "It seems your stitches have been scratched out during a moment of passion. We are going to have to do them all over again." She looks at Donald, "I hope you have good insurance coverage." Nurse Linton gales out of the room.

"Don, what the hell was that about?"

"Dad I..."

"Did it have anything to do with that homo friend of yours?"

"It had nothing to do with him, and he is not a homo, he is androgynous."

"He does not look androgynous to me."

"It's a long story and I don't feel like telling it."

"Well you better tell me how your stitches got ripped out."

"It was a mistake."

"What was a mistake?" Grandmother asks while entering the room.

"The stitches got messed up."

"How did that happen?"

Don is speechless. He does not know what to say. The truth is probably not what is needed here. "I had a visitor."

"Oh so now the truth comes out." Dad says angrily.

"If you imply that I am gay one more time. I'll..."

"You'll what?!"

"Gay?!" Grandma screams.

"Nothing." Don says.

"What is this all about?" Grandma has both hands on her hips and wants an explanation.

"Nothing to get excited about Mom. I just wanted

Don to know that no matter what his sexual preference is, I will always love him." Donald says with a smile.

"Are you saying that Don is..."

"No he is not saying, I am saying, I am not gay! I don't know why he keeps pressing the issue."

"Okay, but what happened to the stitches?" Grandma asks while looking over Don's shoulder.

"I had a visitor yesterday who was a bit excited to see me, and when she hugged me her nails got caught in the stitches."

Grandma takes a look at Don's back. "Where did all of these other scratches come from?" Don is silent as Grandma figures it out. "Was it Lydia? I hope it was." She had a feeling it wasn't because she talked to Lydia on the phone last night. She really likes her, and loves her new found Great Grandson.

"No." Don mumbles, not wanting to see the look of disappointment on his grandmother's face.

"Was it a female?" Dad asks in a low murmur.

"It was two females!" Don blurts out getting angry.

"Yeah, okay son." Donald does not believe his son's story. But Grandma does.

"How could you do that to that sweet girl? Why would you treat your baby mama that way?" Grandma wants to know.

"Pop you are absolutely taking this way too far."

"I'm going too far? Look at all the trouble you have caused. A son we knew nothing about, almost getting killed, and gay sex! I don't know what to expect next."

"Well, if you weren't my father you could expect a swift kick in the mouth."

"How dare you talk to your father that way? I've

never heard you talk like that."

"Dad keeps calling me a homo. He hasn't been with a woman since Mom died and he says I'm gay."

"Oh so now it's my fault? If it weren't for you, your mother would probably still be here!" Donald regrets the words as they leave his mouth. The silence is loud while the three generations soak up what was just said. Donald tries to clean it up. "I didn't mean that son. It wasn't your fault."

His words fall on deaf ears. The damage is done. Donald has cut his son deeper than the knife he took in the back. Don's whole body goes numb and the water embarks from some secret well behind his eyes.

"No Don that is not true," his Grandmother hugs him. "You had nothing to do with that horrible act. We don't know why it happened and maybe we never will. But God does everything for a reason. We just have to learn to accept his ways."

Suddenly Don feels extremely tired and drained. He is overwhelmed as he ponders why God let his mother die. And will God judge him for his mother's death. It is kind of good that all of this has come up because now he does not have to explain about Ebony and Zelda.

Nurse Linton walks in the room with some Doctors and interns on her heels. "And here is our most popular patient Doctors, the visitors never seem to stop coming," she remarks sarcastically. "We need to take a look at your back Mr. Breyer." The physicians bear witness the scratch marks on Don's back with looks of puzzlement, yet they don't ask any questions.

"We are going to need to remove these stitches and reapply new ones," a Doctor states.

205

Dad and Grandma are silent as the Doctors leave to obtain their surgical equipment. Lydia walks in just as Grandma covers up Dons back. He hears her greet his parents as he feigns sleep.

"Is he okay?" Lydia asks after seeing the look of worry on their faces.

"Yes he's fine. There were some problems with his stitches but the Doctor will fix them. How are you sweetie, and where is Damian?"

"Damian is with my Father. I'll have to introduce you to him one day." Lydia and Grandmother talk while Donald stays quiet. They leave the room when the Doctors come in to replace the stitches and Don goes to sleep afterwards and Don drifts off into slumber land for real.

The police arrive at the hospital to take him away. They aggressively pull him off the hospital bed and cuff him. They march him out the building in his hospital clothes and no shoes. He is taken straight to prison and thrown in a courtyard still handcuffed. All the prisoners stop their activities to stare at Don. One very shifty looking character walks over to him.

"You are in a really bad situation here amigo." The guy lights up two cigarettes and puts one into Don's mouth. Even though Don doesn't smoke cigarettes he leaves it there. The shifty character goes on to say, "So tell me my friend how do you want it, conscious or unconscious?"

Don spits the cancer stick out of his mouth. "What you mean man?"

"You know how we treat faggots in here who kill their mothers. It has to be done. So just tell me if you want to be conscious or not. It's all up to you."

Don looks around and realizes that all the inmates

have formed a circle around him. They all have the eager look of pending sexual gratification. Some are even rubbing their crotches. "But I'm not gay!" Don screams.

"It's your choice. I think you should stay conscious, cause if you're not, there is no telling what these cats might do to your body. Plus they might want some head."

"But I'm not gay!"

The inmates bend Don over a pile of bricks and form a line behind him. He begins to cry and scream out "I'm not gay, I'm not gay!"

"Don, wake up son. You're having a bad dream." Don awakes to see his Dad, Grandmother and Lydia looking down on him with deep concern. Donald bends down to whisper in his sons ears. "I know you are not gay son, and I'm sorry for the terrible things I have said. I hope you can find it in your heart to forgive me," He hugs his son.

"Thanks Dad. I would like to apologize also. I said some things out of anger and not truth. You're a great Dad and you're not gay either." They smile but Lydia wonders what the hell is really going on. They yap it up for over an hour when Don's lunch is brought to him. "Don your Grandmother and I are starving. We are going to get something to eat. Lydia would you like to join us?" Dad

"No thanks, I've eaten already. I'll just stay here and hang out with Don for a little while."

"All righty then. Don we will see you later," Dad and Grandmother make their exit.

(Chapter 11)
Nice To Eat You

Killa is brought back to life by a cup of cold water being splashed on his face. "You killed him! Haywire is dead! You cut off his fucking arm and you ate it! What kind of a god damn monster are you?" Johnny is frantic.

"I did not mean to frighten you. If you let me go, I'll explain." Killa is very polite.

"Let you go? Why? So you can try to kill me. Probably want to eat me. You are a demented hood cannibal!"

Killa laughs heartily. He is enjoying the moment as if he is confident of his release. "What can you do? Turn me into the police? You are a wanted criminal." Killa laughs some more.

Johnny smacks Killa across the face. "I can take your life."

Killa recognizes that look on Johnnys face. He is dead serious. His eyes say that he can easily murder a man. "Haywire is not dead." Killa

"Yeah he is. Minus a mother fucking arm. You and Snoop ate it. There is other food here, even dog food. What the hell was you thinking!"

As he watches Johnny flip out, Killa speaks in a calm voice. "I am a killer. I kill people. Hence the name. A lot of people talk about it, but I be about it." He pauses as if he said something profound. "But I am not a typical killer, I'm not going out like no regular low class murderer. Kids will be telling horror stories of me for generations to come. I'm going to be a legend."

"No you are going to be another dead nigger," Johnny smacks Killa across the face again. Killas blood boils and he gets livid. He struggles, screams, orders snoop to attack in vain, and unsuccessfully tries to get loose. His frustration quickly turns into vulnerability, and because he is unable to set himself free, he emotionally ruptures and balls like a baby.

"I just want to be somebody. I know I'm going to die. I know where my soul is going. I just desire to make my mark on this world. I want to be the best at what I do. That's why you have to let me go. I'm not finished. I have to get on with my business." Killa

Snoop walks out the room to get a drink of water. "Tell me what really happened to Snoop? Did you have to cut his throat open to get a bone out?"

Killa giggles. Johnny is on point. "No I did not. Snoop made too much noise. So once again, I did my research to find out how to remove vocal cords and viola, now he is a silent partner." Killa laughs at his own joke.

"They call me evil, but you are downright Satan himself. What about me? If I let you go, what about me?" As Johnny asks the question he feels frightened and alone. He has no friends or anybody he can count on. Then Snoop walks into the room and lies right by his feet.

"We can make a deal. Some kind of truce." Killa looks at Snoop and a chill runs through his body. He knows all the terrible things he has done to that dog. If the dog knew Killa is being incapacitated and cant retaliate, he would probably bite his neck off. In his bid to stay alive, Killa invites Johnny more into his world. "I want to show you something."

"What?"

Killa understands that most criminals get caught because they run their mouths, but he believes he has no choice. He has to get Johnny to let him loose. He has to make him feel that they could be comrades. "I have a box I want you to look through."

"A box? You must think I was born yesterday."

"No, it's important to me. It's my story. Journals, news clippings, video footage, souvenirs, and things. I'm real with this," Killa states proudly. "The box is in the floor model TV right there. Just turn the tube around, and pull the back off."

Johnny contemplates. "If I find one trick, you are as good as dead." He does what Killa says and finds a metal box with a combination lock on it, hidden inside the set.

"The combination is 06-06-98."

Johnny opens the lock, but does not open the box. Instead he places the box in front of Killa and stands behind it while he opens it , "Just in case you rigged it to explode, you will get the brunt of the explosion."

Killa smiles at the thought, "I'm not that good yet."

Johnny looks inside and finds all the items Killa described and more, but the fat bag of weed interests him most. He opens it up to smell it. It has a funny chemical odor. "What kind of weed is this?"

"It's some bullshit smoke. I kept it there because I could not bring myself to throw it away." Killa lies, knowing it's a very potent angel dust. Johnny looks through the rest of the box and finds all kinds of news clippings about the ATM murders to random arson stories. It seems that Killa has had a long history of doing various evil things.

More than willing to discuss every item, Killa runs his mouth about the rapes he has committed, the robberies, and mutilations. He intends on killing Johnny so he feels he can tell all and not worry about the ramifications of being caught. Besides, he is finding it very therapeutic to let go and speak about his experiences.

As Killa is talking, Johnny reflects on the powder he put in Haywire's dessert. "Why do keep saying Haywire isn't dead? I poured water on him and stuck him with a pin. He did not move or flinch one bit." Johnny lightly pushes Haywire and he leans over to the side.

"He's not dead. I went to the library, got on the internet and did some research on how to make a person a zombie. I found the main ingredient came from the Caribbean puffer fish. I got hold of it and tried it for the first time on Haywire. It contains an ingredient that can slow a person's heart rate and make it hard to detect. There were other things I was supposed to add, but I could not get everything."

"So he's going to be like that forever?"

"Maybe, I'm not sure. He may move or even walk. But he most likely won't talk again." Killa is really not sure.

Johnny is horrified. He knows it could have just as easily been him. "So he's going to sleepwalk for the rest of his life with one fucking arm?"

"No he's been zombified. I've never done it before. I don't know what's going to happen. He may come out of it."

As if he was waiting for his cue a muscle spasm makes Haywire sit straight up. Killa is shocked, Snoop runs out the room, and Johnny points a gun at Haywire. "Since he's a goddamn zombie now, he's going to want to eat people like in the movies right?"

"Nah man, I never heard of that." Killa hides his fear because he really isn't sure what's going to happen. He reflects on his dabbling in the black arts and he is totally aware that there are possible repercussions. "But could you let me go, just in case."

"Hell no you crazy fuck. You reap what you sow. You ate him. Now he is coming back for revenge.

Haywire just stares blankly straight ahead. Unblinking and not moving. Five minutes. Ten minutes. Twenty minutes. He is stationary and emotionless. "When is he going to do something?"

"He most likely won't. But then he might. I know that some studies have found that he can hear every word that we are saying and he is conscious of everything around him. He just can't respond."

"I'll bet that you were going to do that zombie shit to me?"

"Of course not. I had a chance to do it, but I didn't, did I?"

Johnny almost wishes he could believe him. He wants so badly to have somebody he can trust and count on. He could really use a friend. A deep look at Haywire reminds him of what Killa does to his friends. "No, but I'm sure you had plans for me. What did you expect to do with Haywire, eat him piece by piece?"

Killa takes a moment to answer because that is exactly what he had planned on doing. With the help of Snoop he was going to eat at least a limb every other day. "I wanted to see if I could cut off each of his limbs and still keep him alive. I wanted to know how much of him could be taken away before he loses the will to live."

"You are a sick bastard."

"Why, because I want to be somebody?"

Johnny observes Haywire some more. Even though he does not like him and vice versa, Johnny believes Haywire is being put through a cruel fate. It's one thing to kill a mother fucker. It's another thing to make a person suffer. But to eat a nigga? Isn't that crossing the line. "After you eat his arms and legs, then what?"

"You really want to know?" Johnny does not answer because he is unsure if he really wants to know. Killa goes on anyway. "First I will remove a few small pieces. Penis, lips, ears, buttocks, stuff like that. When I can't carve him up anymore and if he is still alive I will have to kill him. I will gut him and..." Killa is not able to finish because he is knocked out by a blunt object.

(Chapter 12)
Baby Mama

Don knows Lydia wants information about Fatima. Lydia pulls up a chair to be closer to her man. "Hey Baby," she plants a kiss on his forehead. "I guess you have had a lot of time to think since you've been in the hospital."

"Think?" Don thinks, "I've been busier in here than I have been on the outside, I haven't had any time to think." But, "Yeah I've had a lot on my mind. What have you been thinking about?"

"Well I've been thinking about you and me and..."

"You think it's time for me to settle down and you want us to get married."

"No I was actually going to say that we should give each other more space."

"Are you dumping me?" Don is hurt.

"No, but yes."

"I can't believe this shit. You couldn't wait until I got out of the hospital to tell me this? You have to do this while I am on my deathbed? Kick a man when he is down. That is your style."

"No Don. I love you very much. It's just that I know what I want for my future. You are still searching. You're still growing and I feel I have to step a side and let you learn about life."

"Oh so this is suppose to benefit me? You are doing this for me?"

"You don't want to be with me."

"I do want to be with you."

"Maybe you do, but you want to be with other women too. You are still sowing your royal oats. Not to mention you have no idea what you are going to do with your life."

Don knows she is right, but he tries to defend

himself anyway. "There are a lot of things I can do. I could go to college. I still have my job at the supermarket, I could stay there and work my way up to management. I could be a policeman, a sanitation worker, or even get a job with the post office."

"Yes, you could do all of those things. But the problem is choosing what you want to do. And you are definitely unsure if you want to be with me."

"I do want to be with you."

"I'm not quite so convinced, but I'm still here. I don't know why. I almost killed a girl over you and I'm still trying to figure that shit out."

Don tries to say something comforting, but nothing comes out of his mouth.

"You really don't have to say anything and you probably shouldn't. But there is one question I would like you to answer. All I want is a yes or no. Is that okay?"

"Fine," Don wonders what question she is going to hit him with and just how honest he should be. He has done his share of dirt and it would feel nice to come clean.

"You really gave me a venereal disease and then tried to blame me, didn't you?"

"Oh no, not that," thinks Don. The proper answer to her inquiry can make or break whatever relationship he has left with his baby mama. Saying no would be a flat out lie, and saying yes would condemn him forever. Eternity seems to pass before Don can reply. "I am not completely sure. I mean I have done some scandalous shit, but when I confronted you, I realized it could have gone either way."

Lydia had really hoped Don would confess the truth. Her gut feeling knows Don has given her something, but because she confessed to sleeping with someone else, she will have to take the blame, for now. "So are you saying it could have been you?" She seeks a partial confession.

Don knows she wants affirmation, but she won't get it. At least not today. "No there is no way that it was me."

"But you said it could have fallen either way, what did you mean?"

"I mean that at the time I confronted you, I was not sure what was wrong with me. Once I found out, it could only have been you." Don has to play hard ball to the end. Still he wants to get off the subject, so he switches it. "How is our son?"

An unwilling smile breaks out on her face. If anything good has come out of her relationship with Don it's Damian. She is very happy and proud of her son. The thought of him always brings a smile to her face. Even if she has to raise him all by her self, she will never regret having him. "He is fine. Constantly growing, eating everything, and he gives the best hugs." Her face lights up.

"I've been thinking," Don wants to stray as far away from her question as possible, and talking about their son can keep her yapping for a while. "Isn't it time Damian got into some self defense class?"

"Huh?"

"You know karate, judo, jujitsu. Martial arts."

"Are you kidding? He is much too young. And he doesn't have to defend himself from anybody. He's not even in preschool yet."

"Yeah but if we start early, by the time he is my age, he'll be one bad motherfucker."

"Yeah, and by the time he is twelve, you won't be able to discipline him because he'll be kicking your ass all over the place."

"What? Are you insane? My seed putting his hands on me? Don't make me go out like Marvin Gaye's dad."

"Nigga, are you talking about shooting my son?" Lydia does not know whether to get mad or laugh it off. "Never that. My son and I will always be cool with each other." There is silence. "And besides, we love each other too much to be fighting."

"No martial arts." Lydia

"No martial arts?" Don

"So what happened to your stitches?"

"Some of them came out."

"Damn, they must not have done a good job."

"I guess not. Did I tell you how beautiful you look today? You are blessed."

Lydia starts to figure Don out. He is the master at changing a subject he does not want to talk about. And he definitely is not trying to talk about his stitches. "So did your Dad or Grandmother raise hell? I mean that has to be negligence on the hospital's part. Stitches are not supposed to come out by themselves."

Damn she is persistent. "Well it wasn't totally the hospital's fault. The stitches were itching me bad and because I can't see behind my back, I accidentally loosened a few of them. It's really no big deal. Besides why are you so concerned, aren't you dumping me?"

"If I had of put you through a fraction of the things you have put me through, you would have left me a long time ago."

"You don't know that. That is pure speculation. You have no idea what I would do."

"Bullshit! I almost killed someone over you today, and it was purely self defense. I swear Don if one more crazy shit jumps off with you, I may seriously lose it. I'm going against my better judgment to even be here now. I am just praying that I'm not making a fool of myself by giving you the benefit of the doubt. Don't let me down."

Don wants to go deep into his bag of lies and smooth everything over with Lydia, yet he acknowledges that he has been digging his own grave for quite sometime now. Not wanting to keep making a bigger hole, Don simply replies, "Okay."

"Good, now tell me about Fatima."

All this time he knew she would ask that question and it is still a shock to him. All he can say is "Huh?" He knows it is a sign of being busted and not coming up with anything better to say. "What do you want to know about her for?"

"Are you getting defensive? I almost killed that bitch! What the fuck do you think I want to know about her for? Who the fuck is she?" The fire in her eyes sends beams of hate in his direction.

"Easy baby, take it easy. She is just someone who got the wrong idea."

"Got the wrong idea about what?"

"About us."

"Why would she get the wrong idea about us?"

"I think she felt like she was protecting me."

"Protecting you from what?"

"From you."

"Me? The only reason she would do that is if you were fucking her. And I am sure you were because she came here ready to put it down for her man."

"I wasn't tapping that."

"Then why was she risking her life?"

She probably thought somebody was trying to kill me again."

"Somebody is going to kill you if you keep messing with peoples feelings. You are going to

218

break some girls heart and she is going to trip hard on you!" She stares him up and down. "And it wont be nothing nice."

"You trying to wish bad on me? Put a hex on me or something?"

"Nah, I don't want that kind of karma. Besides you are doing it to yourself. Somebody tried to carve your ass up already, and I'll bet it had something to do with Fatima."

"No not at all." Don says confidently, because it had do with a different girl. "But I do see that you believe I deserved to get stabbed. I must have done some kind of dirt to warrant it. Blame the victim, it must be his fault. This is when you see who is really on your side."

"On your side? Who the hell is sitting on your side right now? Who birthed a life for you? You begged me to keep our son. I was against it, but I trusted the empty promises you made me. And lets face it, I've been raising Damian on my own for the most part. I appreciate all of the things you have done for us, but I have never asked you for anything."

"How do you stand there and talk about you never ask me for anything. Even if you ask me for a cup of water, that is something. And basically you have asked me to be nice to you, and treat you with respect. Not in those exact words, but you know you are an independent woman." Don rambles on, not making much sense. "If you want something, you go get it. If I can provide it, fine. If not, then fuck Don, you'll find another way to attain it. I respect that, and it makes you more desirable. Still please don't make me feel like I can't or don't play a primary role here. I am just as concerned about Damian as you are."

"You better be, because no matter what happens between us, he is your son and he needs you."

"I wish you needed me too."

"Me? To be honest, I can move on with or without you right now. I am very angry, confused and disappointed with you. You put me through a whole lot of heavy, unnecessary bullshit. I really don't know how much more I can take."

Don feels compelled to beg for forgiveness. But to do so would be to admit guilt. There are a lot of head games involved in twisted relationships.

"Lydia, I've made plenty of mistakes, but I do love you and I am trying. Let's just take it day by day. Come lay down next to me." Lydia cuddles next to Don and the sandman quickly arrives to place them both under his spell.

(Chapter 13)
Drama

A little over an hour later, Don feels Lydia pulling away. "Where are you going?"
"I'm hungry and I have to check on Damian."
"Tell him I love him. Will I see you again today?"
"Probably not, but I will be back first thing in the morning."
"Cool." They kiss, Lydia leaves and Don drifts quickly back to sleep.

Two beautiful familiar looking nurses arrive to prepare Don to depart the hospital. They have on extremely short and tight nurse outfits that show all of their curves. Don is the man as he exits the hospital. There are television cameras and a large crowd awaiting his exit on the outside of the hospital.
The buzz on his hospital reality show has made him very popular. When the hospital doors open the crowd screams and yells as if Don is some kind of superstar. He greets his fans warmly and feels euphoria from the love. Everybody wants to shake his hand and hug him.
Suddenly the crowd gets rowdy and begins grabbing him and pulling him in every direction. At first it feels good to have so many people love him. But when his clothes are being ripped off and his hair is pulled from its roots he becomes terrified. He notices Jackie towing on one of his arms. His limb pops out of its socket and someone is trying to literally rip his head off. He looks up and sees it's Johnny who has him in a choke hold. He wants to scream but he can't as he hears his name being called.

"Don baby, wakey wakey."

Don surfaces from his nightmare in the daytime. Someone is talking to him.

"Hi honey. I just wanted to see you and make sure you are okay."

He opens his eyes, "Jackie?"

"What'suppp?" she replies enthusiastically.

"What are you doing here?"

"I came to see you."

"Damn they just let anyone up in here."

"What the hell is that suppose to mean?"

Don sees Jackie did not take to his comment too well. He tries to clean it up. "It's not you so much, I just had a dream that Johnny was out to get me and you were not very nice to me either. Did they catch that him yet?" Don is anxious.

"No he is still on the run."

"Great I just hope he don't run his ass up in here," he screams. "They just let anybody come in here you know."

"I wish you would stop saying that."

"Well I shouldn't be too happy to see you. Besides burning me, you're the reason Johnny tried to kill me in the first place."

"I never forced you to be with me."

"You didn't give me much of a choice either."

"I told you where to put your penis? Are you stupid? You have no control and couldn't say no?" Jackie responds, knowing she was not trying to take no for an answer.

"Yeah I have control. I have enough control to get your ass thrown the fuck out of here. Nurse! Nurse! There's a crazy bitch in here!" He yells.

The same nurse that has been catching Don with his various visitors peeks in, "Is everything okay?"

"Everything is fine. Just a bitch ass nigger here who can't handle the truth," Jackie tells her.

"Okay," the nurse exits.

"I can't believe this shit."

"You! I came here to warn you and you're treating me like I'm the enemy."

"Warn me about what?"

Jackie is hesitant. "Warn you about Johnny.

"What about Johnny?"

"He wants to kill you," she replies very nonchalantly.

"Is that all? Tell me something I don't know."

"I may have inadvertently told him where you are."

Don can hardly believe his ears. "And why would you do that?"

"He called me and was talking trash about you. I told him he wasn't half the man you are."

"But why did you have to tell him where I am?"

"It slipped out when I told him I was going to visit you."

"You did what?"

"Trust me, he would be a real dumb ass motherfucker to bring his stupid butt here. There is a citywide search going on for him."

"Did you go to the police and tell them he called you?"

"Hell nah. I don't want to get involved like that."

"But they could have probably traced the call. What about caller I.D.? You could still give the cops the number."

"Nope it was an unknown number. Besides my parents are angry enough."

"So how the hell are you going to protect me? You got me and you a bullet proof outfit or something?"

"Nigga please. He won't do anything to you as long as I'm around. And I seriously doubt that he is going to come here looking for you."

"You better be right, because I have a feeling that he is angry enough to kill both of us."

"Man you are tense." Jackie starts to massage Don's shoulders. "You have to learn how to relax. I believe Jesus once said that worrying serves no purpose."

"So what am I suppose to do, just chill out while someone tries to eighty six me?"

"No action is important when it is necessary. Right now everything is fine. So let it be." Don closes his eyes and enjoys the rub down he is being given. "That's easy for you to say, It's not your ass on the line."

"My ass is your ass," Jackie takes Don's hand and puts it on her booty.

"Excuse me?" Don inquires, while leaving his hand where she put it.

"Stop fronting, you know how I feel about you."

"How do you feel about me?"

"I love you." Jackie

"Your love is dangerous." Don

"You have to admit we have something illmatic."

"What we have is a tragedy. What has happened between us has hurt a lot of people. It's not about love, and it's bigger than Johnny."

"No it's about me saving your ass. If you would have covered your butt better at school, things would not have gone this far."

"Are you seriously trying to blame me for all of this?" Don

"If the shoe fits." Jackie   "I see you in a whole different light. You are pretty on the outside, but very ugly on the inside."

Jackie is crushed. She has been called a bunch of things, but ugly was never one of them. She does not know what to say, so she lets her tears do the talking.

"Damn," Don thinks. "I sure have a knack for making people cry." Although he feels that he is in the right, Don still undergoes guilt for making her shed tears. "Look Jackie, what's done is done. We can't change the past, but we can prepare for the future. I have caused enough people stress and pain. I do not wish to bring any of it your way. I got mad love for you and before all of this bullshit went down, I considered you a friend. When it all gets said and done, I'm hoping we can still be friends."

"I want to be more than your friend."

"Where is all of this coming from? If anybody knows about my lifestyle, you do. You know I am a hoe. You know how I get down. That's why I am so surprised about what happened between us in the basement. That was totally unexpected."

"I know. And I guess I did not know how I felt about you up until then. Now I think I love you."

"To be honest Jackie, I've always felt that you were out of my league. You have got to be one of the finest girls ever. You can have anybody you desire. You can't walk down the block without turning male and female heads. Why me and what about Johnny?"

"I guess a lot of it had to do with how other girls looked at you. How Fatima brightened up at the mention of your name. I always admired that. And I believe that you have a lot of love in your heart. You are nice to others. Especially when compared to Johnny. You are a good man. Then you whipped it on me in the basement and I was instantly hooked."

"Is that why you took me there a second time?"
"Hell yeah," Jackie smiles. "And I must confess, I was a little bit happy to see you and Fatima break up. I thought that I could really make you mine then."

"And Johnny?"
"You know I was not happy with him. He is rude and abusive. Not to mention, he can't do it like you." Jackie looks him dead in the eye and Don knows she is talking about sex.

"Are you sure you are not confusing good intercourse with love?"

"Good intercourse? You mean great intercourse!" She puts her hand on his private area. "And you have no idea what I can really do yet. When you get out of here I'm going to show you what spectacular love is." Jackie squeezes his genital.

"Keep doing that and you are going to have to climb Mt. Don."

"What, you think I'm scared?" Jackie slides on top of Don before he can protest. Clothes and a bedsheet is between them but he can still feel her warmth and she can feel him growing. "Ain't no shame in my game baby. You got me?" Jackie She feels good to him. She is so smooth with hers and he knows he would look like a winner walking down the block with her. He goes to palm her ass when he hears...

"I can't believe this shit!" It's Lydia.

(Chapter 14)
An Arm For An Arm

Johnny has a hard time deciding what he will do next. Killa is knocked out and Haywire has been turned into a zombie. He looks at Killas possessions and pulls out the bag of marijuana. He rolls a joint, hoping it will help him alleviate some of his stress.

After the first spliff, he doesn't feel anything. But by the time he is in the middle of the second reefer, Snoop starts speaking to him. "You know what you have to do. You have to make things right and even the score."

Johnny recognizes that he is most likely losing his mind. "First of all dogs can't talk. I must be really stressed out." He continues smoking.

"I need your help friend. Killa has done me wrong so many times. I need your help to finally get my revenge." Snoop

"What can I do?"

"Simple. He has fucked me so many times, in so many ways. I want to return the favor."

"You want to take his vocal cords?"

"No! I want to fuck him!" Snoop lifts up his leg and shows off his pink male organ. Then he flashes his set of menacing teeth. "Just keep him unconscious, take his pants down, and bend him over the couch. I'll do the rest."

"But that's rape."

"He has done it to me plenty of times. Besides don't act like it's something you have never done before."

Johnny feels like he has no choice. He does as Snoop has asked him to. Snoop starts by licking Killas ass until it is dripping with his drool and then he mounts him. Even unconscious, Killa makes sounds like he is undergoing some serious violation. Never bearing witness to bestiality Johnny has to turn away. He smokes some more.

Snoop keeps abusing Killa's ass for a few minutes, going to the bathroom to drink some water and then going back to Killas butt. He does this about eight times before Johnny speaks on it. "Isn't that enough revenge? How many times are you going to do it to him?"

"It's just one time, but I'm making it last. Oh by the way, there's some Grey Goose in the kitchen under the sink."

Johnny gets up to get a drink when Killa starts coming out of his induced state and tries to stand up. Quickly Johnny sedates him again. "Okay Snoop, you got one more hour to handle your business. And that's it!" He finds the vodka and pours it straight up.

Snoop contiues to exact his revenge and Johnny continues smoking and sipping on vodka. By the time he is finished his first drink, he is stoned out of his mind and Haywire starts speaking to him. "You got to help me man. You can't leave me like this."

Johnny should be scared but he is not. He simply talks back to Haywire. "There's really nothing I can do for you."

"I need to be whole again. A part of me is missing. Make me whole again."

"I can't. Your arm is gone. It's been digested. Besides, I couldn't put it back if I wanted to."

"Yes you can. You have to try. You owe me. I could have pressed the issue with you using the telephone, but I let you stay anyway. You have to help me."

"How do you know I was on the phone? You

228

wasn't here."

"I wasn't but snoop was." Haywire

"Ain't that some stuff. A snitching dog." Johnny

"Hey bro he asked me, and I didn't see a reason to lie for you." Snoop says.

"How the hell you gonna call me bro?" Johnny asks.

"Okay my dog, he asked me and..."

"You are a funny mother fucker. You knew that was Haywire's arm killa was feeding you and you ate it anyway. I don't know why I did anything for you."

"Don't you ever judge me. You don't know what It's like to be a dog. Especially in a human society. Besides I am part pit. We were created to be vicious and to eat. You should try walking in my paws and then tell me if you can keep from licking your own ass."

"Enough! The dog has had his day. I need mine." Haywire cries out.

"I have to deal with my own issues, I can't help you." Johnny says.

"You have to man. I won't be able to rest in peace if you don't. You must make me complete again."

"I mean really, I can't do nothing for you."

"You know what I need you to do."

"C'mon, you're not saying you want me to..."

"Yes you know exactly what I need."

"I can't. That's crazy. He'll bleed to death."

"I'll help you. I watched him do it. I know how it's done. If you do what I tell you, there won't be much blood at all."

"That's ludicrous! I mean after I do it, how is that going to help you?"

"Give it to me."

"Just give it to you? Put it in your lap and you're

complete again?"

"I'll show you what to do."

"You can't show me shit nigga, you can't move. I don't even know how you can talk to me. Your lips aren't moving."

"I hate to tell you this, but if you don't help me I'll have to haunt you for all eternity."

Johnny thinks about his dilemma, "Aw fuck it, what do I got to lose?" The roach he is toking burns his fingers and he drops it on the floor. "Snoop, wrap it up. There is a surgery about to be performed."

(Chapter 15)
Baby Mama Drama

It seems as if the whole room turns red. Jackie has never seen or met Lydia, yet she instantly comprehends that she is in the danger zone. "I told you that if you kept fucking with people's feelings and trust, that it would bite you in the ass." Lydia pulls a medium sized knife out of her pocket and opens it with a click. Don and Jackie and are too shocked to move, and they are still in their compromising position.

Lydia keeps talking, "I tried to warn you that someone might lose control and try to do you some considerable damage." She grabs the knife by the tip of the blade and pulls her arm back. Never taking her eye off the intended target, she flings her arm forward in Don's direction and lets go at the last second in order to gain maximum speed and accuracy.

Jackie screams and throws up her hands, a move that probably saves Don's life. The knife whizzes through the air and bumps slightly into Jackie's arm, cutting her in the process, but deflecting it just enough to miss Don's neck. It sticks into the headboard next to him.

Jackie pretends to faint and falls off the bed. In one fluid motion she manages to hit the floor and roll under the bed out of Lydia's view.

To Don's surprise he remains calm. He is even a bit flattered that Lydia loves him so much, that she is willing to go to jail for her actions. Still he knows that there is a thin line between love and hate. And right now Lydia's love is so vast that she hates him for hurting her. She is angry enough to kill him. He knows he must choose his words very carefully.

"Lydia honey, I know this looks crazy, and you have every right to be upset..."

"Upset! I'm not upset. I'm furious. And I am not going to hold on to this shit any longer." Lydia pulls out a shiny Biretta.

Now Don feels like pushing the panic button. "No baby. You have to stop and think. Think about Damian. If you do this, he won't have any parent around to take care of him."

"Were you thinking about him while you were spreading your love all over the place? Were you thinking about me or anyone other than yourself?" She puts a bullet in a chamber.

"Baby please, it's not worth it. I'm not worth it. Think about what you are doing," Don pleads.

"You know my daddy is a good man. He always told me that he did not like guns, but there were a few times in his life when he wished he had one. The truth is he had more than one. He taught me how to shoot too. Shoot real good with a gun. I bet that is something you didn't even know about me Don. You never took the time to learn the real me." Lydia walks over to Don, pointing the gun straight at him.

He does not move or make eye contact with her. He simply sits there, staring straight ahead. He has accepted his fate. He won't try to run. He will not try to defend himself or even put up his hands to protect his melon. Don is ready to embrace death. Lydia pulls a pillow from behind Don. She lets the pillow fall out and she holds on to the pillow case. She keeps the gun pointed at Don and walks back to her previous position back in Dons eye view. "Let me finish my story." She begins to carefully wrap the pillowcase around the small caliber weapon. "I never told you my Daddy and I used to target

232

practice in the apartment. Yes I know it's hard to believe, bussing caps in the projects. Yes we did.

It's something I couldn't really talk about you know. But my Daddy is a construction worker. He built a nice size wall. Concrete, metal, padding, and some other shit. And bam, we had our own firing range." She wraps the gun completely in the pillowcase with her finger still on the trigger.

Lydia goes on with her story. "Cool right? Still, there is always the blam factor. That is the volume of the blast. You know how loud the sound can be. A good silencer will kill most of the noise, but if you don't have a silencer a pillowcase or shirt will do just fine." She squares off on him. "How lucky do you feel?"

Don starts to think. In spite of everything he does feel lucky. It probably won't be till the hot lead comes crashing through his flesh that he won't feel so lucky. Still he notices he is not having one of his anxiety attacks despite all that is happening to him. The gun goes "Click," and Don involuntarily cracks a smile at the same time.

"Oh this is some funny shit to you? I have one bullet in a five shooter, and I just shot off one empty chamber. Think you could get lucky one more time?

Don can't believe what is going on. He would have rather she shot him five minutes ago. Why does this shit have to drag out? He contemplates begging her to shot him, but if she has any second thoughts he does not want to discourage her. He knows he could say something but depending on her perception of his comment, she could either put the gun down or pull the trigger again. What does she want him to do or say? He decides silence is his best option.

"You are probably wondering what I want. Well I want answers. I want the truth! You gave me a venereal disease didn't you?"

Don thinks hard. To live or die with a lie.

Lydia fires another shot that does not connect with the bullet. "No more time to think. Just answer the question, yes or no."

"Yes."

"That bitch Fatima, did she have anything to do with it?"

"No."

"Don't lie to me," she starts to pull the trigger but she doesn't. What about that bitch under the bed? She had anything to do with it?"

"Yes." Don drops dime on Jackie. "But no." He tries to save face.

"Well I'll be damned. Just how many girls are you fucking Don?"

"That is not a yes or no question," he gets frustrated.

"Do not get cocky with me nigger," she fires again with no blast. "You have got to be the luckiest man in the universe. Now answer my question. How many?"

"How many? When? Where? Look I enjoy fucking. Women seem to like giving me pussy. I am a god damn pussy magnet. I get more pussy by mistake, than most guys get on purpose. It just comes naturally."

"And what about me? I guess I was just a piece of ass too."

"No. Up until recently, I was real good at not going in unprotected. I didn't want any children, but with you I did. You, I would marry."

"Marry me? Let me tell you something about marriage. It is a union between two people who love each other exclusively. For richer or poor, sickness and health. It's an amalgamation if you will, between a man and woman who decide to be with one another solely. Adultery is not part of a good marriage. Could you ever believe in fidelity?"

"Yes."

"More importantly, could you ever practice it?"

Don does not answer the question. He feels it is a trick question. The answer too which could get him killed.

Lydia wants to reconcile with her man. But because Don does not answer the question she feels that he is incapable of being monogamous. "What's that bitch's name?"

Don briefly forgets Jackie is under the bed and looks around the room. "Who? Jackie?"

"Did Jackie have anything to do with you getting shanked?"

"Yes."

"How?"

"That's not a yes or no question."

"Answer me or let it be the last question you are ever asked."

"Her boyfriend Johnny got the wrong idea about me and her."

"I'll bet he did," Lydia says sarcastically. "Jackie, get your dumb ass from under that bed." No movement. "I'm going to count to three and you better come out from under there or you will get shot. One, two,.." Jackie crawls from under the bed. She stands up and at almost six feet seems to tower over Lydia.

Lydia has the gun and is not the least bit scared as she looks up at Jackie. "Hi Jackie, I'm Lydia. You look like a smart girl, how the hell did you ever get involved with his trifling ass?"

Before Jackie can answer a Nurse Linton walks in. She surveys the situation and faints on the spot. Lydia continues with Jackie, "Never mind my last question. You need to decide real fast, how important your life is. Come over here and turn around and face Don."

Jackie does not move. She is too frightened to move.

"Don't make me say it again."

Jackie walks up close to Lydia and turns around.

"You see that motherfucker over there?" She gestures toward Don. "You either shoot him or take the bullet for him. First of all, do you love him?"

"I, I, I don't know."

It isn't hard for Lydia to coax Jackie into taking the gun. She stands behind her and helps her get a clean aim at him. Don feels in his heart that Jackie will turn the gun on Lydia and save the day. Instead the gun goes "Click."

It is as if time stands still. Don wonders if he is dead and just does not know it. Then Lydia's voice breaks through the silence. "Hot damn!" She is clearly enjoying the excitement. "I guess that only means one thing. The man upstairs has truly been watching over you." Lydia is not going to shoot someone with such good odds. Halfway coming to her senses she reaches to take the gun from Jackie and the trigger gets pressed again. This time the hammer connects with the bullet and it whizzes off. For that precise moment Don can actually see the bullet coming. He just can't move fast enough to avoid it. The ammunition digs into his skin and goes straight through his shoulder. Feeling faint he begins to lose consciousness.

"Now that is some beautiful shit," An unknown presence exclaims with glee. "Hello Jackie. Hello

Don. I believe we have some unfinished business to..." Johnny searches for the right word. "Conclude."

(Chapter 16)
Murder Dem

He staggers onto the 6 train in blood soaked apparel that is mostly camouflaged by his dark clothing. Coming down off a hard trip of Angel Dust he finds a small two seater in the corner to sit down. He puts on his hoody to hide his face and he closes his eyes as the events of the past plays through his mind.

It all starts with him chasing after Don with a knife. He catches up to him and sticks it in his back. He runs from the crime until he is out of breath. Killa gives him a gun, he has a shootout with the cops, and Killa saves him.

They hide at Haywire's place. Haywire doesn't like Johnny. They turn on him. Then Killa turns on Haywire and turns him into a zombie. At that thought, Johnny has to survey his surrounding and wish that those things did not really happen. A good look at all the dried blood on his sneakers tells him it did.

One would think that a young man as disheveled and bloody as he is would arouse a great deal of curiosity, but no one seems to pay any attention to him at all. He goes back to his thoughts, hoping to once again find that the events did not actually happen. But they did.

Snoop really spoke to him. He told him what he wanted from him and where to find things. Even crazier the dog had sex with Killa. Johnny takes a deep breath in exhaustion as he reflects upon the unbelievable dealings that has taken place.

Haywire needed a favor that he felt obligated to oblige. He was instructed to open up a small tool box that contains medical items, pills, needles, liquids, vials, and the likes. "Take out one of those small bottles and a needle," Haywire demands.

"Looks like water," Johnny says, but the bottle says atropine sulfate.

"It's not water. Open the needle, push it through the top of the bottle and pull the liquid inside."

He does what he is told and instinctively he goes to stick Killa with it. "No, wait," Snoop stops him.

"You have to break his arm first."

"What?"

"It's true, you need to pop his arm at the shoulder and then administer the shot." Haywire

"And how the hell am I suppose to break his arm?"

"Just fold his arm behind his back, grab him by his elbow and pull up real hard. Try to lift him off the ground and bring it around his head. If you do it right his bone will snap out of place."

"If I do it right? Nigga, I'd like to see you get up and do it yourself!"

"Don't fuck with me, I got powers you wouldn't believe."

"I'd like to see you do one mother fucking thing."

"Oh yeah."

"Yeah." Johnny starts to believe he is losing his mind because he is arguing with someone who can't talk. Then Haywire lets out a deafening screech. It hurts Johnny's ears. "Stop it."

"Will you help me?"

"Will you stop that awful noise?"

Haywire stops his screaming. "After you break the bone, give him the needle. Then we slice."

They say that a person on PCP can gain the strength of two men, Johnny snaps Killa's arm so easily that it appears as if he can just rip it off. Using way too much pressure Killa's shoulder goes around much more than it was meant to. The bone comes out of its socket and his skin rips. His blood spurts over Johnny's pants, sneakers, and floor. Snoop walks over. "You probably should have given him the needle first," as he starts licking up the life fluid.

With all the blood at his feet and a dog to lap it up, Johnny seems to get more into his role. He picks out the biggest machete in Killa's suitcase. He takes the dangling arm and stretches it out onto the couch He puts it into position for a clean cut. Concentration is the key.

Johnny hits his mark and then some. The blow cuts through Killa, and halfway through the couch. Red soaked feathers float and fall to the ground. Snoop licks up one of the feathers in an effort to get the blood, and the feather gets stuck to his tongue.

"You were supposed to give him the needle to minimize the blood flow." Haywire

"Damn I forgot." Johnny

"You have to cover his wound, and we need to keep him alive." Haywire

"Why?" Johnny

"I just want my arm back. I'm not a murderer."

"There's a more pressing concern," Snoop has something to say. "You cut off the wrong arm."

"Wrong arm? Stay alive?" The rage builds up in Johnny and he cuts off Killas other arm without caring where he cut it.

"Nooooooo." Haywire screams. "You ruined the arm." He screeches.

Johnny picks up a bloody rag off the floor, stuffs it into Haywire's mouth and his scream is muffled. Then he begins to hack away at Haywire, slicing his head clean off and not stopping until there are pieces of Killa and Haywire all over the room. Snoop makes a hasty exit and hides somewhere that he cannot be found.

Johnny finally ends his butchering when there are hardly any pieces big enough to cut left. With nothing more to do, there is one person who keeps coming to his mind. One person he wishes was in that room with him. One person who must die. He can't do it standing in that stinking apartment, so Johnny loads the gun and heads out the door. The air brings his high down a little bit, and by the time he hits the subway he is feeling like he should have stayed in the house and rested. He falls asleep as soon as he sits down. Somehow he wakes up at 103rd Street. Just where he is meant to be.

(Chapter 17)
The Gangs All Here

It is his birthday. It doesn't feel right but he is the man of honor at this event. Music is playing, family, friends, and enemies are dancing and fraternizing.

Everyone seems to be having a good time, only things are very twisted. To begin with, Don's hands are tied behind his back and he is hanging by his ankles upside down from the ceiling. Secondly, there is a strong odor of feces and urine. Still the guests are socializing like a typical party.

He strains his neck in an effort to locate the foul stenches. Right below him is an oddly shaped chocolate cake of various hues, with a single lit large candle in the middle. There is also a punch bowl with some yellow liquid filled to the brim. Johnny walks up to Don, smiles at him and starts pissing in the punch bowl. Don seems to be the only one who thinks what Johnny is doing is insane. Everyone else acts natural and does not pay any attention to him.

After Johnny is done, Lydia steps up and doesn't even look in Don's direction. She pulls down her pants and with Johnny's assistance, positions herself to urinate in the bowl. Then with her ass dangerously close to the lit candle, takes a number two on the cake.

Suddenly Don realizes where the smells are coming from. The punch bowl is filled with urine and the cake is made of feces. Upon further observation, he also notices that the candle is not a candle, but an M80 with a very slow burning fuse. The music stops and the guest surround Don. His Grandma exclaims, "Happy death day Don, it's your day to die." Everyone cheers and they began

*to sing happy death day to the tune of happy
birthday with death being substituted for birth.
Happy death day to you.
Happy death day to you.
Happy death day to you.
Happy death day to you.
How old will you die?
How old will you die?
How old will you die?
How old will you die?
Seemingly right on cue, the M80 explodes and
sends shit flying everywhere, mainly on the man of
the hour. His audience, splattered with doo doo,
squeals with delight. They appear to be overjoyed
with wearing their own dung.
As Fatima is being blind folded, he notices there is
a bat next to what is left of the shit cake. Answar
spins her around three times, gives her the bat and
the crowd steps back to give her room to swing
blindly. She swings like she is trying to hit a home
run, but she does not hit anything.
When she is done, he does not have to get hit to
comprehend that he is the target. He is a human
pi□ata. She is given a cup of urine to splash on
Don.
Next it is Sheena's turn. She is a fellow classmate
of Dons, whom he thinks is attractive. She is
blindfolded, spun around, given the bat and let go.
Her first swing smacks Don hard across his torso.
Her next two swings hurt like hell as she hits Don in
his head and chest. After her last hit, her blindfold
is taken off, and she too is given a warm cup of
smelly liquid body waste to splash on Don. He
assumes everyone will get three chances to knock
his block off, and give him a golden shower.
Unfortunately, he is correct.*

Don is beat to a bloody pulp, as each person gets a turn to blindly bash him with a big stick. Everybody except for his mother. She is unable to take her turn. She and her son understand that if she hits him, he will die. Instead, she weeps for him and refuses to strike him.

The guests do not care one way or the other, but somebody must perish. If not him then her. She desires to take his place, he does not want her to. "No I can't let you die again. Kill me!" He yells. "Kill me!"

"That is the plan." Johnny retorts as he breaks Don out of his daymare.

"It's a very good plan, "Lydia chimes in. She is furious with Don and would like to see him done some bodily harm.

Johnny looks at her. He has never met her before but he is smitten. He expected not to live long after killing Don, now he has a reason to go on living. Not only do they share a common interest, wasting Don, but she is a dime. Small and feisty, just like he likes them. Not tall and intimidating like Jackie. When all of this is done with, he can see himself getting with someone like her. She has other plans.

"So what is your name?" He inquires of her.

"Ellen," she lies.

"Well Ellen, we're going to take care of business here, and let's say you and I go get a bite to eat or catch a movie?"

"Sounds good."

"You got some mother fucking nerve. You never took me to eat or to a mother fucking movie," Jackie steps up.

"You don't deserve nothing bitch. You ain't never been down for your man. You ain't no ride or die bitch." Johnny thinks about his new found female friend. His gut instinct is that she is somebody who will have his back to the very end. When he goes to look at her again, she is not there.

Feeling abandoned, Johnny looks around in a panic, hoping Ellen is still around to hold it down with him. Nurse Linton revives with an air of authority and disgust. She sees Johnny pointing the gun in Don's direction and she stops cold.

"Forget this mess, I quit." Nurse Linton throws down her nurse's cap and walks out of the room, straight down the stairs, and out the hospital doors. All the while she is ranting out loud about how crazy this world is.

"You can't do this. It has to stop. You need to get help," pleads Jackie.

"Who the fuck is going to help me now?" Johnny

"I can help you," B.J. walks in determined not to pull out his gun unless totally necessary. He believes he can talk it over with Johnny. He is not in his uniform so Johnny does not know he is a cop.

"Who the fuck are you?"

"I'm officer Butler Johnson."

"A police officer? The only thing a pig can do for me is die." Johnny lets off four shots. Hitting B.J. with each one. B.J. goes down.

Jackie starts screaming at the top of her lungs.

"Shut up bitch cause I got some for you too." He points the gun at her.

"Mister, we have to stop all of this black on black crime?"

"All these interruptions. Who the fuck are you?"

"His name is Basheem. He is only a kid, please don't hurt him. I'm the one you want," Don speaks.

"Isn't that some shit. You about to die and you are

245

trying to save someone else's life. How fucking nice. After I do you, Jackie can get two, and I'll be sure to save one for little man here."

"No Johnny, he's been through enough already. His mother would be devastated if he came to any harm."

"Like I give a fuck about him or his mother."

"What did you say about my mother?"

"Fuck you and your mother." Johnny points the gun at Basheem.

"Don't Johnny. His mother was recently shot. She is the only ATM victim to survive. She is recovering here at this hospital and she can't take any more pain." Don cries out.

"Ain't that some ironic shit. This is a small world. My cousin shot your mom. I should have been there with him but I got caught up."

"I guess evil just runs in your family," Jackie sobs.

"You know what?" Johnny turns to point the gun at Jackie. "I'm tired of hearing your mouth. I'm a buss a cap in..." He does not get to finish his sentence. He barely hears the shot, and only feels pain for a brief second. Slowly he loses the sensations, functions and abilities of his legs and arms. Then he hits the floor with a bang. Johnny has been shot.

(Chapter 18)
Teach The Children

It's been three months since B.J. was killed. A lot can happen in 90 days. It's easier to see things clearer when you have been clean and sober for a quarter of a year. God is good.

Often times Don feels unworthy of the blessings that have been bestowed upon him. He often contemplates why him? Why did B.J. have to die so he could live? Why did so many people have to get hurt? He prays for forgiveness.

The turnout at B.J.'s funeral was awesome. It seemed as if the whole New York City police force came out to represent for their fallen comrade. Don never thought he could feel comfortable around so many cops. But he did. It felt strange to be on the other side of the law. It's not that Don is a hard core criminal or anything of the sort, but most of his interaction with the NYPD has not been pleasant.

At B.J.'s farewell, he and New York's finest united to pay their respects to a deceased hero. A good man who had a way of making everyone feel like they are part of the team. He definitely brought people together.

The tears flowed for plenty of reasons at B.J.'s funeral. Not only did Don lose a friend and mentor, but a wonderful human being has been lost to the world. Fortunately, heaven has gained another soldier to help fight the war against evil.

Lydia disappeared. She left all her personals items at home and broke out. With Damian by her side, she covered her tracks real good and made herself impossible to find. Don has tried to locate her, and the FBI is allegedly on the case. So far, no leads. Don believes she is hiding because she thinks he is dead.

Mostly, he misses his son. He kind of feels sorry for Lydia since she will most likely lie to Damian about the fate of his father. The questions are going to come. How will she answer?

Dad and especially Grandma are heartbroken over the whole situation. He didn't tell them that Lydia tried to kill him. Basically all they know is that she skipped town without a trace. Poor Grandma. Don can't help but feel responsible.

He knows all too well that he is very much at fault for the messy bed he has made. He dug his own grave, but for some reason, Butler Johnson took his place. Still the search goes on. He is constantly on the internet, looking for traces of his son. Someday he will find him.

Fatima refused to return any of his phone calls. Who could blame her, he did her wrong. She is way too mad at him to ever talk to him again. A few days ago, he went to see D.J., who has been acting real distant with him lately. Don thought it was because he stopped smoking. It was almost as if their friendship was built on weed. Don wanted to change all of that.

He dropped by D.J.'S house to surprise him with some tickets to a Knick game. Don was the one to get the surprise. Fatima was at D.J.'s house putting on her shoes. D.J. must give one hell of a foot massage. Don gave D.J. the tickets and walked out. They look good together anyway.

Johnny is all messed up. The bullet severed his spinal cord and turned him into a paraplegic. And he is being charged with a multitude of crimes. Killa wiped off his prints, and put Johnny's fingers on all the weapons in the house. He did it all while Johnny was knocked unconscious.

Facing charges of shooting at the police, the apartment killings, and the ATM murders, even Atom Killa's real partner in crime finds a way to reduce his sentence by lying on Johnny. He accused Johnny of being the mastermind behind all the crimes. Who could dispute him? Johnny certainly can't.

There was not much of Haywire left to identify him. Still the forensic team joked that he made a good smelling spaghetti. Snoop took more shots than Diallo when the police kicked the door in and he came out of his hiding place. Just more blood to stain the floors of that apartment.

Funny thing happened on the same day Johnny was shot. Mike, a guy Don worked with dropped by. He was a bad influence on Don's life, so Don really did not want to see him. Still Mike and Jackie hit it off and it has been rumored that they are getting married. Good riddance to the both of them.

Don got a letter from Answar apologizing about his behavior. With no return address, he explained that he is leaving New York for someplace on the west coast. There he will have a change to make him a her. He wished Don the best. Don prays everything will turn out good for him/her.

Mrs. Linton left nursing to pursue a career in evangelism. She claims Don showed her the need to preach the gospel. He has been to her church twice already. She gives a fiery sermon.

Ebony enlisted in the navy, and Zelda now goes to Spellman. Don is very proud of both of them. They all write to each other often.

Basheem got charged with using an unregistered fire arm. He was charged with a lot more at first, but after the police confiscated the cameras that 'In Da Hood' left, they brought the charges down. Still

Basheem has to do nine more months in Juvenile detention. Don owes him his life. There has to be a lesson learned from all of this.

Lately however Don has been feeling a comfortable loneliness. He has had his fun and now he feels as if he walks on the outside of the world. He has become anonymous in a lot of ways. No more drinking, smoking, hanging out, or chasing women. Life has slowed down a lot.

the other day he got a letter from the post office for a mail handlers job. He has to go to orientation, be finger printed, and take a drug test. He is not worried about any of it because he is clean. He is going to live a quiet existence as a United States Postal worker... Yeah right!

THE END...

(Almost ☺)

Thank you, for your purchase.
For More Info about this Author and
our other Authors and Writers
please visit out website

www.DNAeBooks.com
and
www.NotJustSex.net

NOT JUST SEX
(Volume 1)
David Theodore

Feel Free to Contact and Email Me:
DavidTheodore@DNAeBooks.com

www.DNAeBooks.com

www.NotJustSex.net

www.ingramcontent.com/pod-product-compliance
Lightning Source LLC
Chambersburg PA
CBHW070051260626
47160CB00004B/1178